A QUEST OF HEROES

(BOOK #1 IN THE SORCERER'S RING)

MORGAN RICE

D1114294

Copyright © 2012 by Morgan Rice

All rights reserved. Except as permitted under the U.S. Copyright Act
of 1976, no part of this publication may be reproduced, distributed or
transmitted in any form or by any means, or stored in a database or
retrieval system, without the prior permission of the author.

This ebook is licensed for your personal enjoyment only. This ebook
may not be re-sold or given away to other people. If you would like to
share this book with another person, please purchase an additional
copy for each recipient. If you're reading this book and did not
purchase it, or it was not purchased for your use only, then please
return it and purchase your own copy. Thank you for respecting the
hard work of this author.

This is a work of fiction. Names, characters, businesses, organizations,
places, events, and incidents either are the product of the author's
imagination or are used fictionally. Any resemblance to actual persons,
living or dead, is entirely coincidental.

ISBN: 978-1-939416-20-9

ACCLAIM FOR MORGAN RICE'S BOOKS

"Grabbed my attention from the beginning and did not let go....This story is an amazing adventure that is fast paced and action packed from the very beginning. There is not a dull moment to be found."
--Paranormal Romance Guild {regarding *Turned*}

"A great plot, and this especially was the kind of book you will have trouble putting down at night. The ending was a cliffhanger that was so spectacular that you will immediately want to buy the next book, just to see what happens."
--The Dallas Examiner {regarding *Loved*}

"A book to rival *Twilight* and *The Vampire Diaries*, and one that will have you wanting to keep reading until the very last page! If you are into adventure, love and vampires this book is the one for you!"
--vampirebooksite.com {regarding *Turned*}

"An ideal story for young readers. Morgan Rice did a good job spinning an interesting twist on what could have been a typical vampire tale. Refreshing and unique, has the classic elements found in many Young Adult paranormal stories."
--The Romance Reviews {regarding *Turned*}

"Rice does a great job of pulling you into the story from the beginning, utilizing a great descriptive quality that transcends the mere painting of the setting....Nicely written and an extremely fast read, this is a good start to a new vampire series sure to be a hit with readers who are looking for a light, yet entertaining story."
--Black Lagoon Reviews {regarding *Turned*}

"Jam packed with action, romance, adventure, and suspense. This book is a wonderful addition to this series and will have you wanting more from Morgan Rice."
--vampirebooksite.com {regarding *Loved*}

"Morgan Rice proves herself again to be an extremely talented storyteller....This would appeal to a wide range of audiences, including younger fans of the vampire/fantasy genre. It ended with an unexpected cliffhanger that leaves you shocked."
--The Romance Reviews {regarding *Loved*}

Books by Morgan Rice

THE SORCERER'S RING
A QUEST OF HEROES (BOOK #1)
A MARCH OF KINGS (BOOK #2)
A FEAST OF DRAGONS (BOOK #3)
A CLASH OF HONOR (BOOK #4)
A VOW OF GLORY (BOOK #5)
A CHARGE OF VALOR (BOOK #6)
A RITE OF SWORDS (BOOK #7)
A GRANT OF ARMS (BOOK #8)
A SKY OF SPELLS (BOOK #9)
A SEA OF SHIELDS (BOOK #10)
A REIGN OF STEEL (BOOK #11)

THE SURVIVAL TRILOGY
ARENA ONE (Book #1)
ARENA TWO (Book #2)

the Vampire Journals
turned (book #1)
loved (book #2)
betrayed (book #3)
destined (book #4)
desired (book #5)
betrothed (book #6)
vowed (book #7)
found (book #8)
resurrected (book #9)
craved (book #10)

"Uneasy lies the head that wears the crown."

--Shakespeare, *Henry IV, Part II*

CHAPTER ONE

The boy stood on the highest knoll of the low country in the Western Kingdom of the Ring, looking north, watching the first of the rising suns. As far as he could see stretched rolling green hills, like camel humps, dipping and rising in a series of valleys and peaks. The burnt-orange rays of the first sun lingered in the morning mist, making them sparkle, lending the light a magic that matched the boy's mood. He rarely woke this early or ventured this far from home—and never ascended this high—knowing it would incur his father's wrath. But on this day, he didn't care. On this day, he disregarded the million rules and chores that had oppressed him for his fourteen years. For this day was different. It was the day his destiny had arrived.

The boy—Thorgrin of the Western Kingdom of the Southern Province of the clan McLeod—known to all he liked simply as Thor—the youngest of four boys, the least favorite of his father, had stayed awake all night in anticipation of this day. He had tossed and turned, bleary-eyed, waiting, *willing*, for the first sun to rise. For a day like this arrived only once every several years, and if he missed it, he would be stuck here, in this village, doomed to tend his father's flock the rest of his days. That was a thought he could not bear.

Conscription Day. It was the one day the King's Army canvassed the provinces, hand-picked volunteers for the King's Legion. As long as he had lived, Thor had dreamt of nothing else. For him, life meant one thing: joining The Silver, the king's elite force of knights, bedecked in the finest armor and the choicest arms anywhere in the two kingdoms. And one could not enter the Silver without first joining the Legion, the company of squires ranging from fourteen to nineteen years of age. And if one was not the son of a noble, or of a famed warrior, there was no other way to join the Legion.

Conscription Day was the only exception, that rare event every few years when the Legion ran low and the king's men scoured the land in search of new recruits. Everyone knew that few commoners were chosen—and that even fewer would actually make the Legion.

Thor stood there, studying the horizon intently, looking for any sign of motion. The Silver, he knew, would have to take this road, the only road into his village, and he wanted to be the first to spot them. His flock of sheep protested all around him, rose up in a chorus of annoying grunts, urging him to bring them back down the mountain, where the grazing was choicer. He tried to block out the noise, and the stench. He had to concentrate.

What had made all of this bearable, all these years of tending flocks, of being his father's lackey, his older brothers' lackey, the one cared for least and burdened most, was the idea that one day he would leave this place. One day, when the Silver came, he would surprise all those who had underestimated him, and be selected. In one swift motion, he would ascend their carriage and say goodbye to all of this.

His father, of course, had never considered him seriously as a candidate for the Legion—in fact, he had never considered him as a candidate for anything. Instead, his father devoted his love and attention to Thor's three older brothers. The oldest was nineteen and the others but a year behind each other, leaving Thor a good three years younger than any of them. Perhaps because they were closer in age, or perhaps because they looked alike and looked nothing like Thor, the three of them stuck together, barely acknowledging Thor's existence.

Worse, they were taller and broader and stronger than he, and Thor, who knew he was not short, nonetheless felt small beside them, felt his muscular legs frail beside their barrels of oak. His father made no move to rectify any of this—and in fact seemed to relish it—leaving Thor to attend the sheep and sharpen weapons, while his brothers were left to train. It was never spoken, but always understood, that Thor would spend his life in the wings, be forced to watch his brothers achieve great things. His destiny, if his father and brothers had their way, would be to stay here, swallowed by this village, and give his family the support they demanded.

Worse still was that Thor sensed that his brothers, paradoxically, were threatened by him, maybe even hated him. Thor could see it in their every glance, every gesture. He didn't understand how, but he aroused something in them, like fear or jealousy. Perhaps it was because he was different from them, didn't look like them or speak with their mannerisms; he didn't even dress like them, his father reserving the best garments—the purple and scarlet robes, the gilded weapons—for his brothers, while Thor was left wearing the coarsest of rags.

Nonetheless, Thor made the best of what he had, finding a way to make his clothes fit, tying the frock with a sash around his waist, and, now that summer was here, cutting off the sleeves to allow his toned arms to be caressed by the breezes. These were matched by coarse linen pants, his only pair, and boots made of the poorest leather, laced up his shins. They were hardly the leather of his brothers' shoes, but he made them work. He wore the typical uniform of a herder.

But he hardly had the typical demeanor: Thor stood tall and lean, with a proud jaw, noble chin, high cheekbones and gray eyes, looking like a displaced warrior. His straight, brown hair fell back in waves on his head, just past his ears, and behind them, his eyes glistened like a minnow in the light.

Thor knew that today his brothers would be allowed to sleep in, be given a hearty meal, sent off for the Selection with the finest weapons and his father's blessing—while he would not even be allowed to attend. He had tried to raise the issue with his father once. It had not gone well. His father had summarily ended the conversation, and he had not tried again. It just wasn't fair.

Thor was determined to reject the fate his father had planned for him: at the first sign of the royal caravan, he would race back to the house, confront his father, and, like it or not, make himself known to the King's Men. He would stand for selection with the others. His father could not stop him. He felt a knot in his stomach at the thought of it.

The first sun rose higher, and when the second sun began to rise, a mint green, adding a layer of light to the purple sky, Thor spotted them.

He stood upright, hairs on end, electrified. There, on the horizon, came the faintest outline of a horse-drawn carriage, its wheels kicking dust into the sky. His heart beat faster as another came into view; then another. Even from here the golden carriages gleamed in the suns, like silver-backed fish leaping from the water.

By the time he counted twelve of them, he could wait no longer. Heart pounding in his chest, forgetting his flock for the first time in his life, he turned and stumbled down the hill, determined to stop at nothing until he made himself known.

*

Thor barely stopped to catch his breath as he sped down the hills, through the trees, scratched by branches and not caring. He reached a clearing and saw his village spread out below: a sleepy country town, packed with one-story, white clay homes with thatched roofs, there were but several dozen families amongst them. Smoke rose from chimneys, and he knew most were up early, preparing their morning meal. It was an idyllic place, just far enough—a full day's ride—from King's Court to deter passersby. Just another farming village on the edge of the Ring, another cog in the wheel of the Western Kingdom.

Thor burst down the final stretch, into the village square, kicking up dirt as he went. Chickens and dogs ran out of his way, and an old woman, squatting outside her home before a cauldron of bubbling water, hissed at him.

"Slow down boy!" she screeched, as he raced passed her, stirring dust into her fire.

But Thor would not slow—not for her, not for anybody. He turned down one side street, then another, twisting and turning the way he knew by heart, until he reached home.

It was a small, nondescript dwelling, like all the others, with its white clay walls and angular, thatched roof. Like most, its single room was divided, his father sleeping on one side, and his three brothers on the other; unlike most, it had a small chicken coop in the back, and it was here that Thor was exiled to sleep. At first he'd slept with his brothers; but over time they had grown bigger and meaner and more exclusive, and made a show of not leaving him room. Thor had been hurt, but now he relished his own space, preferring to be away from their presence. It just confirmed for him that he was the exile in his family that he already knew he was.

Thor ran to his front door and burst through it without stopping.

"Father!" he screamed, gasping for breath. "The Silver! They're coming!"

His father and three brothers sat, hunched over the breakfast table, already dressed in their finest. At his words they jumped up and darted past him, bumping his shoulders as they ran out of the house, into the road.

Thor followed them out, and they all stood there, watching the horizon.

"I see no one," Drake, the oldest, answered in his deep voice. With the broadest shoulders, hair cropped short like his brothers, brown eyes and thin, disapproving lips, he scowled down at Thor, as usual.

"Nor do I," echoed Dross, just a year below Drake, always taking his side.

"They're coming!" Thor shot back. "I swear!"

His father turned to him and grabbed his shoulders sternly.

"And how would you know?" he demanded.

"I saw them."

"How? From where?"

Thor hesitated; his father had him. He of course knew that the only place he could have spotted them was from the top of that knoll. Now Thor was unsure how to respond.

"I...climbed the knoll—"

"With the flock? You know they are not to go that far."

"But today was different. I had to see."

His father glowered down.

"Go inside at once and fetch your brothers' swords and polish their scabbards, so that they look their best before the king's men arrive."

His father, done with him, turned back to his brothers, who all stood in the road, looking out.

"Do you think they'll choose us?" asked Durs, the youngest of the three, a full three years ahead of Thor.

"They'd be foolish not to," his father said. "They are short on men this year. It has been a slim cropping—or else they wouldn't bother coming. Just stand straight, the three of you, keep your chins up and chest out. Do not look them directly in the eye, but do not look away, either. Be strong and confident. Show no weakness. If you want to be in the King's Legion, you must act as if you're already in it."

"Yes, father," his three boys answered at once, getting into position.

He turned and glared back at Thor.

"What are you still doing there?" he asked. "Get inside!"

Thor stood there, torn. He didn't want to disobey his father, but he had to speak with him. His heart pounded as he debated. He decided it would be best to obey, to bring the swords, and then confront his father. Disobeying outright wouldn't help.

Thor raced into the house, out though the back and to the weapons shed. He spotted his brothers' three swords, objects of beauty all of them, crowned with the finest silver hilts, precious gifts his father had toiled for for years. He grabbed all three, surprised as always at their weight, and ran back through the house with them.

He sprinted to his brothers, handed each their sword, then turned to his father.

"What, no polish?" Drake said.

His father turned to him disapprovingly, but before he could say anything, Thor spoke up.

"Father, please. I need to speak with you!"

"I told you to polish—"

"*Please*, father!"

His father glared back, debating. He must have seen the seriousness on Thor's face, because finally, he said: "Well?"

"I want to be considered. With the others. For the Legion."

His brothers' laughter rose up behind him, making his face burn red.

But his father did not laugh; on the contrary, his scowl deepened.

"Do you?" he asked.

Thor nodded back vigorously.

"I'm fourteen. I'm eligible."

"The cutoff is fourteen," Drake said disparagingly, over his shoulder. "If they took you, you'd be the youngest. Do you think they'd choose you over someone like me, five years your elder?"

"You are insolent," Durs said. "You always have been."

Thor turned to them. "I'm not asking you," he said.

He turned back to his father, who still frowned.

"Father, please," he said. "Allow me a chance. That's all I ask. I know I'm young, but I will prove myself, over time."

His father shook his head.

"You're not a soldier, boy. You're not like your brothers. You're a herder. Your life is here. With me. You will do your duties and do them well. One should not dream too high. Embrace your life, and learn to love it."

Thor felt his heart breaking, as he saw his life collapsing before his eyes.

No, he thought. *This can't be.*

"But father—"

"Silence!" he screamed, so shrill it cut the air. "Enough with you. Here they come. Get out of the way, and best mind your manners while they're here."

His father stepped up and with one hand pushed Thor to the side, as if he were an object he'd rather not see. His beefy palm stung Thor's chest.

A great rumbling arose, and townsfolk poured out from their homes, lining the streets. A growing cloud of dust heralded the caravan, and moments later they burst in, a dozen horse-drawn carriages, with a noise like a great thunder.

They came into town like a sudden army, and their caravan came to a halt close to Thor's home. Their horses stood there, prancing, snorting. It took too long for the cloud of dust to settle, and Thor anxiously tried to steal a peek of their armor, their weaponry. He had never been this close to the Silver before, and his heart thumped.

The soldier on the lead horse dismounted his stallion. Here he was, a real, actual member of the Silver, covered in shiny ring mail, a long sword on his belt. He looked to be in his 30s, a real man, stubble on his face, scars on his cheek, and a nose crooked from battle. He was the most substantial man Thor had ever seen, twice as wide as the others, with a countenance that said he was in charge.

The soldier jumped down onto the dirt road, his spurs jingling as he approached the lineup of boys.

All up and down the village stood dozens of boys, at attention, hoping. Joining The Silver meant a life of honor, of battle, of renown, of glory—along with land, title, and riches. It meant the best bride, the choicest land, a life of glory. It meant honor for your family, and entering the Legion was the first step.

Thor studied the large, golden carriages, and knew they could only hold so many recruits. It was a large kingdom, and they had many towns to visit. He gulped, realizing his chances were even more remote than he thought. He would have to beat out all these other boys—many of them substantial fighters—along with his own three brothers. He had a sinking feeling.

Thor could hardly breathe as he watched the soldier pace in the silence, surveying the rows of hopefuls. He began on the far side of the street, then slowly circled. Thor knew all of the other boys, of course. Some of them he knew secretly did not want to be picked, even though their families wanted to send them off. They were afraid; they would make poor soldiers.

Thor burned with indignity. He felt he deserved to be picked, as much as any of them. Just because his brothers were older and bigger and stronger, didn't mean he shouldn't have a right to stand and be chosen. He burned with hatred for his father, and nearly burst out of his skin as the soldier approached.

The soldier stopped, for the first time, before his brothers. He looked them up and down, and seemed impressed. He reached out, grabbed one of their scabbards and yanked it, as if to test how firm it was.

He broke into a smile.

"You haven't yet used your sword in battle, have you?" he asked Drake.

Thor saw Drake nervous for the first time in his life. He swallowed.

"No, my liege. But I've used it many times in practice, and I hope to—"

"In *practice!*"

The soldier roared in laughter and turned to the other soldiers, who joined in, laughing in Drake's face.

Drake turned bright red. It was the first time Thor had ever seen Drake embarrassed—usually, it was Drake embarrassing others.

"Well then I shall certainly tell our enemies to fear you—you who wields your sword *in practice!*"

The crowd of soldiers laughed again.

The soldier then turned to his other brothers.

"Three boys from the same stock," he said, rubbing the stubble on his chin. "That can be useful. You're all a good size. Untested, though. You'll need much training if you are to make the cut."

He paused.

"I suppose we can find room."

He nodded towards the rear wagon.

"Get in, and be quick of it. Before I change my mind."

Thor's three brothers sprinted for the carriage, beaming. Thor noticed his father beaming, too.

But he was crestfallen as he watched them go.

The soldier turned and moved on to the next home. Thor could stand it no longer.

"Sire!" Thor yelled out.

His father turned and glared at him, but Thor no longer cared.

The soldier stopped, his back to him, and slowly turned.

Thor took two steps forward, his heart beating, and stuck out his chest as far as he could.

"You haven't considered me, sire," he said.

The soldier, startled, looked Thor up and down as if he were a joke.

"Haven't I?" he asked, and burst into laughter.

His men burst into laughter, too. But Thor didn't care. This was his moment. It was now or never.

"I want to join the Legion!" Thor said.

The soldier turned and stepped towards Thor.

"Do you now?"

He looked amused.

"And have you even reached your fourteenth year?"

"I did, sire. Two weeks ago."

"*Two weeks ago!*"

The soldier shrieked with laughter, as did the men behind them.

"In that case, our enemies shall surely quiver at the sight of you."

Thor felt himself burning with indignity. He had to do something. He couldn't let it end like this. The soldier turned his back to walk away—but Thor could not allow it.

Thor stepped forward and screamed: "Sire! You are making a mistake!"

A horrified gasp spread through the crowd, as the soldier stopped and slowly turned.

Now, he was scowling.

"Stupid boy," his father said, grabbing Thor by his shoulder, "go back inside!"

"I shall not!" Thor yelled, shaking off his father's grip.

The soldier stepped towards Thor, and his father backed away.

"Do you know the punishment for insulting the Silver?" the soldier snapped.

Thor's heart pounded, but he knew he could not back down.

"Please forgive him, sire," his father said. "He's a young child and—"

"I'm not speaking to you," the soldier said. With a withering look, he forced his father to look away.

He turned back to Thor.

"Answer me!" he said.

Thor swallowed, unable to speak. This was not how he saw it going in his head.

"To insult the Silver is to insult the King himself," Thor said meekly, reciting what he'd learned from memory.

"Yes," the soldier said. "Which means I can give you forty lashes if I choose."

"I mean no insult, sire," Thor said. "I just want to be picked. Please. I've dreamt of this my entire life. Please. Let me join you."

The soldier stood there, and slowly, his expression softened. After a long while, he shook his head.

"You're young, boy. You have a proud heart. But you're not ready. Come back to us when you are weaned."

With that, he turned and stormed off, barely glancing at the other boys. He quickly mounted his horse.

Thor stood there, crestfallen, and watched as the caravan broke into action; as quickly as they'd arrived, they were gone.

The last thing Thor saw was his brothers, sitting in the back of the last carriage, looking out at him, disapproving, mocking. They were being carted away before his eyes, away from here, into a better life.

Inside, Thor felt like dying.

As the excitement faded all around him, villagers slinked back into their homes.

"Do you realize how stupid you were, foolish boy?" Thor's father snapped, grabbing his shoulders. "Do you realize you could have ruined your brothers' chances?"

Thor brushed his father's hands off of him roughly, and his father reached back and backhanded him across the face.

Thor felt the sting of it, and he glared back at his father. A part of him, for the first time, wanted to hit his father back. But he held himself.

"Go get my sheep and bring them back. Now! And when you return, don't expect a meal from me. You will miss your meal tonight, and think about what you've done."

"Maybe I shall not come back at all!" Thor yelled, as he turned and stormed off, away from his home, towards the hills.

"Thor!" his father screamed, as villagers stopped and watched.

Thor broke into a trot, then a run, wanting to get as far away from this place as possible. As he ran, he barely noticed he was crying, tears flooding his face, as every dream he'd ever had was crushed.

CHAPTER TWO

Thor wandered for hours in the hills, seething, until finally he chose a hill and sat, arms crossed over his legs, and watched the horizon. He watched the carriages disappear, watched the cloud of dust that lingered for hours after.

There would be no more visits. Now he was destined to remain here, in this village, for years, awaiting another chance—if they ever returned. If his father ever allowed it. Now it would be just he and his father, alone in the house, and his father would surely let out the full breadth of his wrath on him. He would continue to be his father's lackey, years would pass, and he would end up just like him, stuck here, living a small, menial life—while his brothers gained glory and renown. His veins burned with the indignity of it all: this was not the life he was meant to live. He knew it.

Thor racked his brain for anything he could do, any way he could change it. But he knew there was nothing. These were the cards life had dealt him.

After hours of sitting, he rose dejectedly and began traversing his way back up the familiar hills, higher and higher. Inevitably, he drifted back towards the flock, to the high knoll. As he climbed, the first sun fell in the sky and the second reached its peak, casting a greenish tint. He took his time as he ambled, mindlessly removing his sling from his waist, its leather grip well-worn from years of use. He reached into his sack, tied to his hip, and fingered his collection of stones, each smoother than the next, hand-picked from the choicest creeks. Sometimes he fired on birds, other times, rodents. It was a habit he'd ingrained over years. At first, he missed everything; then, once, he hit a moving target. Since then, his aim was true. Now, hurling stones had become a part of him—and it helped to release some of his anger. His brothers might be able to swing a sword through a log—but they could never hit a flying bird with a stone like he could.

Thor mindlessly placed a stone in the sling, leaned back and hurled it with all he had, pretending he was hurling it at his father. He hit a branch on a far-off tree, taking it down cleanly. Once he'd discovered he could actually kill moving animals, he'd stopped, afraid at his own power and not wanting to hurt anything; now his targets were branches. Unless of course, it was one of the fox that came after his flock; over time, they had learned to stay clear. His flock, as a result, was the safest kept in the village.

Thor thought of his brothers, of where they were right now, and he steamed. After a day's ride they would arrive in King's Court. He could see it. He saw them arriving to great fanfare, people dressed in their finest greeting them. Warriors greeting them. Members of the Silver. They would be taken in, given a place to live in the Legion's barracks, a place to train in the King's fields, given the finest weapons. Each would be named squire to a famous knight. One day, they would become knights themselves, get their own horse, their own coat of arms, and have their own squire. They would partake in all the festivals, and dine at the King's table. It was a charmed life. And it had slipped from his grasp.

Thor felt physically sick, and tried to force it all from his mind. But he could not. There was a part of him, some deep part, that screamed at him. It told him not to give up, that he had a greater destiny than this. He didn't know what it was, but he knew it wasn't here. He felt he was different. Maybe even special. That no one understood him. And that they all underestimated him.

Thor reached the highest knoll and spotted his flock. Well-trained, they were all still gathered, gnawing away contentedly at whatever grass they could find. He counted them, looking for the red marks he had stained on their backs. But he froze as he finished. One sheep was missing.

He counted again, and again. He couldn't believe it: one was gone.

Thor had never lost a sheep before, and his father would not let him live this down. Worse, he hated the idea of one of his sheep lost, alone, vulnerable in the wilderness. He hated to see anything innocent suffer.

Thor scurried to the top of the knoll and scanned the horizon. He spotted it, far-off, several hills away: the lone sheep, the red mark on its back. It was the wild one of the bunch. His heart dropped as he realized the sheep had not only fled, but had chosen, of all places, to head west, to Darkwood.

Thor gulped. Darkwood was forbidden—not just for sheep, but for humans. It was beyond the village limit, and from the time he could walk, Thor knew not to venture there. He never had. Going there, legend told, was a sure death, its woods unmarked and filled with vicious animals.

Thor looked up at the darkening sky, debating. He couldn't let his sheep go. He figured if he could move fast, he could get it back in time.

After one final look back, he turned and broke into a sprint, heading west, for Darkwood, thick clouds gathering in the sky. He had a sinking feeling, yet his legs seemed to carry him on his own. He felt there was no turning back, even if he wanted to.

It was like running into a nightmare.

*

Thor sped down the series of hills without pausing, into the thick canopy of Darkwood. The trails ended where the wood began, and he ran into unmarked territory, summer leaves crunching beneath his feet.

The instant he entered the wood the sky darkened, blocked by the towering pines above. It was colder in here, too, and as he crossed the threshold, he felt a chill. The chill wasn't just from the dark, or the cold—it was from something else. Something he could not name. It was a sense of…being watched.

Thor looked up at the ancient branches, gnarled, thicker than he, swaying and creaking in the breeze. He had barely gone fifty paces into the wood when he began to hear odd animal noises. He turned and could hardly see the opening from which he'd entered; he felt already as if there were no way out. He hesitated.

Darkwood had always sat on the periphery of the town and on the periphery of his consciousness, something deep and mysterious. Every herder who ever lost a sheep to the wood had never dared venture after it. Even his father. The tales about this place were too dark, too persistent.

But there was something different about today that made Thor no longer care, that made him throw caution to the wind. A part of him wanted to push the boundaries, to get as far away from home as possible, and to allow life to take him where it may.

He ventured farther, then paused, unsure which way to go. He noticed markings, bent branches where his sheep must have gone, and turned in that direction. After some time, he turned again.

3

Before another hour had passed, he was hopelessly lost. He turned and tried to remember the direction from which he came—but was no longer sure. An uneasy feeling settled in his stomach, but he figured the only way out was forward, so he continued on.

In the distance, Thor spotted a shaft of sunlight, and made for it. He found himself before a small clearing, and stopped at its edge. He stood there, rooted: he could not believe what he saw before him.

Standing there, his back to him, dressed in a long, blue satin robe, was a man. No—not a man, Thor could sense it from here. He was something else. A druid, maybe. He stood tall and straight, head covered by a hood, perfectly still, as if he did not have a care in the world.

Thor stood there, not knowing what to do. He had heard of druids, but had never encountered one. From the markings on his robe, the elaborate gold trim, this was no mere druid: those were royal markings. Of the King's court. Thor could not understand it. What was a royal druid doing here?

After what felt like an eternity, the druid slowly turned and faced him, and as he did, Thor recognized the face. It took his breath away. It was one of the most famous faces in the kingdom: the King's personal druid. Argon, counselor to kings of the Western Kingdom for centuries. What he was doing here, far from the royal court, in the center of Darkwood, was a mystery. Thor wondered if he were imagining it.

"Your eyes do not deceive you," Argon said, staring right at Thor.

His voice was deep, ancient, as if spoken by the trees themselves. His large, translucent eyes seemed to bore right through Thor, summing him up. He felt an intense energy radiating off of him—as if he were standing opposite the sun.

Thor immediately took a knee and bowed his head.

"My liege," he said. "I'm sorry to have disturbed you."

Thor knew that disrespect towards a King's counselor would result in imprisonment or death. It had been ingrained in him since the time he was born.

"Stand up, child," Argon said. "If I wanted you to kneel, I would have told you."

Slowly, Thor stood and looked at him. Argon took several steps closer. He stood there and stared, until Thor began to feel uncomfortable.

"You have your mother's eyes," Argon said.

4

Thor was taken aback. He had never met his mother, and had never met anyone, aside from his father, who knew her. From what he was told, she had died in childbirth, something for which Thor always felt a sense of guilt. He had always suspected that that was why his family hated him.

"I think you're mistaking me for someone else," Thor said. "I don't have a mother."

"Don't you?" Argon asked with a smile. "Were you born by man alone?"

"I meant to say, sire, that my mother died in birth. I think you mistake me."

"You are Thorgrin, of the Clan McLeod. The youngest of four brothers. The one not picked."

Thor's eyes opened wide. He hardly knew what to make of this. That someone of Argon's stature should know who he was—it was more than he could comprehend. He didn't even imagine that he was known to anyone outside his village.

"How...do you know this?"

Argon smiled back, but did not respond.

Thor was suddenly filled with curiosity.

"How..." Thor added, fumbling for words, "...how do you know my mother? Have you met her? Who was she?"

Argon turned and walked away.

"Questions for another time," he said, his back to him.

Thor watched him go, puzzled. It was such a dizzying and mysterious encounter, and it was all happening so fast. He decided he could not let him leave; he hurried after him.

"What are you doing here?" he asked, hurrying to catch up. Argon, using his staff, an ancient ivory thing, walked deceptively fast. "You were not waiting for *me*, were you?"

"Who else?" Argon asked.

Thor hurried to catch up, following him into the wood, leaving the clearing behind.

"But why me? How did you know I would be here? What is it that you want?"

"So many questions," Argon said. "You fill the air. You should listen instead."

Thor followed him as he continued through the thick wood, doing his best to remain silent.

5

"You come in search of your lost sheep," Argon stated. "A noble effort. But you waste your time. She will not survive."

Thor's eyes opened wide.

"How do you know this?"

"I know worlds you will never know, boy. At least, not yet."

Thor wondered as he hiked to catch up.

"You won't listen, though. That is your nature. Stubborn. Like your mother. You will continue after your sheep, determined to rescue her."

Thor reddened as Argon read his thoughts.

"You are a feisty boy," he added. "Strong-willed. Too proud. Positive traits. But one day it may be your downfall."

Argon began to hike up a mossy ridge, and Thor followed.

"You want to join the King's Legion," he said.

"Yes!" Thor answered, excitedly. "Is there any chance for me? Can you make that happen?"

Argon laughed, a deep, hollow sound that sent a chill up Thor's spine.

"I can make everything and nothing happen. Your destiny was already written. But it is up to you to choose it."

Thor did not understand.

They reached the top of the ridge, and as they did Argon stopped and faced him. Thor stood only feet away, and Argon's energy burned through him.

"Your destiny is an important one," he said. "Do not abandon it."

Thor's eyed widened. His destiny? Important? He felt himself well with pride.

"I do not understand. You speak in riddles. Please, tell me more."

Suddenly, Argon vanished.

Thor could hardly believe it. He looked every which way. He stood there, listening, wondering. Had he imagined it all? Was it some delusion?

Thor turned and examined the wood; from this vantage point, high up on the ridge, he could see farther than before. As he looked, he spotted motion, in the distance. He heard a noise, and felt sure it was his sheep.

He stumbled down the mossy ridge and hurried in that direction, back through the wood. As he went, he could not shake his encounter with Argon. He could hardly conceive it had happened. What was the

King's druid doing here, of all places? He had been waiting for him. But why? And what had he meant about his destiny?

The more Thor tried to unravel it, the less he understood. Argon was both warning him not to continue and at the same time tempting him to do so. Now, as he went, Thor felt an increasing sense of foreboding, as if something momentous were about to happen.

As he turned a bend, he stopped cold in his tracks at the view before him. All of his worst nightmares were confirmed in a single moment. His hair stood on end, and he realized he had made a grave mistake in coming here, this deep into Darkwood.

There, opposite him, hardly thirty paces away, was a Sybold. Hulking, muscular, standing on all fours, nearly the size of a horse, it was the most feared animal of Darkwood, maybe even of the kingdom. Thor had never seen one, but had heard legends. It resembled a lion, but was bigger, broader, its hide a deep scarlet and its eyes a glowing yellow. Legend had it that its scarlet color came from the blood of innocent children.

Thor had heard of few sightings of this beast his entire life, and even these were thought to be dubious. Maybe that was because no one ever actually survived an encounter. Some considered the Sybold to be the God of the Woods, and an omen. What that omen was, Thor had no idea.

He took a careful step back.

The Sybold stood there, its huge jaws half-open, its fangs dripping saliva, staring back with its yellow eyes. In its mouth was Thor's missing sheep: screaming, hanging upside down, half of its body pierced by fangs. It was mostly dead. The Sybold seemed to revel in the kill, taking its time; it seemed to delight in torturing it.

Thor could not stand the sound of the cries. It wiggled, helpless, and he felt responsible.

Thor's first impulse was to turn and run; but he already knew that would be futile. He would never outrun this beast, which could outrun anything. Running would only embolden it. And he could not leave his sheep to die like that.

He stood there, frozen in fear, and knew he had to take action of some sort.

Thor felt his reflexes take over. He slowly reached down, extracted a stone, and placed it in his sling. With a trembling hand, he wound up, took a step forward, and hurled.

The stone sailed through the air and hit its mark. It was a perfect shot. It hit the sheep in its eyeball, driving through to its brain.

The sheep went limp. Dead. Thor had spared this animal its suffering.

The Sybold glared at Thor, enraged that Thor had killed its plaything. It slowly opened its immense jaws and dropped the sheep, which landed with a thump on the forest floor. Then it set its eyes on Thor.

It snarled, a deep, evil sound, rising up from its belly.

As it started hulking towards him, Thor, heart pounding, placed another stone in his sling, reached back, and prepared to fire once again.

The Sybold broke into a sprint, moving faster than anything Thor had ever seen in his life. Thor took a step forward and hurled the stone, praying that it hit, knowing he wouldn't have time to sling another before it arrived.

The stone hit the beast in its right eye, knocking it out. It was a tremendous throw, one that would've brought a lesser animal to its knees.

But this was no lesser animal. The beast was unstoppable. It shrieked at the damage, but never even slowed. Even without one eye, even with the stone lodged in its brain, it continued to charge mindlessly at Thor. There was nothing Thor could do.

A moment later, the beast was on him. It wound up with its huge claw, and swiped his arm.

Thor shrieked. It felt like three knives cutting across his flesh, as he felt hot blood gush out of it.

The beast pinned him to the ground, on all fours. The weight of it was immense, like an elephant standing on his chest. Thor felt his ribcage being crushed.

The beast pulled back its head, opened wide its jaws, revealed its fangs, and began to lower them for Thor's throat.

As it did, Thor reached up and grabbed its neck; it was like grabbing onto solid muscle. Thor could barely hang on. His arms started to shake, as the fangs descended lower. He felt its hot breath all over his face, felt the saliva drip down onto his neck. A rumble came from deep within the animal's chest, burning Thor's ears. He knew he would die.

Thor closed his eyes.

Please God. Give me strength. Allow me to fight this creature. Please. I beg you. I will do anything you ask. I will owe you a great debt.

And then, something happened. Thor felt a tremendous heat rise up within his body, course through his veins, like an energy field racing through him. As he opened his eyes, he saw something that surprised him: from his palms there emanated a yellow light, and as he pushed back into the beast's throat, amazingly, he was able to match its strength, to hold it at bay.

Thor continued to push, and realized he was actually pushing the beast back. His strength grew and he felt a cannonball of energy—and a moment later, the beast went flying backwards, Thor sending it a good ten feet. It landed on its back.

Thor sat up, not understanding what had happened.

The beast regained its feet. Then, in a rage, it charged again—but this time Thor felt different. He felt the energy course through him, and felt more powerful than he had ever been.

As the beast leapt into the air, Thor crouched down, grabbed it by its stomach and hurled it, letting its momentum carry it.

The beast flew through the wood, smashed into a tree, then collapsed to the floor.

Thor turned, amazed. Had he just thrown a Sybold?

The beast blinked twice, then looked at Thor. It charged again.

This time, as the beast pounced, Thor grabbed it by its throat. They both went to the ground, the beast on top of Thor. But Thor rolled over, on top of it. Thor held it, choking it with both hands, as the beast kept trying to raise its head, snap its fangs at him. It just missed. Thor, feeling a new strength, dug his hands in and did not let go. He let the energy course through him. And soon, amazingly, he felt himself stronger than the beast.

Moments later, he realized he was choking the beast to death. Finally, the beast went limp.

Thor did not let go for another full minute.

He stood slowly, out of breath, staring down, wide-eyed, as he held his wounded arm. He could not believe what had just happened. Had he, Thor, just killed a Sybold?

He felt it was a sign, on this day of all days. He felt as if something momentous had happened. He had just killed the most famed and feared beast of his kingdom. Single-handedly. Without a weapon. It did not seem real. No one would believe him.

9

He stood there, reeling, wondering what power had overcome him, what it meant, who he really was. The only people known to have power like that were Druids. But his father and mother were not druids, so he couldn't be one.

Or could he be?

Thor suddenly sensed someone behind him, and spun to see Argon standing there, staring down at the animal.

"How did you get here?" Thor asked, amazed.

Argon ignored him.

"Did you witness what happened?" Thor asked, still unbelieving. "I don't know how I did it."

"But you do know," Argon answered. "Deep inside, you know. You are different than the others."

"It was like…a surge of power," Thor said. "Like a strength I didn't know I had."

"The energy field," Argon said. "One day you will come to know it quite well. You may even learn to control it."

Thor clutched his shoulder, the pain excruciating. He looked down and saw his hand covered in blood. He felt lightheaded, worried what would happen if he didn't get help.

Argon took three steps forward, reached out, grabbed Thor's free hand, and placed it firmly on his wound. He held it there, leaned back, and closed his eyes.

As he did, Thor felt a warm sensation course through his arm. Within seconds, the sticky blood on his hand dried up, and he felt his pain begin to fade.

He looked down, and could not comprehend it: his arm was healed. All that remained were three scars where the claws had cut— but they looked to be several days old. They were sealed. There was no more blood.

Thor looked at Argon in astonishment.

"How did you do that?" he asked.

Argon smiled.

"I didn't. *You* did. I just directed your power."

"But I don't have the power to heal," Thor answered, baffled.

"Don't you?" Argon replied.

"I don't understand. None of this is making any sense," Thor said, increasingly impatient. "Please, tell me."

Argon looked away.

"Some things you must learn over time."

Thor thought of something.

"Does this mean I can join the King's Legion?" he asked, excitedly. "Surely, if I can kill a Sybold, then I can hold my own with other boys."

"Surely you can," he answered.

"But they chose my brothers—they didn't choose me."

"Your brothers couldn't have killed this beast."

Thor stared back, thinking.

"But they have already rejected me. How can I join them?"

"Since when does a warrior need an invitation?" Argon asked.

His words sunk in deep. Thor felt his body warming over.

"Are you saying I should just show up? Uninvited?"

Argon smiled.

"*You* create your destiny. Others do not."

Thor blinked—and a moment later, Argon was gone.

Thor couldn't believe it. He spun around the wood in every direction, but there was no trace of him.

"Over here!" came a voice.

Thor turned and saw a huge boulder before him. He sensed the voice came from up top, and he immediately climbed it.

He reached the top, and was puzzled to see no sign of Argon.

From this vantage point, though, he was able to see above the treetops of Darkwood. He saw where Darkwood ended, saw the second sun setting in a dark green, and beyond that, the road leading to King's Court.

"The road is yours to take," came the voice. "If you dare."

Thor spun but saw nothing. It was just a voice, echoing. But he knew Argon was there, somewhere, egging him on. And he felt, deep down, that he was right.

Without another moment's hesitation, Thor scrambled down the rock and set off, through the wood, for the distant road.

Sprinting for his destiny.

CHAPTER THREE

King MacGil, stout, barrel chested, with a beard too thick with gray, long hair to match, and a broad forehead lined with too many battles, stood on the upper ramparts of his castle, his queen beside him, and overlooked the day's burgeoning festivities. His royal grounds sprawled out beneath him in all their glory, stretching as far as the eye could see, a thriving city walled in by ancient stone fortifications. King's Court. Interconnected by a maze of winding streets sat stone buildings of every shape and size—for the warriors, the caretakers, the horses, the Silver, the Legion, the guards, the barracks, the weapons house, the armory—and among these, hundreds of dwellings for the multitude of his people who chose to live within the city walls. Between these spanned acres of grass, royal gardens, stone-lined plazas, overflowing fountains. King's Court had been improved upon for centuries, by his father, and his father before him—and it sat now at the peak of its glory. Without doubt, it was now the safest stronghold within the Western Kingdom of the Ring.

MacGil was blessed with the finest and most loyal warriors any king had ever known, and in his lifetime, no one had dared attack. The seventh MacGil to hold the throne, he had held it well for his thirty two years of rule, had been a good and wise king. The land had prospered greatly in his reign, he had doubled his army's size, expanded his cities, brought his people bounty, and not a single complaint could be found among his people. He was known as the generous king, and there had never been such a period of bounty and peace since he took the throne.

Which, paradoxically, was precisely what kept MacGil up at night. For MacGil knew his history: in all the ages, there had never been as long a stretch without a war. He no longer wondered *if* there would be an attack—but when. And from whom.

The greatest threat, of course, was from beyond the Ring, from the empire of savages that ruled the outlying Wilds, which had subjugated all the peoples outside the Ring, beyond the Canyon. For MacGil, and the seven generations before him, the Wilds had never

12

posed a direct threat: because of his kingdom's unique geography, shaped in a perfect circle, in a ring, and separated from the rest of the world by a deep canyon a mile wide, and protected by an energy shield within it that had been active since a MacGil first ruled, they had little to fear of the Wilds. The savages had tried many times to attack, to penetrate the shield, to cross the canyon; not once had they been successful. As long as he and his people stayed within the Ring, there was no outside threat.

That did not mean, though, that there was no threat from inside. And that was what had kept MacGil up at night lately. That, indeed, was the purpose of the day's festivities: the marriage of his eldest daughter. A marriage arranged specifically to appease his enemies, to maintain the fragile peace within the Eastern and Western Kingdoms of the Ring.

While the Ring spanned a good five hundred miles in each direction, it was divided down the middle by a mountain range. The Highlands. On the other side of the Highlands sat the Eastern Kingdom, ruling the other half of the Ring. And this kingdom, ruled for centuries by their rivals, the McClouds, had always tried to shatter its fragile truce with the MacGils. The McClouds were malcontents, unhappy with their lot, convinced their side of the kingdom sat on ground less fertile. They contested the Highlands, too, insisting the entire mountain range was theirs, when at least half of it was the MacGil's. There were perpetual border skirmishes, and perpetual threats of invasion.

As MacGil pondered it all, he was annoyed. The McClouds should be happy: they were safe inside the Ring, protected by the Canyon, they sat on choice land, and had nothing to fear. They should just be content with their own half of the Ring. It was only because MacGil had grown his army so strong that, for the first time in history, the McClouds had dared not attack. But MacGil, the wise king he was, sensed something on the horizon; he knew this peace could not last. Thus he had arranged this marriage of his eldest daughter to the eldest prince of the McClouds. And now the day had arrived.

As he looked down, he saw stretched below him thousands of minions, dressed in brightly colored tunics, filtering in from every corner of the kingdom, from both sides of the Highlands. Nearly the entire Ring, all pouring into his fortifications. His people had prepared for months, commanded to make everything look prosperous, strong.

13

This was not just a day for marriage: it was a day to send a message to the McClouds.

MacGil surveyed his hundreds of soldiers, lined up strategically along the ramparts, in the streets, along the walls, more soldiers than he could ever need—and felt satisfied. It was the show of strength he wanted. But he also felt on edge: the environment was charged, ripe for a skirmish. He hoped no hotheads, inflamed with drink, rose up on either side. He scanned the jousting fields, the playing fields, and thought of the day to come, filled with games and jousts and all sorts of festivities. They would be charged. The McClouds would surely show up with their own small army, and every joust, every wrestle, every competition, would take on meaning. If one went awry, it could evolve into a battle.

"My king?"

He felt a soft hand on his, and turned and saw his queen, Krea, still the most beautiful woman he'd ever known. Happily married his entire reign, she had borne him five children, three of them boys, and had not complained once. Moreover, she had become his most trusted counselor. As the years had passed, he had come to learn that she was wiser than all of his men. Indeed, wiser than he.

"It is a political day," she said. "But also our daughter's wedding. Try to enjoy. It won't happen twice."

"I worried less when I had nothing," he answered. "Now that we have it all, everything worries me. We are safe. But I don't feel safe."

She looked back at him with compassionate eyes, large and hazel; they looked as if they held the wisdom of the world. Her eyelids drooped, as they always had, looking just a bit sleepy, and were framed by her beautiful, straight brown hair, which fell on both sides of her face, tinged with gray. She had a few more lines, but she hadn't changed a bit.

"That's because you're not safe," she said. "No king is safe. There are more spies in our court than you'll ever care to know. And that is the way of things."

She leaned in and kissed him, and smiled.

"Try to enjoy it," she said. "It is a wedding after all."

With that, she turned and walked off the ramparts.

He watched her go, then turned and looked back out over his court. She was right; she was always right. He did want to enjoy it. He loved his eldest daughter, and it was a wedding after all. It was the most beautiful day of the most beautiful time of year, spring at its height, and summer dawning, the two suns perfect in the sky, and the slightest of breezes astir. Everything was in full bloom, trees everywhere awash in a broad palette of pinks and purples and oranges and white. There was nothing he'd like more than to go down and sit with his men, watch his daughter get married, and drink pints of ale until he could drink no more.

But he could not. He had a long course of duties before he could even step out of his castle. After all, the day of a daughter's wedding meant obligation for a king: he had to meet with his council; with his children; and with a long a line of supplicants who had a right to see the king on this day. He would be lucky if he left his castle in time for the sunset ceremony.

*

MacGil, dressed in his finest royal garb, velvet black pants, a golden belt, a royal robe made of the finest purple and gold silk, donning his white mantle, shiny leather boots up to his calves, and wearing his crown—an ornate gold band with a large ruby set in its center—strutted down the castle halls, flanked by attendants. He strode through room after room, descending the steps from the parapet, cutting through his royal chambers, through the great arched hall, with its soaring ceiling and rows of stained glass. Finally, he reached an ancient oak door, thick as a tree trunk, and his attendants opened it and stepped aside. The Throne Room.

His advisers stood at attention as MacGil entered, the door slammed shut behind him.

"Be seated," he said, more abrupt than usual. He was tired, on this day especially, of the endless formalities of ruling the kingdom, and wanted to get them over with.

He strode across the Throne Room, which never ceased to impress him, its ceilings soaring fifty feet, one entire wall a panel of stained glass, floors and walls made of stone a foot thick. The room could easily hold a hundred dignitaries. But on days like this, when his council convened, it was just him and his handful of advisers in the cavernous setting. The room was dominated by a vast table, shaped in a semi-circle, behind which his advisors stood.

He strutted through the opening, right down the middle, to his throne. He ascended the stone steps, passed the carved golden lions, then sank into the red velvet cushion lining his throne, carved from a single block of gold. His father had sat on this throne, as had *his* father, and all the MacGils before him. When he sat, MacGil felt the weight of his ancestors, of all the generations, with him.

He surveyed the advisors in attendance. There was Brom, his greatest general, and advisor on military affairs; Kolk, the general of the boys' Legion; Aberthol, the oldest of the bunch, a scholar and historian, mentor of kings for three generations; Firth, his advisor on internal affairs of the court, a skinny man with short, gray hair and hollowed out eyes that never sat still. He was not a man that MacGil had ever trusted, and he never even understood his title. But his father, and his before him, kept an advisor for court affairs, and so he kept it out of respect for them. There was Owen, his treasurer; Bradaigh, his advisor on external affairs; Earnan, his tax collector; Duwayne, his advisor on the masses; and Kelvin, the representative of the nobles.

Of course, the King had absolute authority. But his kingdom was a liberal one, and his fathers had always taken pride in allowing the nobles a voice in all matters, channeled through their representative. It was historically an uneasy power balance between the kingship and the nobles. Now there was harmony, but during other times there had been uprisings, power struggles, between the nobles and royalty. It was a fine balance.

As MacGil surveyed the room he noticed one person missing: the very man he wanted to speak with most. Argon. As usual, when and where he showed up was unpredictable. It infuriated MacGil to no end, but he had no choice but to accept it. The way of druids was inscrutable to him. Without him present, MacGil felt even more haste. He wanted to get through this, get to the thousand other things that awaited him before the wedding.

The group of advisers sat, facing him around the semi-circular table, spread out every ten feet, each sitting in a chair of ancient oak with elaborate carved wooden handles.

"My liege, if I may begin," Owen called out.

"You may. And keep it short. My time is tight today."

"Your daughter will receive a great many gift today, which we all hope will fill her coffers. The thousands of people paying tribute, presenting gifts to you personally, and filling our brothels and taverns, will help fill the coffers, too. And yet the preparation for today's festivities will also deplete a good portion of the royal treasury. I recommend an increase of tax on the people, and on the nobles. A one-time tax, to alleviate the pressures of this great event."

MacGil saw the concern on his treasurer's face, and his stomach sank at the thought of the treasury's depletion. Yet he would not raise taxes again.

"Better to have a poor treasury and loyal subjects," MacGil answered. "Our riches come in the happiness of our subjects. We shall not impose more."

"But my liege, if we do not—"

"I have decided. What else?"

Owen sank back, crestfallen.

"My king," Brom said, in his deep voice. "At your command, we have stationed the bulk of our forces in court for today's event. The show of power will be impressive. But we are stretched thin. If there should be an attack elsewhere in the kingdom, we will be vulnerable."

MacGil nodded, thinking it through.

"Our enemies will not attack us while we are feeding them."

The men laughed.

"And what news from the Highlands?"

"There has been no reported activity for weeks. It seems their troops have drawn down in preparation for the wedding. Maybe they are ready to make peace."

MacGil was not so sure.

"That either means the arranged wedding has worked, or they wait to attack us at another time. And which do you think it is, old man?" MacGil asked, turning to Aberthol.

Aberthol cleared his throat, his voice raspy as it came out: "My liege, your father and his father before him never trusted the McClouds. Just because they lie sleeping, does not mean they will not wake."

MacGil nodded, appreciating the sentiment.

"And what of the Legion?" he asked, turning to Kolk.

"Today we welcomed the new recruits," Kolk answered, with a quick nod.

"My son among them?" MacGil asked.

"He stands proudly with them all, and a fine boy he is."

MacGil nodded, then turned to Bradaigh.

"And what word from beyond the Canyon?"

17

"My liege, our patrols have seen more attempts to bridge the Canyon in recent weeks. There may be signs that the Wilds are mobilizing for an attack."

A hushed whisper spread amongst the men. MacGil felt his stomach tighten at the thought. The energy shield was invincible; still, it did not bode well.

"And what if there should be a full-scale attack?" he asked.

"As long as the shield is active, we have nothing to fear. The Wilds have not succeeded in breaching the Canyon for centuries. There is no reason to think otherwise."

MacGil was not so certain. An attack from outside was long overdue, and he could not help but wonder when it might be.

"My liege," Firth said in his nasally voice, "I feel obliged to add that today our court is filled with many dignitaries from the McCloud kingdom. It would be considered an insult for you not to entertain them, rivals or not. I would advise that you use your afternoon hours to greet each one. They have brought a large entourage, many gifts—and, word is, many spies."

"Who is to say the spies are not already here?" MacGil asked back, looking carefully at Firth as he did—and wondering, as always, if he might be one himself.

Firth opened his mouth to answer, but MacGil sighed and held up a palm, having had enough. "If that is all, I will leave now, to join my daughter's wedding."

"My liege," Kelvin said, clearing his throat, "of course, there is one more thing. The tradition, on the day of your eldest's wedding. Every MacGil has named a successor. The people shall expect you to do the same. They have been buzzing about. It would not be advisable to let them down. Especially with the Dynasty Sword still immobile."

"Would you have me name an heir while I am still in my prime?" MacGil asked.

"My liege, I mean no offense," Kelvin stumbled, looking concerned.

MacGil held up a hand. "I know the tradition. And indeed, I shall name one today."

"Might you inform us as to who?" Firth asked.

MacGil stared him down, annoyed. He was a gossip, and he did not trust this man.

"You will learn of the news when the time is right."

MacGil stood, and the others rose, too. They bowed, turned, and hurried from the room.

MacGil stood there, thinking, for he did not know how long. It was on days like this that he wished he was not king.

*

MacGil stepped down from his throne, boots echoing in the silence, and crossed the room. He opened the ancient oak door himself, yanking the iron handle, and entered a side chamber.

He enjoyed the peace and solitude of this cozy room, as he always had, its walls hardly twenty paces in either direction yet with a soaring, arched ceiling. The room was made entirely of stone, with a small, round piece of stained glass on one wall. Light poured in through its yellows and reds, lighting up a single object in the otherwise bare room.

The Dynasty Sword.

There it sat, in the center of the chamber, lying horizontal, on iron prongs, like a temptress. As he had since he was a boy, MacGil walked close to it, circled it, examined it. The Dynasty Sword. The sword of legend, the source of strength and power of his entire kingdom, from one generation to the next. Whoever had the strength to hoist it would be the Chosen One, the one destined to rule the kingdom for life, to free the kingdom from all threats, in and outside the Ring. It had been a beautiful legend to grow up with, and as soon as he was anointed king, MacGil had tried to hoist it himself, as only MacGil kings were even allowed to try. The kings before him, all of them, had failed. He was sure he would be different. He was sure he would be The One.

But he was wrong. As were all the other MacGil kings before him. And his failure had tainted his kingship ever since.

As he stared at it now, he examined its long blade, made of a mysterious metal no one had ever deciphered. The sword's origin was even more obscure, rumored to have risen from the earth in the midst of a quake.

Examining it, he once again felt the sting of failure. He might be a good king; but he was not The One. His people knew it. His enemies knew it. He might be a good king, but no matter what he did, he would never be The One.

If he had been, he suspected there would be less unrest amongst his court, less plotting. His own people would trust him more and his enemies would not even consider attack. A part of him wished the sword would just disappear, and the legend with it. But he knew it would not. That was the curse—and the power—of a legend. Stronger, even, than an army.

As he stared at it for the thousandth time, MacGil couldn't help but wonder once again who it would be. Who of his bloodline would be destined to wield it? As he thought of what lay before him, his task of naming an heir, he wondered who, if any, would be destined to hoist it.

"The weight of the blade is heavy," came a voice.

MacGil spun, surprised to have company in the small room.

There, standing in the door, was Argon. MacGil recognized the voice before he saw him and was both irritated for his not showing up sooner and pleased to have him here now.

"You're late," MacGil said.

"Your sense of time does not apply to me," Argon answered.

MacGil turned back to the sword.

"Did you ever think I would be able to hoist it?" he asked reflectively. "That day I became king?"

"No," Argon answered flatly.

MacGil turned and stared at him.

"You knew I would not be able to. You saw it, didn't you?"

"Yes."

MacGil pondered this.

"It scares me when you answer directly. That is unlike you."

Argon stayed silent, and finally MacGil realized he wouldn't say anymore.

"I name my successor today," MacGil said. "It feels futile, to name an heir on this day. It strips a king's joy from his child's wedding."

"Maybe such joy is meant to be tempered."

"But I have so many years left to reign," MacGil pleaded.

"Perhaps not as many as you think," Argon answered.

MacGil narrowed his eyes at Argon, wondering. Was it a message?

But Argon added nothing more.

"Six children. Which should I pick?" MacGil asked.

"Why ask me? You have already chosen."

MacGil looked at him. "You see much. Yes, I have. But I still want to know what you think."

"I think you made a wise choice," Argon said. "But remember: a king cannot rule from beyond the grave. Regardless of who you think you choose, fate has a way of choosing for itself."

"Will I live, Argon?" MacGil asked earnestly, asking the question he had wanted to know since he had awakened the night before from a horrific nightmare.

"I dreamt last night of a crow," he added. "It came and stole my crown. Then another carried me away. As it did, I saw my kingdom spread beneath me. It turned black as I went. Barren. A wasteland."

He looked up at Argon, his eyes watery.

"Was it a dream? Or something more?"

"Dreams are always something more, aren't they?" Argon asked.

MacGil was struck by a sinking feeling.

"Where is the danger? Just tell me this much."

Argon stepped close and stared into his eyes, with such an intensity that MacGil felt as if he were staring into another realm itself.

Argon leaned forward, whispered:

"Always closer than you think."

CHAPTER FOUR

Thor hid in the straw in the back of a wagon as it jostled him on the country road. He'd made his way to the road the night before and had waited patiently until a wagon came along large enough for him to board and not be noticed. It was dark by then, and the wagon trotted along just slowly enough for him to gain a good running pace and leap in from behind. He'd landed in the hay, and buried himself inside. Luckily, the driver had not spotted him. Thor hadn't known for certain if the wagon was going to King's Court, but it was heading in that direction, and a wagon this size, and with these markings, could be going few other places.

As Thor rode throughout the night, he had stayed awake for hours, thinking of his encounter with the beast. With Argon. Of his destiny. His former home. His mother. He felt that the universe had answered him, had told him that he had another destiny. He had lay there, hands clasped behind his head, and stared up at the night sky, visible through the tattered canvas. He'd watched the universe, so bright, its red stars so far away. He was exhilarated. For once in his life, he was on a journey. He did not know where, but he was going. One way or the other, he would make his way to King's Court.

When Thor opened his eyes it was morning, light flooding in, and he realized he'd drifted off. He sat up quickly, looking all around, chiding himself for sleeping. He should have been more vigilant—he was lucky he had not been discovered.

The cart still moved, but did not jostle as much. That could only mean one thing: a better road. They must be close to a city. Thor looked down, and saw how smooth the road was, free of rocks, of ditches, and lined with fine white shells. His heart beat faster: they were approaching King's Court.

Thor looked out the back of the cart, and was overwhelmed: the immaculate streets were flooded with activity. Dozens of carts, of all shapes and sizes, carrying all manner of things, filled the roads; one was laden with furs; another, with rugs; another, with chickens.

Amidst them walked hundreds of merchants, some leading cattle, others carrying baskets of goods on their heads. Four men carried a bundle of silks, balancing them on poles. It was an army of people, all heading in one direction.

Thor felt alive. He'd never seen so many people at once, so many goods, so much happening. He'd been in a small village his entire life, and now he was in a hub, engulfed in humanity.

He heard a loud noise, the groaning of chains, the slamming of a huge piece of wood, so strong the ground shook. Moments later, he heard a different sound, of horses' hooves clacking on wood. He looked down, and realized they were crossing a bridge; beneath them passed a moat. A drawbridge.

Thor stuck his head out and saw immense stone pillars, the spiked iron gate above. They were passing through King's Gate.

It was the largest gate he had ever seen. He looked up at the spikes, and marveled that if they came down, they would slice him in half. He spotted four of the king's Silver, guarding the entry, and his heart beat faster.

They passed through a long, stone tunnel, then moments later the sky opened again. They were inside King's Court.

Thor could hardly believe it. There was even more activity here, if possible—what seemed to be thousands of people, milling in every direction. There were vast stretches of grass, perfectly cut, and flowers blooming everywhere. The road widened, and alongside it were booths, vendors, and everywhere, stone buildings. And amidst all of these, the King's men. Soldiers, bedecked in armor. Thor had made it.

In his excitement, he unwittingly stood; as he did, the cart stopped short, and he went flying backwards, landing on his back in the straw. Before he could rise, there was the sound of wood lowered, and he looked up to see an angry old man, bald, dressed in rags, scowling. The cart driver reached in, grabbed Thor by the ankles with his bony hands, and dragged him out the back.

Thor went flying, landing hard on his back on the dirt road, raising up a cloud of dust. Laughter rose up around him.

"Next time you ride my cart, boy, it will be the shackles for you! You're lucky I don't summon the Silver now!"

The old man turned and spat, then hurried back on his cart and whipped his horses on.

Thor, embarrassed, slowly gained his wits and got to his feet. He looked around: one or two passersby chuckled, and Thor sneered back until they looked away. He brushed the dirt off and rubbed his arms; his pride was hurt, but not his body.

His spirits returned as he looked around, dazzled, and realized he should be happy that at least he'd made it this far. Now that he was out of the cart he could look around freely, and an extraordinary sight it was: the court sprawled as far as the eye could see. At its center sat a magnificent stone palace, surrounded by towering, fortified stone walls, crowned by parapets, atop which, everywhere, patrolled the King's army. All around him were fields of green, perfectly maintained, stone plazas, fountains, groves of trees. It was a city. And it was flooded with people.

Everywhere streamed all manner of people—merchants, soldiers, dignitaries—everyone in such a rush. It took Thor several minutes to realize that something special was happening. As he ambled along, he saw preparations being made, chairs placed, an altar erected. It looked like they were preparing for a wedding.

His heart skipped a beat as he saw, in the distance, a jousting lane, with its long dirt path and a rope dividing it. On another field, he saw soldiers hurling spears at far-off targets; on another, archers, aiming at straw. It seemed as if everywhere were games, contests. There was also music, lutes and flutes and cymbals, packs of musicians wandering; and wine, huge vats being rolled out; and food, tables being prepared, banquets stretching as far as the eye could see. It was as if he'd arrived in the midst of a vast celebration.

As dazzling as all this was, Thor felt an urgency to find the Legion. He was already late, and he needed to make himself known.

He hurried to the first person he saw, an older man who seemed, by his blood-stained frock, to be a butcher, hurrying down the road. Everyone here was in such a hurry.

"Excuse me, sir," Thor said, grabbing his arm.

The man looked down at Thor's hand disparagingly.

"What is it, boy?"

"I'm looking for the King's Legion. Do you know where they train?"

"Do I look like a map?" the man hissed, and stormed off.

Thor was taken aback by his rudeness.

He hurried to the next person he saw, a woman kneading flower on a long table. There were several women at this table, all working hard, and Thor figured one of them had to know.

"Excuse me, miss," he said. "Might you know where the King's Legion train?"

They looked at each other and giggled, some of them but a few years older than he.

The eldest turned and looked at him.

"You're looking in the wrong place," she said. "Here, we are preparing for the festivities."

"But I was told they trained in King's Court," Thor said, confused.

The women broke into another chuckle. The eldest put her hands on her hips and shook her head.

"You act as if this is your first time in King's Court. Have you no idea how big it is?"

Thor reddened as the other women laughed, then finally stormed off. He did not like being made fun of.

He saw before him a dozen roads, twisting and turning every which way through King's Court. Spaced out in the stone walls were at least a dozen entrances. The size and scope of this place was overwhelming. He had a sinking feeling he could search for days and still not find it.

An idea struck him: surely, a soldier would know where the others train. He was nervous to approach an actual king's soldier, but realized he had to.

He turned and hurried to the wall, to the soldier standing guard at the closest entrance, hoping he would not throw him out. The soldier stood erect, looking straight ahead.

"I'm looking for the King's Legion," Thor said, summoning his bravest voice.

The soldier continued to stare straight ahead, ignoring him.

"I said I'm looking for the King's Legion!" Thor insisted, louder, determined to be recognized.

After several seconds, the soldier glanced down, sneering.

"Can you tell me where it is?" Thor pressed.

"And what business have you with them?"

"Very important business," Thor urged, hoping the soldier would not press him.

The soldier turned back to looking straight ahead, ignoring him again. Thor felt his heart sinking, afraid he would never receive an answer.

But after what felt like an eternity, he replied: "Take the eastern gate, then head north as far as you can. Take the third gate to the left, then fork right, and fork right again. Pass through the second stone arch, and their ground is beyond the gate. But I tell you you waste your time: they do not entertain visitors."

It was all Thor needed to hear. Without missing another beat, he turned and ran across the field, following the directions, repeating them in his head, trying to memorize them. He noticed the sun higher in the sky, and only prayed that when he arrived, it would not already be too late.

*

Thor sprinted down the immaculate, shell-lined paths, twisting and turning his way through King's Court. He tried his best to follow the directions, hoping he was not being led astray. As he reached the far end of the courtyard, he saw all the gates, and chose the third one on the left. He ran through it and then followed the forks, turning down path after path. He ran against traffic, thousands of people pouring into the city, the crowd growing thicker by the minute. He brushed shoulders with lute players, jugglers, clowns, and all sorts of entertainers, everyone dressed in fineries.

Thor could not stand the thought of the selection process beginning without him, and he tried his best to concentrate as he turned down path after path, looking for any sign of the training ground. He passed through an arch, turned down another road, and then, far off, he spotted what could only be his destination: a mini colosseum, built of stone, in a perfect circle. It had a huge gate in its center, guarded by soldiers. Thor heard a muted cheering from behind its walls and his heart quickened. This was the place.

He sprinted, lungs bursting. As he reached the gate, two guards stepped forward and lowered their lances, barring the way. A third guard stepped forward and held out a palm.

"Stop there," he commanded.

Thor stopped short, gasping for breath, barely able to contain his excitement.

"You…don't…understand," he heaved, words tumbling out between breaths, "I have to be inside. I'm late."

"Late for what?"

"The selection."

26

The guard, a short, heavy man with pockmarked skin, turned and looked at the others, who looked back cynically. He turned and surveyed Thor with a disparaging look.

"The recruits were taken in hours ago, in the royal transport. If you were not invited, you cannot enter."

"But you don't understand. I must—"

The guard reached out and grabbed Thor by the shirt.

"*You* don't understand, you insolent little boy. How dare you come here and try to force your way in? Now go—before I shackle you."

He shoved Thor, who stumbled back several feet.

Thor felt a sting in his chest where the guard's hand had touched him—but more than that, he felt the sting of rejection. He was indignant. He had not come all this way to be turned away by a guard, without even being seen. He was determined to make it inside.

The guard turned back to his men, and Thor slowly walked away, heading clockwise, around the circular building. He had a plan. He waited until he was out of sight, then broke into a jog, creeping his way alongside the walls. He turned to make sure they weren't watching, then picked up speed, sprinting. He kept running until he was halfway around the building and spotted another opening into the arena: high up were arched openings in the stone, blocked by iron bars. One of them, he noticed, was missing its bars. He heard another roar, and lifted himself up onto the ledge and looked.

His heart quickened. There, spread out inside the huge, circular training ground, were dozens of recruits—including his brothers. Lined up, they all faced a dozen of the Silver. The king's men walked amidst them, summing them up.

Another group of recruits stood off to the side, under the watchful eyes of a soldier, hurling spears at a distant target. One of them missed.

Thor's veins burned with indignation. He could have hit those marks; he was just as good as any of them. Just because he was younger, a bit smaller, it wasn't fair that he was being left out.

Suddenly, Thor felt a hand on his back as he was yanked backwards, flying through the air. He landed hard on the ground below, winded.

He looked up and saw the guard from the gate, sneering down.

"What did I tell you, boy?"

Before he could react, the guard leaned back and kicked Thor hard. Thor felt a sharp thump in his ribs, as the guard wound up to kick him again.

This time, Thor caught the guard's foot in mid-air; he yanked it, knocking him off balance and making him fall.

He quickly gained his feet. At the same time, the guard gained his. Thor stood there, staring back, shocked by what he had just done. Across from him, the guard glowered.

"Not only will I shackle you," the guard hissed, "but I will make you pay. No one touches a king's guard! Forget about joining the Legion—now, you will wallow away in the dungeon! You'll be lucky if you're ever seen again!"

The guard pulled out a chain with a shackle at its end. He approached Thor, vengeance on his face.

Thor's mind raced. He could not allow himself to be shackled— yet he did not want to hurt a member of the King's Guard. He had to think of something—and fast.

He remembered his sling. His reflexes took over as he grabbed it, placed a stone, took aim, and hurled.

The stone flew through the air and knocked the shackles from the stunned guard's hand; it also hit the guard's fingers. The guard pulled back and shook his hand, screaming in pain, as the shackles went flying to the ground.

The guard looked up at Thor with a look of death. He pulled his sword from his scabbard. It came out with a distinctive, metallic ring.

"That was your last mistake," he threatened darkly, and charged.

Thor had no choice: this man would just not leave him be. He placed another stone in his sling and hurled it. He aimed deliberately: he did not want to kill him, but he had to stop him. So instead of aiming for his heart, nose, eye, or head, Thor aimed for the one place he knew would stop him, but not kill him.

He aimed between his legs.

He let the stone fly, not at full strength, but enough to put the man down.

It was a perfect strike.

The guard keeled over, dropping his sword, grabbing between his legs as he collapsed to the ground and curled up in a ball.

"You'll hang for this!" he groaned amidst grunts of pain. "GUARDS! GUARDS!"

Thor looked up and in the distance saw several of the King's Guards racing for him.

It was now or never.

Without wasting another moment, he sprinted for the window ledge. He would have to jump through, into the arena, and make himself known. And he would fight anyone who got in his way.

CHAPTER FIVE

MacGil sat in the upper hall of his castle, in his intimate meeting hall, the one he used for personal affairs. He sat on his intimate throne, this one carved of wood, and looked out at his four children standing before him. There was his eldest son, Kendrik, at twenty five years a fine warrior and true gentleman. He, of all his children, resembled MacGil the most—which was ironic, since he was a bastard, MacGil's only issue by another woman, a woman he had long since forgotten. MacGil had raised Kendrik with his true children, despite his Queen's initial protests, on the condition he would never ascend the throne. Which pained MacGil now, since Kendrik was the finest man he'd ever known, a son he was proud to sire, and there would have been no finer heir to the kingdom.

Beside him, in stark contrast, stood his second-born son—yet his firstborn legitimate son—Gareth, twenty-three, thin, with hollow cheeks and large brown eyes which never stopped darting. His character could not be more different than his elder brother's. Gareth's nature was everything his elder brother's was not: where his brother was forthright, Gareth hid his true thoughts; where his brother was proud and noble, Gareth was dishonest and deceitful. It pained MacGil to dislike his own son, and he had tried many times to correct his nature; but after some point in his teenage years, he finally realized his nature was predestined: scheming, power-hungry, and ambitious in every wrong sense of the word. Gareth also, MacGil knew, had no love for women, and had many male lovers. Other kings would have ousted such a son, but MacGil was more open-minded, and for him, this was not a reason not to love him. He did not judge him for this. What he did judge him for was his evil, scheming nature, which was something he could not overlook.

Lined up beside Gareth stood his second-born daughter, Gwendolyn. Having just reached her sixteenth year, she was as beautiful a girl as he had ever laid eyes upon—and her nature outshone even her looks: she was kind, generous, honest—the finest young woman he had ever known. In this regard, she was similar to her eldest brother. She looked at MacGil with a daughter's love for a father, and he'd always felt her loyalty, in every glance. He was even more proud of her than of his sons.

Standing beside her was MacGil's youngest boy, Reece, a proud and spirited young lad who, at fourteen, was just becoming a man. MacGil had watched with great pleasure his initiation into the Legion, and could already see the man he was going to be. One day, he had no doubt, he would be his finest son, and a great ruler. But that day was not now. He was too young yet, and had too much to learn.

MacGil felt mixed feelings as he surveyed his four children, his three sons and daughter, standing before him, felt pride mingled with disappointment. He also felt anger and annoyance, for two of his children were missing. The eldest, his daughter Luanda, of course was preparing for her own wedding, and since she was being married off to another kingdom, she had no business being here, in this discussion of heirs. But his other son, Godfrey, the middle one, eighteen, was absent. MacGil reddened from the snub.

Ever since he was a boy, Godfrey showed such a disrespect for the kingship, it was always clear that he cared not for it, and would never rule. MacGil's greatest disappointment, Godfrey instead chose to waste away his days in ale houses, with miscreant friends, causing the royal family ever-increasing shame and dishonor. He was a slacker, sleeping most of his days, and filling the rest of them with drink. On the one hand, MacGil was relieved he wasn't here; on the other, it was an insult he could not suffer. He had, in fact, expected this, and had sent out his men early to comb the alehouses and bring him back. MacGil sat there silently, waiting, until they did.

The heavy oak door finally slammed open and in marched the royal guards, dragging Godfrey between them. They gave him a shove, and Godfrey stumbled into the room as they slammed the door behind him.

The children turned and stared. Godfrey was slovenly, reeking of ale, unshaven, and half dressed. He smiled back. Insolent. As always.

"Hello father," Godfrey said. "Did I miss all the fun?"

"You will stand with your siblings and wait for me to speak. If you don't, God help me, I'll chain you in the dungeons with the rest of the common prisoners, and you won't see food—much less ale— for three days entire."

Godfrey stood there, defiant, glaring back at his father. In that stare his father detected some deep reservoir of strength, something of himself, a spark of something that might one day serve him well. That is, if he could ever overcome his own personality.

Defiant to the end, Godfrey waited a good ten seconds before finally complying and ambling over to the others.

As they all stood there, MacGil surveyed his five children: the bastard, the deviant, the drunkard, his daughter, and his youngest. It was a strange mix, and he could hardly believe they had all sprung from him. And now, on his eldest daughter's wedding day, the task had fallen on him to choose an heir from this bunch. How was it possible?

It was all, he felt, an exercise in futility: after all, he was in his prime, and could rule for thirty more years; whatever heir he chose today might not even ascend the throne for decades. The entire tradition irked him. It may have been relevant in the times of his fathers, but it had no place now.

He cleared his throat.

"We are gathered here today at the bequest of tradition. As you know, on this day, the day of my eldest's wedding, the task has fallen upon me to name a successor. An heir to rule this kingdom. Should I die, there is no one better fit to rule than your mother. But our kingdom's laws dictate that only the issue of a king may succeed. Thus, I must choose."

MacGil caught his breath, thinking. A heavy silence hung in the air, and he could feel the weight of anticipation. He looked in their eyes, and saw different expressions in each. The bastard looked resigned, knowing he would not be picked. The deviant's eyes were aglow with ambition, as if expecting the choice to naturally fall on him. The drunkard looked out the window; he did not care. His daughter looked back with love, knowing she was not part of this discussion, but loving him nonetheless. The same with his youngest.

"Kendrik, I have always considered you a true son. But the laws of our kingdom prevent me from passing the kingship to anyone of less than true legitimacy."

Kendrik bowed. "Father, I had not expected you would do so. I'm content with my lot. Please do not let this confound you."

MacGil was pained at his response, as he felt how genuine he was and wanted to name him heir all the more.

32

"That leaves four of you. Reece, you're a fine young man, the finest I've ever seen. But you are too young to be part of this discussion."

"I expected as much, father," Reece responded, with a slight bow.

"Godfrey, you are one of my three legitimate sons—yet you choose to waste your days in the ale house, with the filth. You were handed every privilege in life, and have spurned every one. If I have any great disappointment in this life, it is you."

Godfrey grimaced back, shifting uncomfortably.

"Well, then, I suppose I'm done here, and shall head back to the ale house, shan't I, father?"

With a quick, disrespectful bow, Godfrey turned and strutted across the room.

"Get back here!" MacGil screamed. "NOW!"

Godfrey continued to strut, ignoring him. He crossed the room and pulled open the door. Two guards stood there.

MacGil seethed with rage as the guards looked to him questioningly.

But Godfrey did not wait; he shoved his way past them, into the open hall.

"Detain him!" MacGil yelled. "And keep him from the Queen's sight. I don't want his mother burdened by the sight of him on her daughter's wedding day."

"Yes, my liege," they said, closing the door as they hurried off after him.

MacGil sat there, breathing, red-faced, trying to calm down. For the thousandth time, he wondered what he had done to warrant such a child.

He looked back at his remaining children. The four of them stood there, waiting in the thick silence. MacGil took a deep breath, trying to focus.

"That leaves but two of you," he continued. "And from these two, I have chosen a successor."

MacGil turned to his daughter.

"Gwendolyn, that will be you."

There was a gasp in the room; his children all seemed shocked, most of all Gwendolyn.

"Did you speak accurately, father?" Gareth asked. "Did you say Gwendolyn?"

"Father, I am honored," Gwendolyn said. "But I cannot accept. I am a woman."

"True, a woman has never sat on the throne of the MacGils. But I have decided it is time to change tradition. Gwendolyn, you are of the finest mind and spirit of any young woman I've met. You are young, but God be willing, I shall not die anytime soon, and when the time comes, you will be wise enough to rule. The kingdom will be yours."

"But father!" Gareth screamed, his face ashen, "I am the eldest born legitimate son! Always, in all the history of the MacGils, kingship has gone to the eldest son!"

"I am King," MacGil answered darkly, "and I dictate tradition."

"But it's not *fair!*" Gareth pleaded, his voice whining. "I am supposed to be King. Not my sister. Not a woman!"

"Silence your tongue, boy!" MacGil shouted, shaking with rage. "Dare you question my judgment?"

"Am I being passed over then for a woman? Is that what you think of me?"

"I have made my decision," MacGil said. "You will respect it, and follow it obediently, as every other subject of my kingdom. Now, you may all leave me."

His children bowed their heads quickly and hurried from the room.

But Gareth stopped at the door, unable to bring himself to leave.

He turned back, and, alone, faced his father.

MacGil could see the disappointment in his face. Clearly, he had expected to be named heir today. Even more: he had wanted it. Desperately. Which did not surprise MacGil in the least—and which was the very reason he did not give it to him.

"Why do you hate me, father?" he asked.

"I don't hate you. I just don't find you fit to rule my kingdom."

"And why is that?" Gareth pressed.

"Because that is precisely the thing you seek."

Gareth's face turned a dark shade of crimson. Clearly, MacGil had given him an insight into his truest nature. MacGil watched his eyes, saw them burn with a hatred for him that he had never imagined possible.

Without another word, Gareth stormed from the room and slammed the door behind him.

34

In the reverberating echo, MacGil shuddered. He recalled his son's stare and sensed a hatred so deep, deeper than even than those of his enemies. In that moment, he thought of Argon, of his pronouncement, of danger being close.

Could it be as close as this?

CHAPTER SIX

Thor sprinted across the vast field of the arena, running with all he had. Behind him he could hear the footsteps of the King's guards, close on his tail. They chased him across the hot and dusty landscape, cursing as they went. Before him were spread out the members—and new recruits—of the Legion, dozens of boys, just like him, but older and stronger. They were training and being tested in various formations, some throwing spears, others hurling javelins, a few practicing their grips on lances. They aimed for distant targets, and rarely missed. These were his competition, and they seemed formidable.

Among them were dozens of real knights, members of the Silver, standing in a broad semi-circle, watching the action. Judging. Deciding on who would stay and who would be sent home.

Thor knew he had to prove himself, had to impress these men. Within moments the guards would be upon him, and if he had any chance of making an impression, now was the time. But how? His mind raced as he dashed across the courtyard, determined not to be turned away.

As Thor raced across the field, others began to take notice. Some of the recruits stopped what they were doing and turned, and some of the knights did as well. Within moments, Thor felt all the attention focused on him. They looked bewildered, and he realized they must be wondering who he was, sprinting across their field, three of the King's guard chasing him. This was not how he had wanted to make an impression. His whole life, when he had dreamed of joining the Legion, this was not how he had envisioned it happening.

As Thor ran, debating what to do, his course of action was made plain for him. One large boy, a recruit, decided to take it upon himself to impress the others by stopping Thor. Tall, muscle-bound, he was nearly twice Thor's size, and he raised his wooden sword and blocked Thor's way. Thor could see he was determined to strike him down, to make a fool of him in front of everyone, and thereby gain himself advantage over the other recruits.

This made Thor furious. Thor had no bone to pick with this boy, and it was not his fight. But he was making it his fight, just to gain advantage with the others.

As they got closer, Thor could hardly believe this boy's size: he towered over him, scowled down with locks of thick black hair covering his forehead, and the largest, squarest jaw Thor had ever seen. He did not see how he could make a dent against this boy.

The boy charged him with his wooden sword, and Thor knew that if he didn't act quick, he would be knocked out.

Thor's reflexes kicked in. He instinctively took out his sling, reached back, and hurled a rock at the boy's hand. It found its target, and knocked the sword from his hand, just as the boy was bringing it down. It went flying and the boy, screaming, clutched his hand.

Thor wasted no time. He charged, taking advantage of the moment, leapt into the air, and kicked the boy, planting his two front feet squarely on the boy's chest. But the boy was so thick, it was like kicking an oak tree. The boy merely stumbled back a few inches, while Thor stopped cold in his tracks and fell at the boy's feet. This did not bode well, Thor thought, as he hit the ground with a thud, his ears ringing.

Thor tried to gain his feet, but the boy was a step ahead of him: he reached down, grabbed Thor by his back, and threw him, sending him flying, face first, into the dirt.

A crowd of boys quickly gathered in a circle around them and cheered. Thor reddened, humiliated.

Thor turned to get up, but the boy was too fast. He was already on top of him, pinning him down. Before Thor knew it, it had turned into a wrestling match, and the boy's weight was immense.

Thor could hear the muted shouts of the other boys as they formed a circle, screaming, anxious for blood. He looked up and saw the face of the boy, scowling down; the boy reached out his thumbs, and brought them down for Thor's eyes. Thor could not believe it: it seemed this boy really wanted to hurt him. Did he really want to gain advantage that badly?

At the last second, Thor rolled his head out of the way, and the boy's hands went flying by, plunging into the dirt. Thor took the chance to roll out from under him.

Thor gained his feet, and faced the boy, who gained his, too. The boy charged and swung for Thor's face, and Thor ducked at the last second; the air rushed by his face, and he realized if it had hit him, it

37

would have broken his jaw. Thor reached up and punched the boy in the gut—but it hardly did a thing: it was like striking a tree.

Before Thor could react, the boy reached around and elbowed Thor in the face.

Thor stumbled back, reeling from the blow. It was like getting hit by a hammer, and his ears rang.

While he was stumbling, still trying to catch his breath, the boy charged and kicked Thor hard in the chest. Thor went flying backwards and crashed to the ground, landing on his back. The other boys cheered.

Thor, dizzy, began to sit up, but just as he began, the boy charged, reached down and swung and punched him again, hard in the face, knocking him flat on his back again—and down for good.

Thor lay there, hearing the muted cheers of the others, feeling the salty taste of blood running from his nose, the welt on his face. He groaned in pain. He looked up and could see the large boy turn away and walk back towards his friends, already celebrating his victory.

Thor wanted to give up. This boy was huge, fighting him was futile, and he could take no more punishment. But something inside him pushed him. He could not lose. Not in front of all these people.

Don't give up. Get up. Get up!

Thor somehow summoned the strength: groaning, he rolled over and got to his hands and knees, then, slowly, to his feet. He faced the boy, bleeding, his eyes swollen, hard to see, breathing hard, and raised his fists.

The huge boy turned around and stared down at Thor. He shook his head, unbelieving.

"You should have stayed down, boy," he threatened, as he began to walk back to Thor.

"ENOUGH!" yelled a voice. "Elden, stand back!"

A knight suddenly stepped up, getting between them, holding out his palm and stopping Elden from getting closer to Thor. The crowd quieted, as they all looked to the knight: clearly this was a man who demanded respect.

Thor looked up, in awe at his presence: he was tall, with broad shoulders, a square jaw, brown, well-kept hair, in his 20s. Thor liked him immediately. His first-rate armor, a chainmail made of a polished silver, was covered with royal markings: the falcon emblem of the MacGil family. Thor's throat went dry: he was standing before a member of the royal family. He could hardly believe it.

"Explain yourself, boy," he said to Thor. "Why have you charged into our arena uninvited?"

Before Thor could respond, suddenly, the three members of the King's guard broke through the circle. The lead guard stood there, breathing hard, pointing a finger at Thor.

"He defied our command!" the guard yelled. "I am going to shackle him and take him to the King's dungeon!"

"I did nothing wrong!" Thor protested.

"Did you now?" the guard yelled. "Barging into the King's property uninvited?"

"All I wanted was a chance!" Thor yelled, turning, pleading to the knight before him, the member of the royal family. "All I wanted was a chance to join the Legion!"

"This training ground is only for the invited boy," came a gruff voice.

Into the circle stepped a warrior, 50s, broad and stocky, with a bald head a short beard, and a scar running across his nose. He looked like he had been a professional soldier all his life—and from the markings on his armor, the gold pin on his chest, he looked to be their commander. Thor's heart quickened at the site of him: a general.

"I was not invited, sire," Thor said. "That is true. But it has been my life's dream to be here. All I want is a chance to show you what I can do. I am as good as any of these recruits. Just give me one chance to prove it. Please. Joining the Legion is all I've ever dreamt of."

"This battleground is not for dreamers, boy," came his gruff response. "It is for fighters. There are no exceptions to our rules: recruits are chosen."

The general nodded, and the King's guard approached Thor, shackles out.

But suddenly the knight, the royal family member, stepped forward and put out his palm, blocking the guard.

"Maybe, on occasion, an exception may be made," he said.

The guard looked up at him in consternation, clearly wanting to speak out, but having to hold his tongue in deference to a royal family member.

"I admire your spirit, boy," the knight continued. "Before we cast you away, I would like to see what you can do."

"But Kendrick, we have our rules—" the general said, clearly displeased.

"The royal family makes the rules," Kendrick answered sternly, "and the Legion answers to the royal family."

"We answer to your father, the King—not to you," the general retorted, equally defiant.

There was a standoff, the air thick with tension. Thor could hardly believe what he had ignited.

"I know my father, and I know what he would want. He would want to give this boy a try. And that is what we will do."

The general, after several tense moments, finally backed down.

Kendrick turned to Thor, eyes locking on his, brown and intense, the face of a prince, but also of a warrior.

"I will give you one chance," he said to Thor. "Let's see if you can hit that mark."

He gestured at a stack of hay, far across the field, with a small, red stain in its center. Several spears were lodged in the hay, but none inside the red.

"If you can do what none of these others boys could do—if you can hit that mark from here—then you may join us."

The knight stepped aside, and Thor could feel all eyes on him.

He spotted a rack of spears and looked them over carefully: they were of a finer quality than he'd ever seen, made of solid oak, wrapped in the finest leather. His heart was pounding as he stepped forward, wiping the blood from his nose with the back of his hand, feeling more nervous than he had in his life. Clearly, he was being given a nearly impossible task. But he had to try.

Thor reached over and picked one, not too long, or too short. He weighed it in his hand—it was heavy, substantial. Not like the ones he used back home. But it also felt right. He felt that maybe, just maybe, he could find his mark. After all, spear throwing was his finest skill, next to hurling stones, and many long days of roaming the wilderness had given him ample targets. He had always been able to hit targets even his brothers could not.

Thor closed his eyes and breathed deeply. If he missed, he would be pounced upon by the guards and dragged off to jail—and his chances of joining the Legion would be ruined forever. This one moment held everything he had ever dreamt of.

He prayed to God with all he had.

Without hesitating, Thor opened his eyes, took two steps forward, reached back and hurled the spear.

He held his breath as he watched it sail.

Please, God. Please.

The spear cut through the thick, dead silence, and Thor could feel the hundreds of eyes on it.

Then, after an eternity, there came the sound, the undeniable sound of a spear point piercing hay. Thor didn't even have to look. He knew, he just knew, that it was a perfect strike. It was the way the spear felt when it left his hand, the angle of his wrist, that told him it would hit.

Thor dared to look—and saw, with huge relief, that he was right. The spear found its place in the center of the red mark—the only spear in it. He'd done what the other recruits could not.

Stunned silence enveloped him, as he felt the other recruits—and knights—all gaping at him.

Finally, Kendrick stepped forward and clapped Thor hard on the back with his palm, with the sound of satisfaction. He grinned widely.

"I was right," he said. "You will stay!"

"What, my Lord!" screamed the King's guard. "It is not fair! This boy arrived uninvited!"

"He hit that mark. That's invitation enough for me."

"He is far younger and smaller than the others. This is no peewee squad," said the general.

"I would rather a smaller soldier who can hit his mark than an oaf who cannot," the knight replied.

"A lucky throw!" yelled the large boy who Thor had just fought. "If we had more chances, we would hit, too!"

The knight turned and stared down the boy.

"Would you?" he asked. "Shall I see you do it now? Shall we wager your staying here on it?"

The boy, flustered, lowered his head in shame, clearly not willing to take up the offer.

"But this boy is a stranger," protested the general. "We don't even know where he hails from."

"He comes from the lowlands," came a voice.

The others turned to see who spoke, but Thor did not need to—he recognized the voice. It was the voice that had plagued him his entire childhood. The voice of his eldest brother: Drake.

Drake stepped forward, with his other two brothers, and glared down at Thor with a look of disapproval.

"His name is Thorgrin, of the clan McCleod of the Southern Province of the Eastern Kingdom. He is the youngest of four. We all hail from the same household. He tends our father's sheep!"

The entire group of boys and knights burst into a chorus of laughter.

Thor felt his face redden; he wanted to die at that moment. He had never been more ashamed. That was just like his brother, to take away his moment of glory, to do whatever he could to keep him down.

"Tends sheep, does he?" echoed the general.

"Then our foes will surely have to watch out for him!" yelled another boy.

There was another chorus of laughter, and Thor's humiliation deepened.

"Enough!" yelled Kendrick, sternly.

Gradually, the laughter subsided.

"I'd rather have a sheepherder any day who can hit a mark than the lot of you—who seem good at laughing but not much more," Kendrick added.

With that, a silence descended on the boys, who weren't laughing anymore.

Thor was infinitely grateful to Kendrick. He vowed to find out who he was, to pay him back any way he could. Regardless of what happened to him, this man had, at least, restored his honor.

"Don't you know, boy, that it is not a warrior's way to tattle on his friends—much less his own family, his own blood?" the knight asked Drake.

Drake looked down, flustered, one of the rare times that Thor had seen him out of sorts.

But one of his other brothers, Dress, stepped forward and protested: "But Thor wasn't even chosen. *We* were. He is merely following us here."

"I'm not following you," Thor insisted, finally speaking up. "I'm here for the Legion. Not for you."

"It doesn't matter why he's here," the general said, annoyed, stepping forward. "He's wasting all of our time. Yes it was a good hit of the spear, but he still cannot join us. Has no knight to sponsor him, and no squire willing to partner with him."

"I will partner with him," called out a voice.

Thor spun, along with the others. He was surprised to see, standing a few feet away, a boy his age, who actually looked like him, except with blond hair and bright green eyes, wearing the most beautiful royal armor he had ever seen, chainmail covered with scarlet and black markings—clearly, another member of the King's family.

"Impossible," the general said. "The royal family does not partner with commoners."

"I can do as I choose," the boy shot back. "And I say that Thorgrin will be my partner."

"Even if we sanctioned it," the general said. "It does not matter. He has no knight to sponsor him."

"I shall sponsor him," came a voice.

Everyone turned in the other direction, and there came a muffled gasp amongst the others.

Thor turned to see a knight, mounted on a horse, bedecked in the most beautiful shining armor he had ever seen, wearing all manner of weaponry on his belt. He positively shined, and it was like looking at the sun. Thor could tell by his demeanor, his bearing, and by the markings on his helmet, that he was different than the others. He was a champion.

Thor recognized this knight. He had seen paintings of him, and had heard of his legend. Erec. He couldn't believe it. He was the greatest knight in the Ring.

"But my lord, you already have a squire," the general protested.

"Then I shall have two," Erec answered, in a deep, confident voice.

A stunned silence pervaded the group.

"Then there is nothing left to say," Kendrick said. "Thorgrin has a sponsor and a partner. The matter is resolved. He is now a member of the Legion."

"But you have forgotten about me!" the King's guard screamed, stepping forward. "None of this excuses the fact that the boy has struck a member of the King's guard, and that he must be punished. Justice must be done!"

"Justice will be done," Kendrick responded, steely. "But it will be at my discretion. Not yours."

"But my liege, he must be put in the stocks! An example must be made of him!"

"If you keep up your talk, then *you* shall be the one going to the stocks," Kendrick said back to the guard, glaring him down, steel in his voice.

Finally, the guard backed down; reluctantly, he turned and walked away, red-faced, glaring at Thor.

"Then it is official," Kendrick called out in a loud voice. "Welcome, Thorgrin, to the King's Legion!"

The crowd of knights and boys let out a cheer. They then turned away, back to their training.

Thor felt numb with shock. He could hardly believe it. He was now a member of the King's Legion. It was like a dream.

Thor turned to Kendrick, more grateful to him than he could ever say. He had never had anyone in his life before who cared about him, who went out of his way to look out for him, to protect him. It was a funny feeling. He already felt closer to this man than to his own father.

"I don't know how to thank you," Thor said. "I am deeply indebted to you."

Kendrick smiled down. "Kendrick is my name. You shall get to know it well. I am the King's eldest son. I admire your courage. You shall be a fine addition to this lot."

Kendrick turned and hurried off, and as he did, the huge boy that Thor had fought shuffled by.

"Watch your back," the boy said. "We sleep in the same barracks, you know. And don't think for a moment you're safe."

The boy turned and stormed off before Thor could respond; he could hardly believe he had already made an enemy.

He was beginning to wonder what was in store for him here, when suddenly the King's youngest son hurried over to him.

"Don't mind him," he said to Thor. "He's always picking fights. I'm Reece."

"Thank you," Thor said, reaching out his hand, "for choosing me as your partner. I don't know what I would have done without it."

"I'm happy to choose anyone who stands up to that brute," Reece said happily. "That was a nice fight."

"Are you kidding?" Thor asked, wiping dried blood from his face and feeling his welt swell up. "He killed me."

"But you didn't give up," Reece said. "Impressive. Any of the others of us would have just stayed down. And that was one hell of a spear throw. How did you learn to throw like that? We shall be partners for life!" He looked at Thor meaningfully as he shook his hand. "And friends, too. I can sense it."

As Thor shook his hand, he couldn't help but feel that he was making a friend for life.

Suddenly, he was poked from the side.

He spun and saw an older boy standing there, with pockmarked skin and a long and narrow face.

"I am Feithgold. Erec's squire. You are now his *second* squire. Which means you answer to me. And we have a tournament in minutes. Are you going to just stand there when you been made squire to the most famous knight in the kingdom? Follow me! Quickly!"

Reece had already turned away, and Thor turned and hurried after the squire as he ran across the field. He had no idea where they were going—but he didn't care. He was singing inside. He had made it.

He could hardly believe it.

He had made it.

CHAPTER SEVEN

Gareth hurried across King's court, dressed in his royal fineries, pushing his way amidst the masses who poured in from all directions for his sister's wedding, and he fumed. He was still reeling from his encounter with his father. How was it possible that he was skipped over? That his father would not choose him as king? It made no sense. He was the firstborn legitimate son. That was the way it had always worked. He had always, from the time he was born, assumed he would reign—he had no reason to think otherwise.

It was unconscionable. Passing him over for a younger sibling—and a girl, no less. When word spread, he would be the laughingstock of the kingdom. As he walked, he felt as if the wind had been knocked out of him, and he did not know how to catch his breath.

He stumbled his way with the masses towards the wedding ceremony of his elder sister. He looked about, saw the multitude of colored robes, the endless streams of people, all the different folk from all the different provinces. He hated being this close to commoners. This was the one time when the poor could mingle with the rich, the one time those savages from the Eastern Kingdom, from the far side of the Highlands, had been allowed in, too. Gareth still could hardly conceive that his sister was being married off to one of them. It was a shrewd political move by his father, a pathetic attempt to make peace between the kingdoms.

Even stranger, somehow, his sister seemed to actually like this creature. Gareth could hardly conceive why. Knowing her, it was not the *man* she liked, but the title, the chance to be queen of her own province. She would get what she deserved: they were all savages, those on the other side of the Highlands. In Gareth's mind, they lacked his civility, his refinery, his sophistication. It was not his problem. If his sister was happy, let her be married off. It was just one less sibling to have around that might stand in his way to the throne. In fact, the farther away she was, the better.

46

Not that any of this was his concern anymore. After today, he would never be king. Now, he would be relegated to being just another anonymous prince in his father's kingdom. Now, he had no path to power; now he was doomed to a life of mediocrity.

His father had underestimated him—he always had. His father considered himself politically shrewd—but Gareth knew that he was much shrewder, and always had been. For instance, this marrying off of Luanda to a McCloud: his father thought himself a master politician. But Gareth was more far-sighted than his father, was able to consider more of the ramifications, and was already looking one step farther. He knew where this would lead. Ultimately, this marriage would not appease the McClouds, but embolden them. They were brutes, so they would see this peace offering not as a sign of strength, but of weakness. They would not care for a bond between the families, and as soon as his sister was taken away, Gareth felt certain they would plan an attack. It was all a ruse. He had tried to tell his father, but he would not listen.

Not that any of this was his concern anymore. After all, now he was just another prince, just another cog in the kingdom. Gareth positively burned at the thought of it, and he hated his father at that moment with a hatred he never knew was possible. As he crammed in, shoulder to shoulder with the masses, he imagined ways he could take revenge, and ways he could get the kingship after all. He could not just sit idly by, that was for certain. He could not let the kingship go to his younger sister.

"There you are," came a voice.

Gareth turned and saw Firth, walking up beside him, wearing a jolly smile, revealing his perfect teeth. 18, tall, thin, with a high voice and smooth skin and ruddy cheeks, Firth was his lover of the moment. Gareth was usually happy to see him, but was in no mood for him now.

"I think you have been avoiding me all day," Firth added, linking one arm around his as they walked.

Gareth immediately shook off his arm, and checked to make sure no one had seen.

"Are you stupid?" Gareth chastised. "Don't you ever link arms with me in public again. *Ever.*"

Firth look down, red-faced. "I'm sorry," he said. "I didn't think."

"That's right, you didn't. Do it again, and I shall never see you again," Gareth scolded.

Firth turned redder, and looked truly apologetic. "I'm sorry," he said.

Gareth checked again, felt confident no one had seen, and felt a little bit better.

"What gossip from the masses?" Gareth asked, wanting to change the subject, to shake his dark thoughts.

Firth immediately perked up and regained his smile.

"Everyone waits in expectation. They all wait for the announcement that you have been named successor."

Gareth's face dropped. Firth examined him.

"Haven't you?" Firth asked, skeptical.

Gareth reddened as he walked, not meeting Firth's eyes.

"No."

Firth gasped.

"He passed me over. Can you imagine? For my sister. My younger sister."

Now Firth's face fell. He looked astonished.

"That is impossible," he said. "You are firstborn. She is a woman. It's not possible," he repeated.

Gareth looked at him, stone cold. "I do not lie."

The two of them walked for some time in silence, and as it grew even more crowded, Gareth looked around, starting to realize where he was and really take it all in. King's Court was absolutely jammed—there must have been thousands of people swarming in, from every possible entrance. They all shuffled their way towards the elaborate wedding stage, around which were set at least a thousand of the nicest chairs, with thick cushions, covered in a red velvet, and with golden frames. An army of servants strode up and down the aisles, seating people, carrying drinks.

On either side of the endlessly long wedding aisle, strewn with flowers, sat the two families—the MacGils and McClouds—the line sharply demarcated. There were hundreds on either side, each dressed in their finest, the MacGils in the deep purple of their clan, and the McClouds in their burnt-orange. To Gareth's eye, the two clans could not look more different: though they were each dressed in fineries, he felt as if the McClouds were merely dressing up, pretending. They were brutes beneath their clothes—he could see it in their facial expressions, in the way they moved, jostled each other, the way they laughed too loudly. There was something beneath their surface that royal clothing could not hide. He resented having them within their

48

gates. He resented this entire wedding. It was yet another foolish decision by his father.

If he were king, he would have executed a different plan: he would have called this wedding, too. But then he would have waited until late in the night, when the McClouds were steeped in drink, barred the doors to the hall, and burned them all in a great fire, killed them all in one clean swoop.

"Brutes," Firth said, as he examined the other side of the wedding aisle. "I can hardly imagine why your father let them in."

"It should make for interesting games, afterwards," Gareth said. "He invites our enemy into our gates, then arranges wedding day competitions. Is that not a recipe for skirmish?"

"Do you think?" Firth asked. "A battle? Here? With all these soldiers? On her wedding day?"

Gareth shrugged. He put nothing past the McClouds.

"The honor of a wedding day means nothing to them."

"But we have thousands of soldiers here."

"As do they."

Gareth turned and saw a long line of soldiers—MacGils and McClouds—lined up on either side of the battlements. They would not have brought so many soldiers, he knew, unless they were expecting a skirmish. Despite the occasion, despite the fine dress, despite the lavishness of the setting, the endless banquets of food, the summer solstice in full bloom, the flowers—despite everything, there still hung a heavy tension in the air. Everyone was on edge—Gareth could see it by the way they bunched up their shoulders, held out their elbows. No one trusted each other.

Maybe he would get lucky, Gareth thought, and one of them would stab his father in his heart. Then maybe he could become king after all.

"I suppose we can't sit together," Firth said, disappointment in his voice, as they approached the seating area.

Gareth shot him a look of contempt. "How stupid are you?" he spat, venom in his voice.

He was seriously beginning to wonder whether he had made a good idea to choose this stable boy as his lover. If he didn't get him over his sappy ways quick, he might just out them both.

Firth looked down in shame.

"I will see you afterwards, in the stables. Now be gone with you," he said, and gave him a small shove. Firth disappeared into the crowd.

Suddenly, Gareth felt an icy grip on his arm. For a moment his heart stopped, as he wondered if he was discovered; but then he felt the long nails, the thin fingers, plunge into his skin, and he knew it right away to be the grasp of his wife. Helena.

"Don't embarrass me on this day," she hissed, hatred in her voice.

He turned and studied her: she looked beautiful, all done up, wearing a long white satin gown, her hair piled high with pins, wearing her finest diamond necklace, and her face smoothed over with makeup. Gareth could see objectively that she was beautiful, as beautiful as she was on the day he married her. But still he felt no attraction to her. It had been another idea of his father's—to try to marry him out of his nature. But all it had done was give him a perpetually sour companion—and stir up even more court speculation about his true inclinations.

"It is your sister's wedding day," she rebuked. "You can act as if we are a couple—for once."

She locked one arm through his and they walked to a reserved area, roped off with velvet. Two royal guards let them through and they mingled with the rest of the royals, at the base of the aisle.

A trumpet was blown, and slowly, the crowd quieted. There came the gentle music of a harpsichord, and as it did, more flowers were strewn along the aisle, and the royal procession began to walk down, couples arm in arm. Gareth was tugged by Helena, and he began marching down the aisle with her.

Gareth felt more conspicuous, more awkward than ever, hardly knowing how to make his love seem genuine. He felt hundreds of eyes on him, and couldn't help but feel as if they were all evaluating him, though he knew they were not. The aisle could not be short enough; he could not wait to reach the end and stand near his sister at the altar, and get this over with. He also could not stop thinking about his meeting with his father: he wondered if all these onlookers already knew the news.

"I received ill news today," he whispered to Helena as they finally reached the end, and the eyes were off him.

"Do you think I don't know that already?" she snapped.

He turned and looked at her, surprised.

She looked back with contempt. "I have my spies," she said.

He narrowed his eyes, wanting to hurt her. How could she be so nonchalant?

"If I am not king, then you shall never be queen," he said.

"I never expected to be queen," she answered.

That surprised him even more.

"I never expected him to name you," she added. "Why would he? You are not a leader. You are a lover. But not *my* lover."

Gareth felt himself reddening.

"Nor are you mine," he said to her.

It was her turn to redden. He was reminding her that she was not the only one that had a secret lover. He had heard rumors, had spies of his own that told him of her exploits. He had let her get away with it so far—as long as she kept it quiet, and left him alone.

"It's not like you give me a choice," she answered. "Do you expect me to remain celibate the rest of my life?"

"You knew who I was," he answered. "Yet you chose to marry me. You chose power, not love. Don't act surprised."

"Our marriage was arranged," she said. "I did not choose a thing."

"But you did not protest," he answered.

They were at a stalemate, and Gareth lacked the energy to argue with her today. She was a useful prop, a puppet wife. He could tolerate her, and she could be useful on occasion—as long as she did not annoy him too much.

Gareth watched with supreme cynicism as everyone turned to watch his eldest sister being walked down the aisle by his father, that creature. The gall of him—he even had the nerve to feign sadness, wiping a tear as he walked her. An actor to the last. But in Gareth's eyes, he was just a bumbling fool. He couldn't imagine his father felt any genuine sadness for marrying off his daughter, who, after all, he was throwing to the wolves of the McCloud kingdom. He felt an equal disdain for Luanda, who seemed to be enjoying the whole thing. She seemed to hardly care that she was being married off to a lesser people. She, too, was after power. Cold-blooded. Calculated. In this way, she, of all his siblings, was most like him. In some ways he could relate to her, though they never had much warmth for each other.

Gareth shifted on his feet, impatient, waiting for it all to end.

He suffered through the ceremony, as Argon presided over the blessings, reciting the spells, performing the rituals. It was all a charade, and it made him sick. It was just the union of two families for political reasons. Why couldn't they just call it what it was?

51

Soon enough, thank heavens, it was over. The crowd rose up in a huge cheer as the two kissed. A great horn was blown, and the perfect order of the wedding dissolved into controlled chaos. They all made their way back down the aisle, and over to the reception area.

Even Gareth, as cynical as he was, was impressed by the site: his father had spared no expense this time. Stretching out before them were all manner of tables, banquets, vats of wine, an endless array of roasting pigs and sheep and lamb.

Behind them, they were already preparing for the main event: the games. There were targets being prepared for stone hurling, spear throwing, bows and arrows—and, at the center of it all, the jousting lane. Already, the masses were crowding around it.

Crowds were already parting for the knights on both sides. For the MacGils, the first to enter, of course, was his brother, Kendrick, up on his horse, bedecked in armor, followed by dozens of the Silver. But it was not until Erec arrived, set back from the others, on his white horse, that the crowd quieted in awe. He was like a magnet for attention: even Helena leaned forward, and Gareth saw her lust for him, like all the other women.

"He's nearly of selection age, yet he's not married. Any woman in the kingdom would marry him. Why does he choose none of us?"

"And what do you care?" Gareth asked, feeling jealous, despite himself. He too, wanted to be up there, in armor, on a horse, jousting for his father's name. But he was not a warrior. And everyone knew it.

Helena ignored him with a dismissive wave of her hand. "You are not a man," she said, derisively. "You do not understand these things."

Gareth blushed. He wanted to let her have it, but now was not the time. Instead, he accompanied her as she took a seat in the stands, with the others, to watch the day's festivities. This day was going from worse to worse, and Gareth already felt a pit in his stomach. It would be a very long day, a day of endless chivalry, of pomp, of pretense. Of men wounding or killing each other. A day he was completely excluded from. A day that represented everything he hated.

As he sat there, he brooded. He wished silently that the festivities would erupt into a full-fledged battle, that there would be full-scale bloodshed before him, that everything good about this place be destroyed, torn to bits.

One day he would have his way. One day he would be king.

One day.

CHAPTER EIGHT

Thor did his best to keep up with Erec's squire, hurrying to catch up as he weaved his way through the masses. It had been such a whirlwind since the arena, he could hardly process what was happening all around him. He was still trembling inside, could still hardly believe he had been accepted into the Legion, and he had been named second squire to Erec.

"I told you boy, keep up!" Feithgold snapped.

Thor resented him calling him "boy," especially as he was hardly a few years older. He nearly lost sight of him as he darted in out of the crowd, almost as if he were trying to lose Thor.

"Is it always this crowded here?" Thor called out, trying to catch up.

"Of course not!" Feithgold yelled back. "Today is not only the summer solstice, the biggest day of the year, but also the day the king chose for his daughter's wedding—and the only day in history we've opened our gates to the McClouds. There has never been such a crowd here as now. It is unprecedented. I hadn't expected this! I fear we will be late!" he said, all in a rush, as he sped through the crowd.

"Where are we going?" Thor asked.

"We're going to do what every good squire does: to help our knight prepare!"

"Prepare for what?" Thor pressed, nearly out of breath. It was getting hotter by the minute, and he wiped the sweat from his brow.

"Why, the royal joust!"

They finally reached the edge of the crowd. They stopped before a king's guard, who recognized Feithgold and gestured to the others to let them pass.

They slipped under a rope and stepped into a clearing, free from the masses. Thor could hardly believe it: there, up close, were the jousting lanes. Behind the ropes stood mobs of spectators, and up and down the dirt lanes stood huge warhorses—the largest Thor had ever seen—mounted by knights in all manner of armor. Mixed among the

54

Silver were knights from all over the two kingdoms, from every province, some in black armor, others in white, wearing helmets and donning weapons of every shape and size. It looked as if the entire world had descended on these jousting lanes.

There were already some competitions were in progress, knights from places Thor did not recognize charging each other, clanging lances and shields, followed always by a short cheer from the crowd. Up close, Thor could not believe the strength and speed of the horses, the sound the weapons made. It seemed like a deadly business.

"It hardly seems like a sport!" Thor said to Feithgold as he followed him along the perimeter of the lanes.

"That's because it is not," Feithgold yelled back, over the sound of a clang. "It is a serious business, masked as a game. People die here, every day. It is battle. Lucky are the ones who walk away unscathed. They are far and few between."

Thor looked up as two knights charged each other and moments later, collided at full speed. There was an awful crash of metal on metal, and one of them went flying off his horse, and landed on his back, just feet away from Thor.

The crowd gasped. The knight did not stir, and Thor looked down and saw a piece of a wooden shaft stuck in his ribs, piercing his armor. He cried out in pain, and blood poured from his mouth. Several squires ran over and attended him, dragging him off the field. The winning knight paraded slowly, raising his lance to the cheer of the crowd.

Thor was amazed. He had not envisioned the sport to be so deadly.

"What those boys just did—that is your job now," Feithgold said. "You are squire now. More precisely, second squire."

He stopped and came in close—so close, Thor could smell his bad breath.

"And don't you forget it. I answer to Erec. And you answer to me. Your job is to assist me. Do you understand?"

Thor nodded back, still trying to take it all in. He had imagined it all going differently in his head, and still didn't know exactly what was in store for him. He could feel how threatened Feithgold was by his presence, and felt he had made an enemy.

"It is not my intention to interfere with your being Erec's squire," Thor said.

Feithgold let out a short, derisive laugh.

"You couldn't interfere with me, boy, if you tried. Just stay out of my way and do as I tell you."

With that, Feithgold turned and hurried down a series of twisting paths behind the ropes. Thor followed as best he could, and soon found himself in a labyrinth of stables. He walked down a narrow corridor, all around him warhorses strutting, squires tending nervously to them. Feithgold twisted and turned and finally stopped before a giant, magnificent horse. Thor stopped and looked up, and had to catch his breath. He could hardly believe that something so big and beautiful was real, and that it could be contained behind a fence. It looked as if it were ready for war.

"Warkfin," Feithgold said. "Erec's horse. Or one of them—the one he prefers for jousting. Not an easy beast to tame. But Erec has managed. Open the gate," Feithgold ordered.

Thor looked at him, puzzled, then looked back at the gate, trying to figure it out. He stepped forward, pulled at a peg between the slats, and nothing happened. He pulled harder and it budged, and he gently swung open the wooden gate.

The second he did, Warkfin neighed, leaned back and kicked the wood, just grazing the tip of Thor's finger. Thor yanked back his hand in pain.

Feithgold laugh.

"That's why I had you open it. Do it quicker next time, boy. Warkfin waits for no one. Especially you."

Thor was fuming; Feithgold was already getting on his nerves, and he hardly saw how he would be able to put up with him.

He quickly open the wooden gates, stepping out of the way this time of the horse's flailing legs.

"Shall I bring him out?" Thor asked with trepidation, not really wanting to grab his reigns as he stomped and swayed.

"Of course not," Feithgold said. "That is my role. Your role is to feed him—when I tell you to. And to shovel his waist."

Feithgold grabbed Warkfin's reigns and began to lead him down the stables. Thor swallowed, watching him. This was not the initiation he had in mind. He knew he had to start somewhere, but this was degrading. He had pictured war and glory and battle, training and competition among boys his own age. He never saw himself as a servant in waiting. He was starting to wonder if he had made the right decision.

They finally burst out of the dark stables and back into the bright light of day, back in the jousting lanes. Thor squinted at the bright light, and was momentarily overcome by the thousands of people cheering, the noise of opposing knights as they smashed into one other. He'd never heard such a clang of metal, and the earth tremored from the horses' gait.

All around him were dozens of knights and their squires, preparing. Squires polished their knight's armor, greased up weapons, checked saddles and straps and double-checked weapons as knights mounted their steeds, grabbed their weapons, and waited for their names to be called.

"Elmalkin!" an announcer called out.

A knight from a province Thor did not recognize, a broad fellow in red armor, galloped out the gate. Thor turned and jumped out of the way just in time. He charged down the narrow lane, and Thor watched as his lance brushed off the shield of a competitor. They clanged, and the other knight's lance struck, and Elmalkin went flying backwards, landing on his back. The crowd cheered.

The knight immediately gathered himself, though, jumping to his feet, spinning around, and reaching out a hand to his squire, who stood beside Thor.

"My mace!" the knight yelled out.

The squire beside Thor jumped into action, grabbing a mace off the weapons rack and sprinting out towards the center of the lane. He ran towards his knight, but the other knight had circled back, and was charging again. Just as the squire was reaching him, just as he was placing the mace into his hand, the other knight thundered down upon them. The squire did not reach the knight in time: the other knight brought his lance down—and as he did, his lance swiped the squire's head. The squire, reeling from the below, spun around quickly and went down to the dirt, face first.

He was not moving. Thor could see blood oozing from his head, even from here, staining the dirt.

Thor swallowed.

"It's not a pretty sight, is it?"

Thor turned to see Feithgold standing beside them, staring back.

"Steel yourself boy. This is battle. And we're right in the middle of it."

The crowd suddenly grew quiet, as the main jousting lane was opened. Thor could sense anticipation in the air, as all the other jousts stopped in anticipation of this one. On one side, out came Kendrik, walking out on his horse, lance in hand.

On the far side, facing him, out walked a knight in the distinctive armor of the McClouds.

"MacGils versus McClouds," Feithgold whispered to Thor. "We've been at war for a thousand years. And I very much doubt this match will settle it."

Each knight lowered his visor, a horn sounded, and with a shout, the two charged each other.

Thor was amazed at how much speed they picked up, and moments later they collided with such a clang, Thor nearly raised his hands to his ears. The crowd gasped as both fighters fell from their horses.

They each jumped to their feet and threw off their helmets, as their squires ran out to them, handing them short swords. The two knights sparred with all they had. Watching Kendrick swing and slash had Thor mesmerized: it was a thing of beauty. But the McCloud was a fine warrior, too. Back and forth they went, each exhausting the other, neither giving ground.

Finally their swords met in one momentous clash, and they each knocked each other's swords from their hands. Their squires ran out, maces in hand, but as Kendrick was reaching for his mace, the McCloud's squire ran up behind him and struck him in the back with a mace, the blow sending him to the ground, to the horrified gasp of the crowd.

The McCloud knight stepped forward and pointed his sword to Kendrick's throat, pinning him to the ground. Kendrick was left with no choice.

"I concede!" he yelled.

There was a victorious shout among the McClouds—but a shout of anger from the MacGils.

"He cheated!" yelled out the MacGils.

"He cheated! He cheated!" echoed a chorus of angry cries.

The mob was getting angrier and angrier, and soon there was such a chorus of protests that the mob began to disperse, and both sides—the MacGils and McClouds—began to approach each other on foot.

"This isn't good," Feithgold said to Thor, as they stood on the side, watching.

Moments later, the crowd erupted: blows were thrown, and it became an all-out brawl. It was chaos. Men were swinging wildly, grabbing each other in locks, driving each other to the ground. The crowd was swelling, and it was threatening to blow up into an all-out war.

A horn sounded, and guards from both sides marched in, and managed to split up the crowd. Another, louder, horn sounded, and silence fell as King MacGil stood from his throne.

"There will be no skirmishers today!" he boomed in his kingly voice. "Not on this day of celebration! And not in my court!"

Slowly, the crowd calmed.

"If it is a contest you wish for between our two great clans, it will be decided by one fighter, one champion, from each side."

MacGil looked to King McCloud, who sat on the far side, seated with his entourage.

"Agreed?" MacGil yelled out.

McCloud stood solemnly.

"Agreed!" he echoed.

The crowd cheered on both sides.

"Choose your best man!" MacGil yelled.

"I already have," McCloud said.

There emerged from the McCloud side a formidable knight, the biggest man Thor had ever seen, mounted on his horse. He looked like a boulder, all bulk, with a long beard, and a scowl that looked permanent.

Thor sensed movement beside him, and right next to him, Erec stepped up, mounted Warfkin and walked forward. Thor swallowed. He could hardly believe this was happening all around him. He swelled with pride for Erec.

Then he was overcome with anxiety, as he realized that he was on duty. After all, he was squire and this was his knight who was about to fight.

"What do we do?" Thor asked Feithgold in a rush.

"Just stand back and do as I tell you," he answered.

Erec strode forward into the jousting lane, and the two knights stayed there, facing each other, their horses stomping in a tense standoff. Thor felt his heart pounding in his chest as he waited and watched.

A horn sounded, and the two charged each other.

59

Thor could not believe the beauty and grace of Warfkin as he watched him move. It was like watching a fish jump from the sea. The other man was huge, but Erec was the most graceful and sleek fighter Thor had ever seen. He cut through the air, his head low, his silver armor rippling, more polished than any armor he had laid his eyes upon.

As the two men met, Erec held his lance with perfect aim, and leaned to the side. He managed to knock the knight in the center of shield and at the same time, to dodge his blow.

The huge mountain of a man tumbled backwards, onto the ground. It was like a boulder landing.

The MacGil crowd cheered as Erec rode past, turned and circled back. He held the tip of his lance to the man's throat.

"Yield!" Erec yelled down.

The knight spit.

"Never!"

The knight then reached into a hidden satchel on his waist, pulled out a handful of dirt, and before Erec could react, he threw it up into Erec's face.

Erec, stunned, reached up and grabbed for his eyes, dropping his lance, and fell from his horse.

The MacGil crowd booed and hissed and cried in outrage as Erec fell, clutching his eyes. The knight, wasting no time, hurried over and kneed him in the ribs.

Erec rolled over, and the knight grabbed a huge rock, picked it up high and prepared to bring it down on Erec's skull.

"NO!" Thor screamed, stepping forward, unable to control himself.

Thor watched in horror as the knight brought down the rock. At the last second, Erec somehow rolled out of the way. The stone lodged deep into the ground, right where his skull had been.

Thor was amazed at Erec's dexterity. He was already back on his feet, facing this dirty fighter.

"Short swords!" the Kings cried out.

Feithgold suddenly wheeled and stared at Thor, wide-eyed.

"Hand it to me!" he yelled.

Thor's heart pounded in panic. He spun around, searching Erec's weapons rack, looking desperately for the sword. There was a dizzying array of weapons before him. He reached out, grabbed it, and thrust it into Feithgold's palm.

"Stupid boy! That is a medium sword!" Feithgold yelled.

Thor felt his throat go dry, felt the whole kingdom staring at him. His vision was blurry with anxiety, as he spiraled into panic, not knowing which sword to choose. He could barely focus.

Feithgold stepped forward, shoved Thor out of the way, and grabbed the short sword himself. He then raced out into the jousting lane.

Thor watched as he ran, feeling useless, horrible. He also tried to imagine if it were himself running out there, in front of all those people, and his knees grew weak.

The other knight's squire reached him first, and Erec had to jump out of the way, as the knight swung for him, unarmed, barely missing. Finally, Feithgold reached Erec and placed the short sword into his hand. As he did, the knight charged Erec. But Erec was too fast: he waited until the last moment, then jumped out of the way.

The knight kept charging, though, and ran right into Feithgold, standing, to his bad luck, in the place where Erec had just been. The knight, filled with rage at missing Erec, kept charging and grabbed Feithgold with both hands by his hair, and head butted him hard across the face.

There was a cracking of bone, as blood squirted from Feithgold's nose, and he collapsed to the ground, limp.

Thor stood there, mouth open in shock. He could not believe it. Neither could the crowd, which booed and hissed.

Erec swung around with his sword, just missing the knight, and the two faced each other again.

As Thor stood there, he suddenly realized: he was Erec's only squire now. He gulped. What was he supposed to be doing? He was not prepared for this. And the whole kingdom was watching.

The two knights attacked each other viciously, going blow for blow. Clearly the McCloud knight was much stronger than Erec—yet Erec was the better fighter, faster and more agile. They swung and slashed and parried, neither able to gain advantage.

Finally, MacGil stood.

"Long spears!" he yelled.

Thor's heart pounded. He knew this meant him: he was on duty.

He spun and looked at the rack, and grabbed the weapon that seemed most appropriate. As he grabbed its leather shaft, he prayed he chose correctly.

He burst onto the lane and could feel thousands of eyes on him. He ran and ran, for all he was worth, wanting to reach Erec, and finally placing it into his hand. He was proud to see he reached him first.

Erec took his spear and spun, prepared to face the other knight. Erec, being the honorable warrior that he was, waited until the other knight was armed before attacking. Thor hurried off to the side, out of the men's way, not wanting to repeat Feithgold's mistake. As he did, he grabbed Feithgold's limp body and dragged him back, out of harm's way.

As Thor watched, he sensed something was wrong. The knight took his spear, raised it straight up, then began to bring it down in a strange motion. As he did, suddenly, Thor felt his world go into focus in a way he never had. He intuited that something wrong. His eyes locked on the knight's spear tip, and as he looked closely, he realized it was loose. The knight was about to use the tip of his spear as a throwing knife.

As the knight brought down his spear, the tip became detached and went flying through the air. It tumbled through the air, end over end, and was heading right for Erec's heart. In moments, Erec would be dead—and there was no way he could react in time.

In that moment, Thor felt his whole body warming. He felt a tingling sensation—it was the same sensation he'd experienced back in Darkwood, before the Sybold. His whole world slowed. He was able to see the tip spinning in slow motion, was able to feel an energy, a heat, rising within him—one he didn't know he had.

He stepped forward and felt bigger than the spear. In his mind, he willed it to stop. He demanded it to stop. He did not want to see Erec hurt. Especially not this way.

"NO!"" Thor shrieked.

He took another step, and held out his palm, aimed at the spear tip.

As he did, suddenly, the tip stopped and hung there, in mid-air, right before reaching Erec's heart.

It then dropped harmlessly to the ground.

The two knights both turned and looked at Thor—as did the two kings, as did the thousands of spectators. He felt the whole world staring down at him, and realized they all just witnessed what he did. They all knew he was not normal, that he had some sort of power, that he had influenced the games, had saved Erec—and changed the fate of the kingdom.

Thor stood there, rooted in place, wondering what just happened.

He knew now that he wasn't the same as all these people. He was different.

But who was he?

CHAPTER NINE

Thor found himself swept up, ushered through the crowd by Reece, the King's youngest son and his newfound sparring partner. Ever since the jousting match, it had been a blur. Whatever he had done back there, whatever power he had used to stop that spear point from killing Erec, it had caught the attention of the entire kingdom. The match had been stopped after that, called off by both kings, and a truce called. Each fighter retired to his side, the masses broke up in an agitated stir, and Thor had found himself grabbed by the arm, and ushered off by Reece.

He'd been swept away in a royal entourage, cutting the back way through the masses, Reece tugging at his arm as he went. Thor was still shaking from the day's events. He hardly understood what he had just done back there, how it had influenced things. He had just wanted to be anonymous, just another one of the King's legion. He had not wanted to be the center of attention.

Worse, he didn't know where he was being led, if he was going to be punished somehow for interfering. Of course, he had saved Erec's life—but he had also interfered with a Knight's battle, which he knew was forbidden for a squire. He didn't know if he would be rewarded or rebuked.

"How did you do that?" Reece asked, as he yanked him along. Thor followed blindly, trying to process it all himself. As he went, the masses gawked, staring at him as if he were some kind of freak.

"I don't know," Thor answered truthfully. "I just wanted to help him and…it happened."

Reece shook his head.

"You saved Erec's life. Do you realize that? He is our most famed knight. And you saved him."

Thor felt good as he turned Reece's words over in his head, felt a wave of relief. He had liked Reece from the moment he'd met him; he had a calming effect, always knowing what to say. As he pondered it, he realized maybe he was not in for punishment after all. Maybe, in some ways, they would view him as a sort of hero.

"I didn't try to do anything," Thor said. "I just wanted him to live. It was just…natural. It was no big deal."

"No big deal?" Reece echoed. "I couldn't have done it. None of us could have."

They turned the corner, and Thor saw before them the king's castle, sprawled out, reaching high into the sky. It looked monumental. The King's army stood at attention, lining the cobblestone road leading over the drawbridge, keeping the masses at bay. They stepped aside to allowed Reece and Thor past.

The two of them walked along the road, soldiers on either side, right to the huge arched doors, covered in iron bolts. Four soldiers pulled it open and stepped aside, at attention. Thor could not believe the treatment he was receiving: he felt as if he were a member of the royal family.

They entered the castle, the doors closing behind them, and Thor was amazed at the sight before him: the inside was immense, with soaring stone walls a foot thick and vast, open rooms. Before him milled hundreds of members of the royal court, rambling about in an excited stir. He could sense the buzz and excitement in the air, and all eyes turned and looked at him as he entered. He felt overwhelmed by the attention.

They all huddled close, seemed to gawk as he went with Reece down the castle corridors. He had never seen so many people dressed in such fineries. He saw dozens of girls, of all ages, dressed in elaborate outfits, locking arms and whispering in each other's ears and giggling at him as he went. He felt self-conscious. He couldn't tell if they liked him, or if they were making fun of him. He was not used to being the center of attention—much less in a royal court—and hardly knew how to handle himself.

"Why are they laughing at me?" he asked Reece.

Reece turned and chuckled. "They're not laughing at you," he said. "They have taken a liking to you. You're famous."

"Famous?" he asked, stunned. "What do you mean? I just got here."

Reece laughed and clasped a hand on his shoulder. He was clearly amused by Thor.

"Word spreads faster in the royal court than you might imagine. And a newcomer like yourself—well, this does not happen every day."

"Where are we going?" he asked, realizing he was being led somewhere.

"My father wants to meet you," he said, as they turned down a new corridor.

Thor swallowed.

"Your father? You mean…the King?" Suddenly, he was nervous. "Why would he want to meet me? Are you sure?"

Reece laughed.

"I am quite sure. Stop being so nervous. It's just my dad."

"Just your dad?" Thor said, unbelieving. "He's the King!"

"He's not that bad. I have a feeling it will be a happy audience. You saved Erec's life, after all."

Thor swallowed hard, his palms sweaty, as another large door opened, and they entered a vast hall. He looked up in awe at the ceiling, arched, covered in an elaborate design and soaring high. The walls were lined with arched, stained glass windows, and if possible, even more people were crammed into this room. There must have been a thousand of them, and the room positively swarmed. Banquet tables stretched across the room, as far as the eye could see, people sitting on endlessly long benches, dining. Between these was a narrow aisle with a long, red carpet, leading to a platform on which sat the royal throne. The crowd parted ways as Reece and Thor walked down the carpet, towards the King.

"And where do you think you're taking him?" came a hostile, nasally voice.

Thor looked up to see a man standing over him, not much older than he was, dressed in a royal garb, clearly a prince, blocking their way and scowling down.

"It's father's orders," Reece snapped back. "Better get out of our way, unless you want to defy them."

The prince stood his ground, frowning, looking as if he'd bit into something rotten as he examined Thor. Thor did not like him at all: there was something he did not trust about him, with his lean, unkind features and eyes which never stopped darting.

"This is not a hall for commoners," the prince replied. "You should leave the riffraff outside, where it came from."

Thor felt his chest tighten. Clearly this man hated him, and he had no idea why.

"Shall I tell father you said that?" Reece defended, standing his ground.

66

Grudgingly, the prince turned and stormed away.

"Who was that?" Thor asked Reece, as they continued walking.

"Never mind him," Reece replied. "He's just my older brother—or one of them. Gareth. The oldest. Well, not really the oldest—he's just the oldest legitimate one. Kendrick, who you met on the battleground—he is really the oldest."

"Why does Gareth hate me? I don't even know him."

"Don't worry—he doesn't only reserve his hate for you. He hates everybody. And anyone who gets close to the family, he sees as a threat. Never mind him. He is but one of many."

As they continued walking, Thor felt increasingly grateful to Reece, who, he was realizing, was becoming a true friend.

"Why did you stand up for me?" Thor asked, curious.

Reece shrugged.

"I was ordered to bring you to father. Besides, you're my sparring partner. And it's been a long time since someone came through my age here who I thought could be worthy."

"But what makes me worthy?" Thor asked.

"It's the fighter's spirit. It cannot be faked."

As they continued to walk down the aisle, towards the king, Thor felt as if he'd always known him—it was strange, but in some ways he felt as if he were his own brother. He had never had a brother—not a real brother, and it felt good.

"My other brothers are not like him, don't worry," Reece said as people flocked around them, trying to catch a glimpse of Thor. "My brother Kendrick, the one you met—he's the best of all. He's my half-brother, but I consider him a true brother—even more than Gareth. Kendrick is like a second father to me. He will be to you, too, I am sure of it. There is nothing he would not do for me—or for anyone. He is the most loved of our royal family among the people. It is a great loss that he is not allowed to become king."

"You said 'brothers.' You have another brother, too?" Thor asked.

Reece took a deep breath.

"I have one other, yes. We are not that close. Godfrey. Unfortunately, he wastes his days in the alehouse, with the commoners. He's not a fighter, like us. He's not interested in it—he's not interested in anything, really. Except ale—and the ladies."

Suddenly, they stopped short, as a girl blocked their way. Thor stood there, transfixed. Perhaps a couple of years older than him, she stared back with blue, almond eyes, perfect skin, and long, strawberry hair. She was dressed in a white satin dress, bordered by lace, and her eyes positively glowed, dancing with joy and mischief. She locked her eyes on his, and it held him completely captivated. He couldn't move if he wanted to. She was the most beautiful person he had ever seen.

She smiled, displaying perfect white teeth—and as if he weren't transfixed already, her smile held him there, lit up his heart in a single gesture. He never felt so alive.

Thor stood there, speechless, unable to speak. Unable to breathe. It was the first time in his life that he'd ever felt this way.

"And aren't you going to introduce me?" she asked Reece. Her voice went right into him—it was even more sweet than her appearance.

Reece sighed.

"And then there's my sister," he said with a smile. "Gwen, this is Thor. Thor, Gwen."

Gwen curtsied.

"How do you do?" she asked with a smile.

Thor stood there, frozen. Finally, Gwen giggled.

"Not so many words at once, please," she said with a laugh.

Thor felt himself redden; he cleared his throat.

"I am...I... am...sorry," he said. "I'm Thor."

Gwen giggled.

"I know that already," she said. She turned to her brother. "My, Reece, your friend certainly has a way with words."

"Father wants to meet him," he said impatiently. "We are going to be late."

As Thor stood there, he wanted to speak to her, to tell her how beautiful she was, how happy he was to meet her, how grateful he was that she had stopped. But his tongue was completely tied. He had never been this nervous in his life. So, instead, all that came out was:

"Thank you."

Gwen giggled, laughing harder.

"Thank you for what?" she asked. Her eyes lit up. Clearly, she was enjoying this.

Thor felt himself redden again.

"Um...I don't know," he mumbled.

Gwen laughed harder, and Thor felt humiliated. Reece elbowed him, prodded him on, and the two continued to walk. After a few steps, Thor checked back over his shoulder. Gwen still stood there, staring back at him.

Thor felt his heart pounding. He wanted to talk to her, to find out everything about her. He was so embarrassed for his loss of words. But he had never been exposed to girls, really, in his small village—and certainly never exposed to a girl so beautiful. He had never been taught exactly what to say, how to act.

"She talks a lot," Reece said, as they continued, approaching the king. "Never mind her."

"What is her name?" Thor asked.

Reece gave him a funny look. "She just told you!" he said with a laugh.

"I'm sorry…I…uh…I forgot," Thor said, embarrassed.

"Gwendolyn. But everyone calls her Gwen."

Gwendolyn. Thor turned her name over and over in his head. Gwendolyn. *Gwen.* He did not want to let it go. He wanted it to linger in his consciousness. He wondered if he would have a chance to see her again. He guessed probably not, being a commoner. The thought hurt him.

The crowd grew quiet as Thor looked up and realized they were now close to the King. King MacGil sat on his throne, dressed in his royal purple mantle, wearing his crown, and looked imposing.

Reece kneeled before him, and the crowd quieted. Thor followed. A silence blanketed the room.

The king cleared his throat, a deep, hearty noise. As he spoke, his voice boomed throughout the room.

"Thorgrin of the Lowlands of the Southern Province of the Western Kingdom," he began. "Do you realize that today you interfered with the King's royal joust?"

Thor felt his throat go dry. He hardly knew how to respond; it was not a good way to begin. He wondered if he was going to be punished.

"I am sorry, my liege," he finally said. "I didn't mean to."

MacGil leaned forward and raised one eyebrow.

"You didn't mean to? Are you saying you didn't mean to save Erec's life?"

Thor was flustered. He realized he was just making it worse.

"No my liege. I did mean to—"

"So then you admit you did mean to interfere?"

Thor felt his heart pounding. What could he say?

"I am sorry, my liege. I guess I just...wanted to help."

"Wanted to *help*?" MacGil boomed, then leaned back and roared with laughter.

"You wanted to help! Erec! Our greatest and most famed knight!"

The room erupted with laughter, and Thor felt his face redden, one too many times for one day. Could he do nothing right here?

"Stand and come closer boy," MacGil ordered.

Thor looked up in surprise to see the king smiling down, studying him, as he stood and approached.

"I spot nobility in your face. You are not a common boy. No, not common at all...."

MacGil cleared his throat.

"Erec is our most loved knight. What you have done today is a great thing. A great thing for us all. As a reward, from this day, I take you in as part of my family, with all the same respects and honors due to any of my sons."

The King leaned back and boomed: "Let it be known!"

There came a huge cheer and stomping of feet throughout the room.

Thor looked around, flustered, hardly able to process all that was happening to him. Part of the king's family. It was beyond his wildest dreams. All he had wanted was to be accepted, to be given a spot in the Legion. Now, this. He was so overwhelmed with gratitude, with joy, he hardly knew what to do.

Before he could respond, suddenly the room broke into song and dance and feast, people celebrating all around him. It was mayhem. He looked up at the king, saw the love in his eyes, the adoration and acceptance, and hardly knew what he had done to deserve it. He had never felt the love of a father figure in his life. And now here he was, loved not just by a man, but by the King no less. Overnight, his world had changed. He only prayed that all of this was real.

*

Gwendolyn hurried through the crowd, pushing her way, wanting to catch site of the boy before he was ushered out of the royal court. *Thor*. Her heart beat faster at the thought of him, and she could not stop turning his name over in her head. She had been unable to stop thinking about him from the moment she had encountered him. He was younger than her, but not by more than a year or two— and besides, he had an air about him that made him seem older, more mature than the others, more profound. From the moment she had seen him, she had felt she had known him. She smiled to herself as she remembered meeting him, how flustered he was. She could see in his eyes that he felt the same way about her.

Of course, she did not even know the boy. But she had witnessed what he had done on the jousting lane, had seen what a liking her younger brother had taken to him. She had watched him ever since, sensing there was something special about him, something different than the others. When she met him, it had only confirmed it. He was different than all these royal types, different than all the people born and bred here. There was something refreshingly genuine about him. He was an outsider. A commoner. But oddly, with a royal bearing. It was as if he were too proud for what he was.

Gwen shoved her way to the upper balcony's edge, and looked down: below was spread out the royal court, and she caught a last glimpse of the boy as he was ushered out, her brother, Reece, by his side. They were surely heading to the barracks, to train with the other boys. She felt a pang of regret, already wondering, scheming, how she could arrange to see him again.

Gwen had to know more about him. She had to find out. For that, she would have to speak to the one woman who knew everything about anyone and everything going on in the kingdom: her mother.

Gwen turned and cut her way back through the crowd, twisting through the back corridors of the castle she knew by heart. Her head spun. It had been a dizzying day. First, the morning's meeting with her father, his shocking news that he wanted her to rule his kingdom. She was completely caught off guard, had never expected it in a million years. She still could hardly process it now. How could she ever possibly rule a kingdom? She pushed the thought from her mind, hoping that day would never come. After all, her father was healthy and strong, and more than anything, all she wanted was for him to live. To be here, with her. To be happy.

But she could not push the meeting from her mind. Somewhere, back there, lurking, was the seed planted that one day, whenever that day should come, *she* would be next. She would succeed him. Not any of her brothers. But her. It terrified her; it also gave her a sense of importance, of confidence, unlike any she'd ever had. He had found

71

her fit to rule, her—*her*—to be the wisest of them all. She wondered why.

It also, in some ways, worried her. She assumed it would stir up a huge amount of resentment and envy, her, a girl, being chosen to rule. Already, she could feel Gareth's envy. And that scared her. She knew her older brother to be terribly manipulative, and completely unforgiving. She knew he would stop at nothing until he got what he wanted. And she hated the idea of being in his sights. She had tried to talk to him after the meeting, but he would not even look at her.

Gwen ran down the spiral staircase, twisting and turning, her shoes echoing on the stone. She turned down another corridor, passed through the rear chapel, through another door, passed several guards, and entered the private chambers of the castle. She had to speak with her mother, and she knew she would be resting here, as she saw her slipping out of the feast. Her mother had little tolerance for these long social affairs anymore. She knew that she liked to slip out to her private chambers and rest as often as possible.

Gwen passed another guard, went down another hall, then finally stopped before the door to her mother's dressing room. She was about to open it, but then she stopped. Behind the open door, she heard muted voices, their pitch rising, and sensed something wrong. It was her mother, arguing. She listened closely, and heard her father's voice. They were fighting. But why?

Gwen knew she should not be listening—but she could not help herself. She reached out and gently pushed open the heavy oak door, grabbing it by its iron knocker. She opened it just a crack and listened.

"He won't stay in my house," her mother snapped, on edge.

"You rush to judgment, when you don't even know the entire story."

"I know the story," she snapped back. "Enough of it."

Gwen heard venom in her mother's voice, and was taken aback. She rarely heard her parents fight—just a few times in her life—and she had never heard her mother so worked up. She could not understand why.

"He will stay in the barracks, with the other boys. I do not want him under my roof. Do you understand?" she pressed.

"It is a big castle," her father spat back. "His presence will not be noticed by you."

"I don't care if it is noticed or not. I don't want him here. He's your problem. It was you who chose to bring him in."

"You are not so innocent either," her father retorted.

She heard footsteps, watched her father strut across the room and out the door on the other side, slamming it behind him so hard that the room shook. Her mother stood there, alone in the center of the room, and began to cry.

Gwen stood there and felt terrible. She didn't know what to do. On the one hand, she thought it best to slip away, but on the other, she couldn't stand the sight of her mother crying, couldn't stand to leave her there like that. She also, for the life of her, could not understand what they were arguing about. She assumed they were arguing about Thor. But why? Why would her mother even care? Dozens of people lived under their roof.

Gwen couldn't bring herself to just walk away, not with her mother in that state. She had to comfort her. She reached up and gently pushed the door open.

It creaked, and her mother wheeled, caught off guard. She scowled back.

"Do you not knock?" she snapped. Gwen could see how upset she was, and felt terrible.

"What's wrong mother?" Gwen asked, walking towards her gently. "I don't mean to pry, but I heard you arguing with father."

"You are right: you shouldn't pry," her mother retorted.

Gwen was surprised: her mother was often a handful, but was rarely like this. The force of her anger made Gwen stop in her tracks, a few feet away, unsure.

"Is it about the new boy? Thor?" she asked.

Her mother turned and looked away, wiping a tear.

"I don't understand," Gwen pressed. "Why would you care where he stayed?"

"My matters are of no concern to you," she said coldly, clearly wanting to end the matter. "What do you want? Why have you come here?"

Gwen was nervous now. She wanted her mother to tell her everything about Thor, but she couldn't have picked a worse moment. She cleared her throat, hesitant.

"I...actually wanted to ask you about him. What do you know of him?"

Her mother turned and narrowed her eyes at her, suspicious.

"Why?" she asked, with deadly seriousness. Gwen could feel her summing her up, looking right through her, and seeing with her

73

uncanny perception that Gwen liked him. She tried to hide her feelings, but knew it was no use.

"I'm just curious," she said, unconvincingly.

Suddenly, the queen took three steps towards her, grabbed her arms roughly, and stared into her face.

"Listen to me," she hissed. "I'm only going to say this once. Stay away from that boy. Do you hear me? I don't want you anywhere near him, under any circumstance."

Gwen was horrified.

"But why? He's a hero."

"He is not one of us," her mother answered. "Despite what your father might think. I want you to keep away from him. Do you hear me? Vow to me. Vow to me right now."

"I will not vow," Gwen said, yanking her arm away from her mother's too strong grip.

"He is a commoner, and you are Princess," her mother yelled. "You are a *Princess*. Do you understand? If I hear of you going anywhere near him, I will have him exiled from here. Do you understand?"

Gwen hardly knew how to respond. She had never seen her mother like this.

"Do not tell me what to do, mother," she said, finally.

Gwen did her best to put on a brave voice, but deep inside she was trembling. She had come here wanting to know everything; now, she felt terrified. She did not understand what was happening.

"Do as you wish," her mother said. "But his fate lies in your hands. Don't forget it."

With that, her mother turned, strutted from the room, and slammed it behind her, leaving Gwen all alone in the reverberating silence, her good mood shattered. She stood there and wondered. What could possibly elicit such a strong reaction from her mother and her father?

Who   was   this   boy?

CHAPTER TEN

MacGil sat in the banquet hall, watching over his subjects, he at one end of the table and Cloud at the other, and hundreds of men from both clans between them. The wedding revelries had been going on for hours, and finally, the tension between the clans had settled down from the day's jousting. As MacGil suspected, all the men needed was wine and meat—and women—to make them forget their differences. Now they all mingled at the same table, like brothers in arms. In fact, looking them over, MacGil could no longer even tell they were of two separate clans.

MacGil felt vindicated: his master plan was working after all. Already, the two clans seemed closer. He had managed to do what a long line of MacGil kings before him could not: to unify both sides of the ring, to make them, if not friends, then at least peaceful neighbors. He spotted his daughter, Luanda, arm in arm with her new husband, the McCloud prince, and she seemed content. His guilt lessened. He might have given her away—but he did, at least, give her a queenship.

MacGil thought back to all the planning that preceded this event, recalled the long days of arguing with his advisors. He had gone against the advice of all his counselors in arranging this union. He knew it was not an easy peace. He knew that, in time, the McLouds would settle in on their side of the Highlands, that this wedding would be long forgotten, and that one day they would stir with unrest. He was not naïve. But now, at least, there was a blood tie between the clans—and especially when a child was born, that could not be so easily ignored. If that child flourished, and one day even ruled, a child born of two sides of the Ring, then perhaps, one day, the entire ring could be united, the Highlands would no longer be a border of contention, and the land could prosper under one rule. That was his dream. Not for himself, but for his descendants. After all, the Ring had to stay strong, needed to stay unified in order to protect the Canyon, to fight off the hordes of the world beyond. As long as the two clans remained divided, they presented a weakened front to the rest of the world.

"A toast," MacGil shouted, and stood.

The table grew quiet as hundreds of men stood, too, raising their casks.

"To the wedding of my eldest child! To the union of the MacGils and McClouds! To peace throughout the Ring!"

"HERE HERE!" came a chorus of shouts, and everyone drank and the room once again filled with the noise of laughter and feasting.

MacGil sat back and surveyed the room, looking for his other children. There, of course, was Godfrey, drinking with two fists, a girl on each shoulder, surrounded by his miscreant friends. This was probably the one royal event he had ever willingly attended. There was Gareth, sitting too closely to his lover, Firth, whispering in his ear; MacGil could see from his darting, restless eyes, that he was plotting something. The thought of it made his stomach turn, and he looked away. There, on the far side of the room, was his youngest son, Reece, feasting at the squires' table, with the new boy, Thor. He already felt like a son, and he was pleased to see his youngest was fast friends with him.

He scanned the faces for his younger daughter, Gwendolyn, and finally found her, sitting off to the side, surrounded by her handmaids, giggling. He followed her gaze, and noticed she was watching Thor. He examined her for a long time, and realized she was smitten. He had not foreseen this, and he was not quite sure what to make of it. He sensed trouble there. Especially from his wife.

"All things are not what they seem," came a voice.

MacGil turned to see Argon sitting by his side, watching the two clans dining together.

"What do you make of all this?" MacGil asked. "Will there be peace in the kingdoms?"

"Peace is never static," Argon said. "It ebbs and flows, like the tides. What you see before you is the veneer of peace. You see one side of its face. You're trying to force peace on an ancient rivalry. But there are hundreds of years of spilled blood. The souls cry out for vengeance. And that cannot be appeased with a single marriage."

"What are you saying?" MacGil asked, taking another gulp of his wine, feeling nervous, as he often did around Argon.

Argon turned and stared at him with an intensity so strong, it struck panic into MacGil's heart.

"There will be war. The McClouds will attack. Prepare yourself. All of the house guests you see before you will soon be doing their best to murder your family."

MacGil gulped.

"Did I make the wrong decision to marry her off to them?"

Argon was silent for a while, until finally he said: "Not necessarily."

Argon looked away, and MacGil could see that he was finished with the topic. He was disappointed, because there were a million questions he wanted answered: but he knew his sorcerer would not answer them until he was ready. So instead, he watched Argon's eyes, and realized that they were watching his other daughter. Gwendolyn. He looked, too, and saw Gwendolyn watching Thor.

"Do you see them together?" MacGil asked, suddenly curious to know.

"Perhaps," Argon answered. "There is still much yet to be decided."

"You speak in riddles."

Argon shrugged and looked away, and MacGil realized he wouldn't get any more from him.

"You saw what happened on the field today?" MacGil prodded. "With the boy?"

"I saw it before it happened," Argon replied.

"And what do you make of it? What are the source of the boy's powers? Is he like you?"

Argon turned and stared into MacGil's eyes, and the intensity of his stare almost made him look away.

"He is far more powerful than me."

MacGil stared back, shocked. He had never heard Argon speak like this.

"More powerful? Than you? How is that possible? You are the king's sorcerer—there is no one more powerful than you in all the land."

Argon shrugged.

"Power does not only come in one form," he said. "The boy has powers beyond what you can imagine. Powers beyond what he knows. He has no idea who he is. Or where he hails from."

Argon turned and stared at MacGil.

"But you do," he added.

MacGil stared back, wondering.

77

"Do I?" MacGil asked. "Tell me. I need to know."

Argon shook his head.

"Search your feelings. They are true."

"What will become of him?" MacGil asked.

"He will become a great leader. And a great warrior. He will rule kingdoms in his own right. Far greater kingdoms than you. And he will be a far greater king than you. It is his destiny."

For a brief moment, MacGil burned with envy. He turned and examined the boy, laughing harmlessly with his son, at a table for squires, the commoner, the weak outsider, the youngest of the bunch. He didn't imagine how it was possible. Looking at him now, he looked barely eligible to join the Legion. He wondered for a moment if Argon was wrong.

But he knew that Argon had never been wrong, and that he never made pronouncements without a reason.

"Why are you telling me this?" MacGil asked.

Argon turned and stared at him.

"Because it is your time to prepare. The boy needs to be trained. He needs to be given the best of everything. It is your responsibility."

"Mine? And what of his father?"

"What of him?" Argon asked.

CHAPTER ELEVEN

Thor peeled open his eyes, disoriented, wondering where he was. He lay on the floor, on a mound of straw, his face planted sideways, his arms dangling over his head. He lifted his face, wiping the drool off, and immediately felt a stab of pain in his head, behind his eyes. It was the worst headache of his life. He remembered the night before, the king's feast, the drinking, his first taste of ale. The room was spinning. His throat was dry, and at that moment he vowed he would never drink again.

Thor looked around, trying to get his bearings in the cavernous barracks. Everywhere were bodies, lying on heaps of straw, the room filled with snoring; he turned the other way, and saw Reece, a few feet away, passed out, too. It was then he realized: he was in the barracks. The Legion's barracks. All around him were boys about his age, and there looked to be about fifty of them.

Thor vaguely remembered Reece showing him the way, in the late hours of the morning, and his crashing on the mound of straw. Early morning light flooded in through the open windows, and Thor soon realized he was the only one yet awake. He looked down and saw he had slept in his clothes, and reached up and ran a hand through his greasy hair. He would give anything for a chance to bathe—although he had no idea where. And he would do anything for a pint of water. His stomach rumbled, and he wanted food, too.

It was all so new to him. He barely knew where he was, where life would take him next, what the routines were of the king's Legion. He was happy. It had been a dazzling night, one of the finest of his life. He had found a close friend in Reece, and he had caught Gwendolyn looking at him once or twice. He had tried to speak with her, but each time he approached, his courage failed. He felt the pain of regret as he thought about it. There had been too many people around. If it was ever just the two of them, he would gain the courage. But would there be a next time?

Before Thor could finish the thought, there was a sudden banging on the wooden doors of the barracks, and a moment later, they crashed open, light flooding in.

"To your feet, squires!" came a shout.

In marched a dozen members of the King's Silver, chain mail rattling, banging on the wooden walls with metal staffs. The noise was deafening, and all-around Thor, the other boys jumped to their feet.

Leading the group was a particularly fierce-looking soldier, the one Thor recognized from the arena of the day before, the one Reece had told him was named Kolk, broad and stocky, with a bald head a short beard, and a scar running across his nose.

He seemed to be scowling right at Thor as he raised a finger and pointed it at him.

"You there boy!" he screamed. "I said on your feet!"

Thor was confused. He was already standing.

"But I'm already on my feet, sire," Thor answered.

Kolk stepped forward and backhanded Thor across the face. Thor stung with the indignation of it, as all eyes were on him.

"Don't you talk back to your superior again!" Kolk reprimanded.

Before Thor could respond the men moved on, roaming through the room, yanking one boy after another to his feet, kicking some in the ribs who were too slow to get up.

"Don't worry," came a reassuring voice.

He turned and saw Reece standing there.

"It is not personal to you. It is just their way. Their way of breaking us down."

"But they didn't do it to you," Thor said.

"Of course, they won't touch me, because of my father. But they won't exactly be polite, either. They want us in shape, that's all. They think this will toughen us up. Don't pay much attention to them."

The boys were all marched out of their barracks and Thor and Reece fell in with them. As they stepped outside, the bright sunlight struck Thor and he squinted and held up his hands. Suddenly, he was overwhelmed with a wave of nausea, and he turned, bent over, and threw up.

He could hear the snicker of boys all around him. A guard pushed him, and Thor stumbled forward, back in line with the others, wiping his mouth. Thor had never felt more awful.

Beside him, Reece smiled.

"Rough night, was it?" he asked Thor, grinning widely, elbowing him in the ribs. "I told you to stop after the second cask."

Thor felt queasy as the light pierced his eyes; it had never felt so strong as today. It was a hot day already, and he could feel drops of sweat forming beneath his leathermail.

Thor tried to remember back, to Reece's warning of the night before—but for the life of him, he could not remember.

"I don't remember any such advice," Thor retorted.

Reece grinned wider. "Precisely. That is because you did not listen."

Reece chuckled.

"And those ham-handed attempts to speak to my sister," he added. "It was positively pathetic," laughed. "I don't think I've ever seen a boy so fearful of a girl in my life."

Thor reddened as he tried to remember. But he could not. It was all hazy to him.

"I mean you no offense," Thor said. "With your sister."

"You cannot offend me. If she should choose you, I would be thrilled."

The two of them marched faster, as the group turned up a hill. The sun seemed to be getting stronger with each step.

"But I must warn you: every hand in the kingdom is after her. The chances of her choosing you... Well, let's just say they are remote."

As they walked faster, marching across the rolling green hills of King's Court, Thor felt reassured. He felt accepted by Reece. It was amazing to Thor, but he continued to feel that Reece was more of a brother to him than he'd ever had. As they walked, Thor noticed his three real brothers, marching close by. One of them turned and scowled back to him, then nudged his other brother, who looked back with a mocking grin. They shook their heads, and turned away. They had not so much as one kind word for Thor. But he hardly expected anything else.

"Get in line, Legion! Now!"

Thor looked up and saw several more of the Silver crowd around them, pushing the fifty of them into a tight line, double file. One man came up behind and struck the boy in front of Thor with a large bamboo rod, cracking him hard on the back; the boy cried out, and fell more tightly in line. Soon they were in two neat rows, marching steadily through the King's ground.

"When you march into battle, you march as one!" called out Kolk, walking up and down the sides. "This is not your mother's yard. You are marching to war!"

Thor marched and marched beside Reece, sweating in the sun, wondering where they were being led. His stomach still turned from the ale, and he wondered when he would have breakfast, when he would get something to drink. Once again, he cursed himself for drinking the night before.

As they went up and down the hills, through an arched stone gate, they finally reached the surrounding fields. They passed through another arched stone gate, and finally entered a coliseum of sorts. Clearly, the training ground for the Legion.

Before them were all sorts of targets, for throwing spears, firing arrows, hurling rocks, and piles of straw for slashing swords. Thor's heart quickened at the sight of it. He wanted to get in there, to use the weapons, to train.

But as Thor made his way towards the training area, suddenly he was elbowed in the ribs from behind, and a small group of six boys, most of them younger, like Thor, were herded off the main line. He found himself being split from Reece, being led to the other side of the field.

"Think you're going to train?" Kolk asked mockingly as they forked from the others, away from the targets. "It's horses for you today."

Thor looked up, and saw where they were headed: on the far side of the field, several horses pranced about. Kolk smiled down with an evil smile.

"While the others hurl spears and wield swords, today you will tend horses and clean their waste. We all have to start somewhere. Welcome to the Legion."

Thor's heart fell. This was not how he had seen it going at all.

"You think you're special boy?" Kolk asked, walking beside him, getting close to his face. Thor sensed that he was trying to break him. "Just because the king and his son have taken a liking to you, doesn't mean crap to me. You're in *my* command now. You understand me? I don't care about whatever fancy you pulled on the jousting ground. You're just another little boy. Do you understand me?"

Thor swallowed as he sensed that he was in for a long, hard training.

Making matters worse, as soon as Kolk drifted away to torture someone else, the boy in front of Thor, a short stocky kid with a flat nose, turned and sneered at him.

"You don't belong here," he said. "You cheated your way in. You weren't selected. You're not one of us. Not really. None of us like you."

The boy beside him also turned and sneered at Thor.

"We're going to do everything we can to make sure you drop out," he said. "Getting in is easy next to *staying* in."

Thor recoiled at their hatred. He couldn't believe he already had enemies, and didn't understand what he'd done to deserve it. All he'd ever wanted was to join the Legion.

"Why don't you mind for yourself," came a voice.

Thor looked over and saw a tall, skinny redhead boy, with freckles across his face and small green eyes, sticking up for him. "You two are stuck here shoveling with the rest of us," he added. "You're not so special, either. Go pick on someone else."

"You mind your business, lackey," one of the boys shot back, "or we'll be after you, too."

"Try it," the redhead snapped.

"You'll talk when I tell you to," Kolk yelled at one of the boys, smacking him hard upside the head. The two boys in front of Thor, thankfully, turned back around.

Thor hardly knew what to say; he fell in beside the redhead, so grateful to him.

"Thank you," Thor said.

The redhead turned and smiled at him.

"Name is O'Connor. I'd shake your hand, but they'd smack me if I did. So take this as an invisible handshake."

He smiled wider, and Thor instantly liked him.

"Don't mind them," he added. "They're just scared. Like the rest of us. None of us quite knew what we were signing up for."

Soon their group reached the end of the field, and Thor looked up and saw six horses, prancing about.

"Take up the reins!" Kolk commanded. "Hold them steady, and walk them around the arena until they break. Do it now!"

Thor stepped forward to grab the reins from the horse's mouth, and as he did, the horse stepped back and pranced, nearly kicking him. Thor, startled, stumbled back, and the others in the group laughed at him. He felt himself smacked hard in the back of the head, and saw Kolk, and felt like turning and hitting him back.

"You are a member of the Legion now. You never retreat. From anybody. No man, no beast. Now take those reins!"

Thor steeled himself, stepped forward, and grabbed the reins from the prancing horse. He managed to hang on, while the horse yanked and pulled, and began to lead him around the wide dirt field, getting in line with the others. His horse tugged at him, resisting, but Thor tugged back, not giving up so easily.

"It gets better, I hear."

Thor turned to see O'Connor coming up beside him, smiling. "They want to break us, you know?"

Suddenly, Thor's horse stopped. No matter how much he yanked it, this time, it would not budge. Then Thor smelled something awful; he looked back, and saw more waste coming from the horse than he ever imagined possible. It did not seem to end.

Thor felt a small shovel cast into his palm, and looked over to see Kolk beside him, smiling down.

"Clean it up!" he snapped.

CHAPTER TWELVE

Gareth stood in the crowded marketplace, wearing a cloak despite the midday sun, sweating beneath it, and trying to remain anonymous. He always tried to avoid this part of King's Court, these crowded alleyways, which stank of humanity and common man. All around him were people haggling, trading, trying to get one up on each other. Gareth stood at a corner stall, feigning interest in a vendor's fruit, keeping his head low, his cloak on. Standing just a few feet away was Firth, at the end of the dark alleyway, doing what they had come here to do.

Gareth stood within earshot of the conversation, keeping his back to him so as not to be seen. Firth had told him of a man, a mercenary, who would sell him a poison vial. Gareth wanted something strong, something certain to do the trick. No chances could be taken. After all, his own life was on the line.

It was hardly the sort of thing he could ask the local apothecary for. He had set Firth to the task, who had reported back to him after testing out the black market. After much pointing of the way, Firth had lead them to this slovenly character, who he spoke with now, furtively, at the end of the alleyway. Gareth had insisted on coming along for their final transaction, to make sure everything went smoothly, to make sure he was not being swindled and given a false potion. Plus, he was still not completely assured of Firth's competence. Some matters, he just had to take care of himself.

They had been waiting for this man for half an hour now, Gareth getting jostled in the busy market, praying he was not recognized. Even if he was, he figured, as long as he kept his back to the alley, if someone should know who he was, he could merely walk away, and no one would make the connection.

"Where is the vial?" Firth, just a few feet away, asked the cretin.

Gareth turned just a bit, so as not to be noticed, and peaked from the corner of his cloak. Standing there, opposite Firth, was an evil-looking man, slovenly, too thin, with sunken cheeks and huge black

85

eyes. He looked something like a rat. He stared down at Firth, unblinking.

"Where's the money?" he responded.

Gareth hoped Firth would handle this well: he usually managed to screw things up somehow.

"I shall give you the money when you give me the vial," Firth held his ground.

Good, Gareth thought, impressed.

There was a thick moment of silence, then:

"Give me half the money now, and I will tell you where the vial is."

"Where it is?" Firth echoed, his voice rising in surprise. "You said I would have it."

"I said you would have it, yes. I did not say I would bring it. Do you take me for a fool? Spies are everywhere. I know not what you intend—but I assume it is not trivial. After all, why else buy a vial of poison?"

Firth paused, and Gareth knew he was caught off guard.

Finally, Gareth heard the distinct noise of coins clacking, and peeked over and saw the royal gold pouring from Firth's pouch, into the man's palm.

Gareth waited, the seconds stretching forever, increasingly worried they were being had for.

"You'll take the Blackwood," the man finally responded. "At your third mile, fork on the path that leads up the hill. At the top, fork again, this time to the left. You will go through the darkest would you have ever seen, then arrive at a small clearing. The witch's cottage. She will be waiting for you—with the vial you desire."

Gareth peeked from his hood, and saw Firth prepare to leave. As he did, the man reached out, and suddenly grabbed him hard by his shirt.

"The money," the man growled. "It is not enough."

Gareth could see the fear spread across Firth's face, and regretted having sent him for this task. This slovenly character must have detected his fear—and now he was taking advantage. Firth was just not cut out for the sort of thing.

"But I gave you precisely what you asked for," Firth protested, his voice rising too high. He sounded effeminate. And this seemed to embolden the man.

The man grinned back, evil.

"But now I ask for more."

Firth's eyes opened wide with fear, and uncertainty. Then, suddenly, Firth turned and looked right at him.

Gareth turned away, hoping it was not too late, hoping he was not spotted. How could Firth be so stupid? He prayed he had not given him away.

As Gareth stood there, his back to them, his heart pounded as he waited. He anxiously fingered the fruit, pretending to be interested. There was an interminable silence behind him, as Gareth imagined all the things that might go wrong.

Please, don't let him come this way, Gareth prayed to himself. *Please. I'll do anything. I'll abandon the plot.*

Then, suddenly, he felt a rough palm slap him on his back. He spun and looked.

The cretin stared back, his large black, soulless eyes staring into his.

"You didn't tell me you had a partner," the man growled. "Or are you a spy?"

The man reached out before Gareth could react, and yanked down Gareth's hood. He got a good look at Gareth's face, and his eyes opened wide in shock.

"The Royal Prince," the man stumbled. "What are you doing here?"

A second later, the man's eyes narrowed in recognition, and he answered himself, with a small, satisfied smile, piecing together the whole plot instantly. He was much smarter than Gareth had hoped.

"I see," the man said. "This vial—it was for you, wasn't it? You aim to poison someone, don't you? But who? Yes, that is the question…"

Gareth's face flushed with anxiety. This man—he was too quick. It was too late. His whole world was unraveling around him. Firth had screwed it up. If this man gave Gareth away, he would be sentenced to death.

"Your father, maybe?" the man asked, his eyes lighting in recognition. "Yes, that must be it, mustn't it? You were passed over. Your father. You aim to kill your father."

Gareth had had enough. Without hesitating, he stepped forward, pulled a small dagger from inside his cloak, and plunged it into the man's chest. The man gasped.

Gareth didn't want any passersby to witness this: he grabbed the man by his tunic and pulled him close, ever closer, until their faces were almost touching, until he could smell his rotten breath. With his free hand, he reached up and clamped the man's mouth shut, before he could cry out. Gareth felt the man's hot blood trickling on his palm, running through his fingers.

Firth came up beside him and let out a horrified cry.

Gareth held the man there, like that, for a good sixty seconds, until finally, he felt him slumping in his arms. He let him collapse, limp, a heap on the ground.

Gareth spun all around, wondering if he had been seen; luckily, no heads turned in this busy marketplace, in this dark alley. He removed his cloak, and threw it over the lifeless heap.

"I am so sorry, so sorry, so sorry," Firth kept repeating, like a little girl, crying hysterically and shaking as he approached Gareth. "Are you okay? Are you okay?"

Gareth reached up and backhanded him.

"Shut your mouth and be gone from here," he hissed.

Firth turned and hurried off.

Gareth prepared to leave, but then stopped and turned back. He had one thing left to do: he reached down, grabbed his sack of coins from the dead man's hand, and stuffed it back into his waistband.

The man would not be needing this.

CHAPTER THIRTEEN

Gareth walked quickly through the forest trail, Firth beside him, his hood pulled over his head, despite the heat. He could hardly conceive that he now found himself in exactly the situation he had wanted to avoid. Now there was a dead body, a trail. Who knows who that man may have talked to. Firth should have been more circumspect in his dealings with the man. Now, the trail could end up leading back to Gareth.

"I'm sorry," Firth said, hurrying to catch up beside him.

Gareth ignored him, doubling his pace, seething.

"What you did was foolish, and weak," Gareth said. "You never should have glanced my way."

"I didn't mean to. I didn't know what to do when he demanded more money."

Firth was right: it was a tricky situation. The man was a selfish, greedy pig and he changed the rules of the game and deserved to die. Gareth shed no tears over him. He only prayed that no one had witnessed the murder. The last thing he needed was a trail. There would be tremendous scrutiny in the wake of his father's assassination, and he could not afford even the smallest trail of clues left to follow.

At least they were now in Blackwood. Despite the summer sun, it was nearly dark in here, the towering eucalyptus trees blocking out every shaft of light. It matched his mood. Gareth hated this place. He continued hiking down the meandering trail, following the dead man's directions. He hoped the man was telling the truth, not leading them astray. The whole thing could be a lie. Or it could be he was leading them to a trap, to some friend of his waiting to rob them of more money.

Gareth chided himself. He had put too much trust in Firth. He should have handled this all himself. Like he always did.

"You better just hope that this trail leads us to the witch," Gareth quipped, "and that she has the poison."

They continued down trail after trail, until finally they reached a fork, just as the man said they would. It boded well, and Gareth was slightly relieved. They followed it to the right, climbed a hill, and soon forked again. His instructions were true, and before them was, indeed, the darkest patch of wood that Gareth had ever seen. The trees were impossibly thick, mangled.

Gareth entered them, and felt an immediate chill up his skin, could feel the evil hanging in the air. He could hardly believe it was still daylight.

Just as he was getting scared, thinking of turning back, before him the trail ended in a small clearing. It was lit up by a single shaft of sunlight that broke through the wood. In its center was a small stone cottage. The witch's cottage.

Gareth's heart quickened. As he entered the clearing, he looked around to make sure no one was watching, to make sure it was not a trap.

"You see, he was telling the truth," Firth said, excitement in his voice.

"That means nothing," Garrett chided. "Remain outside, and stand guard. Knock if anyone enters. And keep your mouth shut."

Gareth didn't bother to knock on the small, arched wooden door before him. Instead, he grabbed the iron handle, yanked open the two-foot thick door, and ducked his head as he entered, closing it behind him.

It was dark in here, lit only by scattered candles in the room. It was a single room cottage, devoid of windows, and he immediately felt enveloped by a heavy energy. He stood there, stifled by the thick silence, preparing himself for anything. He could feel the evil in here. It made his skin crawl.

From out of the shadows he detected motion, then a noise.

Hobbling towards him there appeared an old woman, shriveled up, hunchback. She raised a candle and lit her face, and he could see it was covered in warts and lines. She looked ancient, older than the gnarled trees that hovered over her cottage.

"You wear a hood, even in blackness," she said, wearing a sinister smile, her voice sounding like crackling wood. "Your mission is not innocent."

"I've come for a vial," Gareth said quickly, trying to sound brave and confident, but hearing the quivering in his voice. "Sheldrake Root. I'm told you have it."

There was a long silence, followed by a horrific hackle. It echoed in the small room.

"Whether or not I have it is not the question. The question is: why do you want it?"

Gareth's heart pounded as he tried to formulate an answer.

"Why should you care?" he finally asked.

"It amuses me to know who you are killing," she said.

"That's no business of yours. I've brought money for you."

Gareth reached into his waistband, took out the bag of gold, in addition to the bag of gold he had given the dead man, and banged them both down on her small wooden table. The sound of metallic coins rang in the room.

He prayed it would pacify her, that she would give him what he wanted and he could leave this place.

The witch reached out a single finger with a long, curved nail, picked up one of the bags and inspected it. Gareth held his breath, hoping she would ask no more.

"This might be just enough to buy my silence," she said.

She turned and hobbled into the darkness. There was a hissing noise, and beside a candle Gareth could see her mixing liquid into a small, glass vial. It bubbled over, and she put a cork on it. Time seemed to slow as Gareth waited, increasingly impatient. A million worries raced through his mind: what if he was discovered? Right here, right now? What if she gave him the wrong vial? What if she told someone about him? Had she recognized him? He couldn't tell.

Gareth was having increasing reservations about this whole thing. He never knew how hard it could be to assassinate someone.

After what felt like an interminable silence, finally, she returned. She held out the vial, so small it nearly disappeared into his palm.

"Such a small vial?" he asked. "Can this do the trick?"

She smiled.

"You'd be amazed at how little it takes to kill a man."

Gareth turned and began to head for the door, when suddenly he felt a cold finger on his shoulder. He had no idea how she had managed to cross the room so quickly, and it terrified him. He stood there, frozen, afraid to turn and look at her.

She stood there, inches away, grinning back. She leaned in so close, an awful smell emanating from her, then suddenly reached up with both hands, grabbed his cheeks, and kissed him, pressing her shriveled lips hard against his.

Gareth was revolted. It was the most disgusting thing that had ever happened to him. Her lips were like the lips of a lizard, her tounge, which she pressed onto his, like that of a reptile. He tried to pull away, but she held his face tight, pulling him harder, kissing him on the mouth.

Finally, he managed to yank himself away. He wiped his mouth with the back of his hand, as she leaned back and chuckled.

"The first time you kill a man is the hardest," she said. "You will find it much easier the next time around."

*

Gareth burst out of the cottage, back into the clearing, to find Firth standing there, waiting for him.

"What's wrong? What happened?" Firth asked, concerned. "You look as if you've been stabbed. Did she hurt you?"

Gareth stood there, breathing hard, wiping his mouth again and again. He hardly knew how to respond.

"Let's get away from this place," he said. "Now!"

As they began to move, to head out of the clearing into the black wood, suddenly the sun was obscured by clouds, racing across the sky, making the beautiful day cold and dark. Gareth looked up, and had never seen such thick, black clouds appear so quickly. He knew that whatever was happening, it was not normal. He worried about how deep the powers were of this witch, as he felt the cold wind rise in the summer day, creep up the back of his neck. He couldn't help but think that she had somehow possessed him with that kiss, cast some sort of curse on him.

"What happened in there?" Firth pressed.

"I don't want to talk about it," Gareth said. "I don't want to think about this day—ever again."

The two of them hurried back down the trail, down the hill, soon entering the main forest trail to head back towards King's Court. Just as Gareth was beginning to feel more relieved, preparing to shove the whole episode to the back of his mind, suddenly, he heard another set of boots. He turned and saw a group of men walking towards them. He couldn't believe it.

His brother. Godfrey. The drunk. He was walking towards them, laughing, surrounded by the villainous Harry, and two other of his miscreant friends. Of all times and places, for his brother to run into him here. In the woods, in the middle of nowhere. Gareth felt as if his whole plot were cursed.

Gareth turned away, pulled the hood over his face, and hiked twice as fast, praying he had not been discovered.

"Gareth?" called out the voice.

Gareth had no choice. He froze in his tracks, pulled back his hood, and turned and looked at his brother, who came waltzing merrily towards him.

"What are you doing here?" Godfrey asked.

Gareth opened his mouth, but then closed it, stumbling, at a loss for words.

"We were going for a hike," Firth volunteered, rescuing him.

"A hike, were you?" one of Godfrey's friends mocked Firth, in a high, feminine voice. His friends laughed, too. Gareth knew that his brother and his friends all judged him for his predisposition—but he hardly cared about that now. He just needed to change the topic. He didn't want them to wonder what he was doing out here.

"What are *you* doing out here?" Gareth asked, turning the tables.

"A new tavern opened, by Southwood," Godfrey answered. "We had just been trying it out. The best ale in all the kingdom. Want some?" he asked, holding out a cask.

Gareth shook his head quickly. He knew he had to distract him, and he figured the best way was to change the topic, to rebuke him.

"Father would be furious if he caught you drinking during the day," Gareth said. "I suggest you set down that and return to court."

It worked. Godfrey glowered, and clearly he was no longer thinking about Gareth, but about father, and himself.

"And since when did you care about father's needs?" he retorted.

Gareth had had enough. He hadn't time to waste with a drunkard. He succeeded in what he wanted, distracting him, and now, hopefully, he wouldn't think too deeply about why he had run into him here.

Gareth turned and hurried down the trail, hearing their mocking laughter behind him as he went. He no longer cared. Soon, it would be he who had the last laugh.

CHAPTER FOURTEEN

Thor sat before the wooden table, working away at the bow and arrow laid out in pieces. Beside him sat Reece, along with several other members of the Legion. They were all hunched over their weapons, hard at work on carving the bows and tightening the strings.

"A warrior knows how to string his own bow," Kolk yelled out, as he walked up and down the rows of boys, leaning over, examining each one's work. "The tension must be just right. Too little, and your arrow will not reach its mark. Too much, and your aim will not be true. Weapons break in battle. Weapons break on journeys. You must know how to repair them as you go. The greatest warrior is also a blacksmith, a carpenter, a cobbler, a mender of all things broken. And you don't really know your own weapon until you've repaired it yourself."

Kolk stopped behind Thor and leaned over his shoulder. He reached out and yanked the wooden bow out of Thor's grasp, the string hurting his palm as he did.

"The string is not taught enough," he chided. "It is crooked. Use a weapon like this in battle, and you will surely die. And your partner will die besides you."

Kolk slammed the bow back down, then moved on; several other boys snickered. Thor reddened as he grabbed the string again, pulled it as taught as he possibly could, and wrapped it around the notch in the bow. He'd been at work on this for hours, the cap to an exhausting day of labor and menial tasks.

Most of the others were out and about, training, sparring, sword fighting. He looked out and in the distance saw his brothers, the three of them, laughing as they clacked wooden swords; as usual, Thor felt that they were gaining the upper hand and he was being left behind, in their shadow. Thor thought it unfair. He felt increasingly that he was unwanted here, as if he were not a true member of the Legion.

"Don't worry, you'll get the hang of it," O'Connor said beside him.

Thor's palms were chafed from trying; he pulled back the string one last time, this time with all his might, and finally, to his surprise, it clicked. The string fit neatly in the notch, as he pulled with all his might, sweating. He felt a great sense of satisfaction, as the bow finally felt as strong as it should be.

The sun grew longer in the sky and he looked up, wiped his forehead with the back of his hand, and wondered how much longer this would go on. He contemplated what it meant to be a warrior. In his head, he had seen it differently. He had only imagined training, all the time. But, he guessed, this was also a form of training.

"This was not what I signed up for, either," O'Connor said, as if reading his mind.

Thor turned, and was reassured to find his constant smile.

"I come from the Northern Province," he continued. "I, too, dreamed of joining the Legion my entire life. I guess I imagined constant sparring, battle. Not all of these menial tasks. But it will get better. It is just because we are new. It is a form of initiation. There seems to be a hierarchy here. We are also the youngest. I don't see the nineteen-year-olds doing this. This can't last forever. Besides, it's a useful skill to learn."

A horn sounded. Thor looked over and saw the rest of the Legion gathering together, beside a huge stone wall in the middle of the field. Ropes were draped across it, spaced every ten feet. The wall must have rose thirty feet and piled at its base were stacks of hay.

"What are you waiting for?" Kolk screamed. "MOVE!"

The Silver appeared all around them, screaming, and before Thor knew it he and all the others jumped from their benches and ran across the field, for the wall.

Soon they were all gathered there, standing before the ropes. There was an excited buzz in the air, as all of the Legion members stood there, together. Thor was ecstatic to finally be included with the others, and he found himself gravitating to Reece, who stood with another friend of his. O'Connor joined them.

"You will find in battle that most towns are fortified," Kolk boomed out, looking over the faces of the boys. "Breaching fortifications is the work of a soldier. In a typical siege, ropes and grappling hooks are used, much like the ones we have thrown over this wall, and climbing a wall is one of the most dangerous things you will encounter in battle. In few cases will you be more exposed, more vulnerable. The enemy will pour down molten lead on you. They will shoot down arrows. Drop rocks. You don't climb a wall until the moment is perfect. And when you do, you must climb for your life—or else risk death."

Kolk took a deep breath, then screamed out: "BEGIN!"

All around him the boys broke into action, each charging for a rope. Thor sprinted for a free rope; he was about to grab it, when an older boy reached it first, bumping him out of the way. Thor scrambled, and grabbed the closest one he could find. He grabbed the thick knotted twine, his heart pounding, as he began to scramble his way up the wall.

The day had turned misty, and Thor's feet slipped on the stone as he climbed. Still, he made good time, and he couldn't help but notice that he was faster than many of the others, nearly taking the lead as he scrambled his way up. He was, for the first time today, starting to feel good, starting to feel a sense of pride.

Suddenly, he felt something hard slam into his shoulder. He looked up, and saw members of the Silver at the top of the wall, throwing down small rocks, sticks, all manner of debris. The boy on the rope beside Thor reached up with one hand to block his face and lost his grip and fell backwards, down to the ground. He fell a good twenty feet, and landed in the pile of hay below.

Thor was losing his grip, too, but somehow managed to hang on. A club hailed down and hit Thor hard on the back, but he continued to climb. He was making good time and was starting to think he might even be the first one to the top, when suddenly, he felt himself kicked hard in the ribs. He couldn't even understand where it came from, until he looked over and saw one of the boys beside him, swinging sideways. Before Thor could react, the boy kicked him again.

Thor lost his grip this time and found himself hurling backwards, through the air, flailing. He landed on his back in the hay, shocked, but unhurt.

Thor scrambled to his hands and knees, catching his breath, and looked about: all around him, boys were dropping like flies from the ropes, landing in the hay, kicked or shoved by each other—or if not, then kicked off by members of the Silver up top. Those who weren't had their ropes cut, so they went flying, too. Not a single member reached the top.

"On your feet!" yelled Kolk. Thor jumped up, as did the others. "SWORDS!"

The boys ran as one to a huge rack of wooden swords. Thor joined them and grabbed one, shocked at how heavy it was. It weighed twice as much as any weapon he had lifted. He could barely hold it.

"Heavy swords, begin!" came a shout.

Thor looked up and saw that huge oaf, Elden, the one who had first attacked him when he met the Legion. Thor remembered him too well: his face was still hurting from the bruises he had given him. He was bearing down on him, sword held high, a look of fury on his face.

Thor raised his sword at the last moment; he managed to block Elden's blow, but the sword was so heavy, he was barely able to hold it back. Elden, bigger and stronger, reached around and kicked Thor hard in the ribs.

Thor dropped to his knees, in pain. Elden swung around again, to crack him in the face, but Thor managed to reached up and block the blow with a moment to spare. But Elden was too quick and strong, and he swung around and slashed Thor in the leg, knocking him down on his side.

A small crowd of boys gathered around them, cheering and hollering, as clearly their fight was becoming the center of attention. It seemed as if they were all rooting for Elden.

Elden came down with his sword again, slashing down hard, and Thor rolled out of the way, the blow barely missing his back. Thor had a moment's advantage, and he took it: he swung around and hit the oaf hard behind the knee. It was a soft spot, and enough to knock him back, then down, stumbling onto his rear.

Thor used the chance to scramble to his feet. Elden rose, red-faced, more furious than ever, and now the two faced off.

Thor knew he couldn't just stand there; he charged and swung. But this practice sword was made of a strange wood and just too heavy; his move was telegraphed. Elden blocked it easily, then jabbed Thor hard in the ribs.

It hit a soft spot, and Thor keeled over and dropped his sword, the wind knocked out of him.

The other boys screamed in delight. Thor kneeled there, unarmed, and felt the tip of Elden's sword jammed into the base of his throat.

"Yield!" Elden demanded.

Thor glared up at him, feeling the salty taste of blood on his lip.

"Never," he muttered, defiant.

Elden grimaced, raised his sword, and prepared to bring it down. There was nothing Thor could do. He knew that he was in for a mighty blow.

As the sword came down, Thor closed his eyes and concentrated. He felt the world slowing down, felt himself transported to another realm. He was suddenly able to feel the swing of the sword in the air, its motion, and he willed the universe to stop it.

He felt his body warming, tingling, and as he focused, he felt something happening. He felt himself able to control it.

Suddenly the sword freezed in mid-air. Thor had somehow managed to stop it using his power.

As Elden stood there, holding the sword, confused, Thor then used his mind power to grasp and squeeze Elden's wrist. He squeezed harder and harder in his mind, and in moments, Elden cried out and dropped the sword.

All the boys quieted, as they stood there, frozen, looking down at Thor, wide-eyed in surprise and fear.

"He's a demon!" one yelled out.

"A sorcerer," another yelled.

Thor was overwhelmed. He had no grasp of what he had just done. But he knew it was normal. He was both proud and embarrassed, emboldened and afraid.

Kolk stepped forward, into the circle, standing between Thor and Elden.

"This is no place for spells, boy, whoever you are," he chastised Thor. "It is a place for battle. You defied our rules of fighting. You will think about what you have done. I will send you to a place of true danger, and we shall see how well your spells defend you there. Report to guard patrol at the Canyon."

There was a gasp among the Legion, and they all quieted. Thor did not understand exactly what that meant, but he knew that whatever it was, it could not be good.

"You can't send him to the Canyon!" Reece protested. "He is too new. He could get hurt."

"I shall do whatever I choose to boy," Kolk grimaced at Reece. "Your father is not here to protect you now. Or him. And I run this Legion. And you better mind your tongue—just because you are royalty, don't think you can speak out of line again."

"Fine," Reece responded. "Then I shall join him!"

"As will I!" O'Connor chimed in, stepping forward.

Kolk looked them over, and slowly shook his head.

"Fools. That is your choice. Join him if you wish."

Kolk turned and looked at Elden. "Don't think you get off so easy, either," he said to him. "You started this fight. You must pay the price, too. You will join them on patrol tonight."

"But sire, you can't send me to the Canyon!" Elden protested, eyes wide in fear. It was the first time Thor had seen him afraid of anything.

Kolk took a step forward, close to Elden, and raised his hands on his hips. "Can't I?" he said. "Not only can I send you there— I can also send you away for good, out of this Legion, and to the farthest reaches of our kingdom, if you continue to talk back to me."

Elden looked away, too flustered to respond.

"Anyone else want to join them?" Kolk called out.

The other boys, bigger and older and stronger, all looked away in fear. Thor gulped as he looked around at the nervous faces, and wondered just how bad the Canyon could be.

CHAPTER FIFTEEN

Thor walked along the well-trodden, dirt road, flanked by Reece, O'Connor and Elden. The four of them had barely said a word to each other since they left, still in shock. Thor looked over at Reece and O'Connor with a feeling of gratitude he had never known before. He could hardly believe that they had put themselves on the line for him like that. He felt that he had found true friends, more like brothers. He had no idea what lay in store for them at the Canyon, but whatever they should face, he was happy to have them at his side.

Elden, he tried not to look at. He could see him, kicking rocks, smoldering with rage, could see how annoyed and upset he was to be here, on patrol with them. But Thor felt no pity for him. As Kolk had said, he had started the whole thing. It served him right.

The four of them, a ragtag group, proceeded down the road, following directions. They had been walking for hours, it was getting late in the afternoon, and Thor's legs were growing weary. He was also hungry. Had been given only a small bowl of barley for lunch, and he hoped some food might be waiting for them wherever they were going.

But he had bigger worries than that. He looked down at his new armor, and knew that it would not have been given to him if there were not an important reason. Before sending them off, the four of them had been given new squire's armor, leather, dressed in chainmail, given short swords of a course metal. It was hardly the fine iron used to forge a knight's sword, but it was certainly better than nothing. It felt good to have a substantial weapon at his waist—in addition, of course, to his sling, which he still carried. Though he knew that if they were to encounter real trouble tonight, the weapons and armor they were given might not suffice. He longed for the superior armor and weapons of his cohorts in the Legion: medium and long swords of the finest metal, short spears, maces, daggers, halberds. But these belonged to the boys of fame and honor, from famous families, who could afford such a thing. This was not Thor, a simple shepherd's son.

As they all marched down the interminable road, into the second sunset, far from the welcoming gates of King's Court, towards the distant divide of the Canyon, Thor could not help but feel as if this were all his fault. For some reason, some of the other members of the Legion had seemed to not taking a liking to him, as if they resented his presence. It didn't make any sense. And it gave him a sinking feeling. His whole life he had wanted nothing more than to join them. Now, he felt he had crashed into it by cheating, and he wondered if he would ever be truly accepted by his peers.

Now, on top of everything, he was singled out to be marched away for Canyon duty. It was unfair. He hadn't started the fight, and when he had used his powers, whatever they were, it had not been on purpose. He still didn't understand them, didn't know where they came from, how he summoned them, or how to turn them off. He shouldn't be punished for that.

Thor had no idea what Canyon duty meant, but from the looks of the others, clearly, it was not desirable. He wondered if he were being marched off to be killed, if this was their way of forcing him out of the Legion. He was determined not to give up.

"How much farther can the Canyon be?" O'Connor asked, breaking the silence.

"Not far enough," answered Elden. "We wouldn't be in this mess if it weren't for Thor."

"You started the fight, remember?" Reece interrupted.

"But I fought cleanly, and he did not," Elden protested. "Besides, he deserved it."

"Why?" Thor asked, wanting to know the answer that had been burning inside for a while. "Why did I deserve it?"

"Because you don't belong here, with us. You stole your position in the Legion. The rest of us, we were picked. You fought your way in."

"But isn't that what the Legion is about? Fighting?" Reece answered. "I would argue that Thor deserves his spot more than any of us. We were merely picked. He struggled and fought to gain what was not given him."

Elden shrugged, unimpressed.

"The rules are the rules. He was not picked. He shouldn't be with us. That's why I fought him."

"Well, you are not going to make me go away," Thor responded, shakiness in his voice, determined to be accepted.

"We'll see about that," Elden muttered darkly.

"And just what you mean by that?" O'Connor asked.

But Elden did not volunteer anymore; he continued walking silently. Thor's stomach tightened. He couldn't help but feel as if he had made too many enemies, and he did not understand why. He did not like the feeling.

"Don't pay any attention to him," Reece said to Thor, loudly enough to be heard. "You did nothing wrong. They sent you to Canyon duty because they see potential in you. They want to toughen you up. Or else they wouldn't bother. You're also on the radar because my father singled you out. That's all."

"But what is Canyon duty?" he asked.

Reece cleared his throat, looking anxious.

"I've never been on it myself. But I've heard stories. From some of the older kids, and from my brothers. It is patrol duty. But on the other side of the Canyon."

"The other side?" O'Connor asked, terror in his voice.

"What do you mean the other side?" Thor asked, not understanding.

Reece studied him.

"Have you never been to the Canyon?"

Thor could feel the others looking at him, and he shook his head, self-conscious.

"You're kidding," Elden snapped.

"Really?" O'Connor pressed. "Not once in your life?"

Thor shook his head, reddening. "My father never took us anywhere. I've heard of it."

"You've probably never been outside your village, boy," Elden said. "Have you?"

Thor shrugged, silent. Was it that obvious?

"He hasn't," Elden added, incredulous. "Unbelievable."

"Shut up," Reece said. "Leave him alone. That doesn't make you any better than him."

Elden sneered at Reece and raised his hand briefly to his scabbard; but then relaxed it. Apparently, even though he was bigger than Reece, he didn't seem to want to provoke the king's son.

"The Canyon is the only thing keeping our kingdom of the Ring safe," Reece explained. "Nothing else stands between us and the hordes of the world. If the savages of the Wilds were to breach it, we would all be finished. The entire Ring looks to us, the King's men, to protect them. We have patrols guarding it all the time—mostly on this side, and occasionally, on the other. There is only one bridge across, only one way in or out, and the most elite of the Silver stand watch around-the-clock."

Thor had heard of the Canyon his entire life, had heard horrifying stories of the evils that lurked on the other side, the massive evil empire that surrounded the Ring, and how close they all lived to terror. It was one of the reasons why he had wanted to join the King's Legion: to help protect his family and his kingdom. He hated the idea that other men were out there, protecting him around-the-clock, while he lived comfortably in the arms of the kingdom. He wanted to do his service and help fight off the evil hordes. He could imagine nothing braver than those men who guarded the Canyon passageway.

"The Canyon is a mile wide, and surrounds the entire Ring," Reece explained. "It is not easy to breach. But of course our men are not the only thing keeping the hordes at bay. There are millions of those creatures out there, and if they wanted to overrun this Canyon, by sheer force of will, they could in a moment. Our manpower only helps supplement the energy shield of the Canyon. The real power that keeps them at bay is the power of the Sword."

Thor turned. "The Sword?"

Reece looked at him.

"The Destiny Sword. You know the legend?"

"This country rube probably never even heard of it," Elden chimed in.

"Of course I know it," Thor snapped back, defensive. Not only did he know it, but he had spent many days pondering the legend throughout his life. He had always wanted to see it. The fabled Destiny Sword, the magical sword whose energy protected the Ring, filled the Canyon with a potent force that protected the Ring from invaders.

"The sword lives in King's Court?" Thor asked.

Reece nodded.

"It has lived amongst the royal family for generations. Without it, the kingdom would be nothing. The Ring would be overrun."

"If we are protected, then why bother patrol the Canyon at all?" Thor asked.

"The Sword only blocks the major threats," Reece explained. "A small and isolated evil creature can slip in, here and there. That is why our men are needed. A single creature could cross the Canyon, or even a small group of them—they might be so bold as to try to cross the bridge, or they may act with stealth and climb down the Canyon walls on one end and up on the other. It is our job to keep them out. A single creature can cause a lot of damage. Years ago, one of them slipped in, and murdered half the children of a village before he was caught. The Sword does the bulk of the work, but we are an indispensable part."

Thor took it all in, wondering. The Canyon seemed so grand, their duty so important, he could hardly believe that he would be part of this great purpose.

"But even with all that, I haven't explained it very well," Reece said. "There's more to the Canyon than just that," he said, then fell silent.

Thor looked at him and saw something like fear or wonder in his eyes.

"How can I explain it?" Reece said, clearly struggling. He cleared his throat. "The Canyon is far bigger than all of us. The Canyon is…"

"The Canyon is a place for men," came a resounding voice.

They all turned at the sound of the voice, the sound of a horse.

Thor could not believe it. There, trotting up beside them, bedecked in full chainmail, with long gleaming weapons hanging over the side of his incredible horse, was Erec. He smiled down at them, keeping his eyes fixed on Thor.

Thor looked up, in shock.

"It is a place that will make you a man," Erec added, "if you are not one already."

Thor had not seen Erec since his jousting match, and felt so relieved at his presence, to have a real knight here with them as they headed for the Canyon—no less, Erec himself. He felt invincible having him, and prayed he was coming with them.

"What are you doing here?" Thor asked. "Are you accompanying us?" he asked, hoping he didn't sound too eager.

Erec leaned back and laughed.

"Not to worry, young one," he said. "I'm going with you."

"Really?" Reece asked.

"It is tradition for a member of the Silver to accompany members of the Legion on their first patrol. I volunteered."

Erec turned and looked down at Thor.

"After all, you helped me yesterday."

Thor felt his heart warm, buoyed by Erec's presence. He also felt lifted up in the eyes of his friends. Here he was, being accompanied by the greatest knight of the kingdom, as they headed towards the Canyon. Much of his fear was falling away.

"Of course, I shall not go out on patrol with you," Erec added. "But I will lead you across the bridge, and to your camp. It will be your duty to venture out on patrol, alone, from there."

"It is a great honor, sire," Reece said.

"Thank you," O'Connor and Elden echoed.

Erec looked down at Thor and smiled.

"After all, if you're going to be my first squire, I can't let you die just yet."

"First?" Thor asked, his heart skipping a beat.

"Feithgold broke his leg in the jousting match. He will be out for at least eight weeks. You are my first squire now. And our training might as well begin, shan't it?"

"Of course, sire," Thor responded.

Thor's mind was swimming. He could hardly believe it. For the first time in a while, he felt as if luck was finally turning his way. Now he was first squire to the greatest knight of all. He felt as if he had leapfrogged over all his friends; he could hardly believe it.

The five of them continued on, heading west into the setting sun, Erec walking slowly on his horse beside them.

"I assume you have been to the Canyon, sire?" Thor asked.

"Many times," Erec responded. "My first patrol, I was your age, in fact."

"And how did you find it?" Reece asked.

All four boys turned and stared at him as they went, rapt with attention. Erec rode on for some time in silence, looking straight ahead, his jaw set.

"Your first time is an experience you never forget. It is hard to explain. It is a strange and foreign and mystical and beautiful place. On the other side lie unimaginable dangers. The bridge to cross it is long and steep. There are many of us patrolling—but always, you feel alone. It is nature at its best. It crushes man to be in its shadow. Our men have patrolled it for hundreds of years. It is a rite of passage. You do not fully understand danger without it; you cannot become a knight without it."

He fell back into silence. The four boys looked at each other, queasy.

"Should we expect a skirmish on the other side then?" Thor asked.

Erec shrugged.

"Anything is possible, once you reach the Wilds. Unlikely. But possible."

Erec looked down at Thor.

"Do you want to be a great squire, and one day, a great knight?" he asked, looking right at Thor.

Thor's heart beat faster.

"Yes, sire, more than anything."

"Then there are things you must learn," Erec said. "Strength is not enough; agility is not enough; being a great fighter is not enough. There is something else, something more important than all of them."

Erec fell back into silence, and Thor could wait no longer.

"What?" Thor asked. "What is most important?"

"You must be of a sound spirit," Erec replied. "Never afraid. You must enter the darkest wood, the most dangerous battle, with complete equanimity. You must carry this equanimity with you, always, whenever and wherever you go. Never fearful, always on guard. Never restful, always diligent. You don't have the luxury of expecting others to protect you anymore. You're no longer a citizen. You're now one of the King's men. The greatest qualities for a warrior are courage, and equanimity. Be not afraid of danger. Expect it. But do not seek it.

"This Ring we live in," Erec added, "our kingdom. It seems as if we, with all our men, protect it against the hordes of the world. But we do not. We are protected only by the Canyon, and only by the sorcery within it. We live in a sorcerer's ring. Don't forget it. We live and die by magic. There is no security here, boy, on either side of the canyon. Take away sorcery, take away magic, and we have nothing."

They walked on in silence for quite some time, as Thor turned Erec's words over in his head, again and again. He felt as if Erec were giving him a hidden message: he felt as if he were telling him that, whatever power he had, whatever magic he might be summoning, it was nothing to be ashamed of. In fact, it was something to be proud of, and the source of all energy in the kingdom. Thor felt better. He had felt he was being sent out here, to the Canyon, as a punishment for his using his magic, and had felt guilty about it; but now he felt that his powers, whatever they were, might become a source of pride.

As the other boys drifted ahead, and Erec and Thor fell back, Erec looked down at him.

"You've already managed to make some powerful enemies at Court," he said, an amused smile on his face. "As many enemies as you have friends, it seems."

Thor reddened, shamed.

"I don't know how, sire. I didn't intend to."

"Enemies are not gained by intentions. They are often gained by envy. You have managed to create a great deal of it. That is not necessarily a bad thing. You are the center of much speculation."

Thor scratched his head, trying to understand.

"But I don't know why."

Erec still looked amused.

"The queen herself is chief among your adversaries. You have somehow managed to get on her wrong side."

"My mother?" Reece asked, turning. "Why?"

"That is the very question I've been wondering myself," Erec said.

Thor felt terrible. The Queen? An enemy? What had he done to her? He could hardly conceive it. How could he even be important enough for her to take notice of? He hardly knew what was happening around him.

Suddenly, something dawned on him.

"Is she the reason that I was sent out here? To the Canyon?" he asked.

Erec turned and looked straight ahead, his face growing serious.

"She might be," he said, contemplative. "She just might be."

Thor wondered at the extent and depth of the enemies he had made. He had stumbled into a court he knew nothing about. He had just wanted to belong. He had just followed his passion and his dream, and had done whatever he could to achieve it. He did not think that by doing so, he might raise envy or jealousy. He turned it over and over in his mind, like a riddle, but could not get to the bottom of it.

As Thor was mulling these thoughts, they reached the top of a knoll, and as the site spread out before them, all thoughts of anything else fell away. Thor's breath was taken away—and not just by the strong gust of wind.

There, stretching out before them, as far as the eye could see, lay the Canyon. It was the first time Thor had ever seen it, and the site shocked him so thoroughly, he stood rooted to his place, unable to move. It was the grandest and most majestic thing he had ever seen. The huge chasm in the earth seemed to stretch for eternity, and was spanned only by a single, narrow bridge, lined with soldiers. The bridge seemed to stretch to the end of the earth itself.

The Canyon was alight with greens and blues from the second setting sun, and they bounced off its walls, sparkling. As he felt his legs again, Thor began to walk with the others, closer and closer to the bridge, and was able to look down, deep into the Canyon's cliffs: they seemed to plummet down into the bowels of the earth. Thor could not even see the bottom, and didn't know if that was because it had no bottom, or if it was because it was covered in mist. The rock that lined the cliffs looked to be a million years old, formed with patterns that storms must have left centuries before. It was the most primordial place he had ever seen. He had no idea his planet was so vast, so vibrant, so alive.

It was as if he had come to the beginning of creation.

Thor heard the others gasp all around him, too.

The thought of the four of them patrolling this Canyon seemed laughable. They were dwarfed even by the site of it.

As they walked towards the bridge, soldiers stiffened on either side, at attention, making way for the new patrol. Thor felt his heart quicken.

"I don't see how the four of us can possibly patrol this?" O'Connor said.

Elden snickered.

"There are tons of patrols beside us. We are merely one cog in the machine."

As they walked across the bridge, the only sound to be heard was that of the whipping wind, and of their boots, and of Erec's horse, walking along. The hoofs left a hollow and reassuring sound, the only real thing that Thor could hang onto in this surreal place.

None of the soldiers, who all stiffened at attention in Erec's presence, said a word as they stood guard. They must have passed hundreds of them.

As they went, Thor could not help but notice, on either side of them, impaled on spikes every few feet along the railing, were the heads of barbarian invaders. Some still fresh, still dripping with blood.

Thor looked away. It made it all too real. He did not know if he was ready for this. He tried not to imagine the many skirmishes that must have produced those heads, the lives that had been lost, what awaited them on the other side. For the first time, he wondered if they would make it back. Was that the purpose of this whole expedition? To kill him off?

He looked over the edge, at the endlessly disappearing cliffs, and heard the screech of a distant bird; it was a sound he had never heard before. He wondered what kind of bird it was, and what other exotic animals lurked on the other side.

But it was not really the animals that bothered him, or even the heads on spikes. More than anything, it was the feeling of this place. He could not tell if it was the mist, or the howling wind, or the vastness of the open sky, or the light of the setting sun—but something about this place was so surreal, it transported him. Enveloped him. He felt a heavy magical energy hanging over them. He wondered if it was the protection of the Sword, or some other ancient energy. He felt as if he were crossing not just a mass of land, but crossing into another realm of existence.

He could hardly believe that, for the first time in his life, he would spend the night, unprotected, on the other side of the Canyon.

CHAPTER SIXTEEN

As the sun began to fade from the sky—a dark scarlet mixed with blue that seemed to envelop the universe—Thor walked with Reece, O'Connor, and Elden down the trail that led into the forest of the Wilds. Thor had never been so on edge in his life. Now it was just the four of them, Erec having remained behind at camp, and despite all their bickering with each other, Thor sensed they now needed each other more than ever. They had to bond, and to learn how to do it on their own, without Erec. Before they'd parted, Erec had told them not to worry, that he would stay at base and hear their screams, and would be there if they needed him.

That gave Thor little assurance now.

As the woods narrowed in on them, Thor looked around at this exotic place, the forest floor lined with thorns and strange fruits. The branches were gnarled and ancient, nearly touching each other, so close that Thor needed to duck his head in places. They had thorns instead of leaves, and they protruded everywhere. Yellow vines hung down in places, and Thor had made the mistake of reaching up to push a vine from his face only to realize it was a snake. He had yelled and jumped out of the way, just in time.

He had expected the others to laugh at him, but they, too, were humbled with fear. All around them were the foreign noises of exotic animals. Some were low and guttural, some high-pitched and shrieking. Some of them echoed from far-off; others seemed impossibly close. Twilight came on too fast, as they all headed deeper into the forest. Thor felt certain that at any moment they could be ambushed. As the sky grew darker, it was getting harder to even see the faces of his compatriots. He gripped his sword hilt so tightly, his knuckles white. His other hand clutched his slingshot. He saw the others gripping their weapons, too.

Thor willed himself to be strong, to be confident and courageous as a good knight should. As Erec had instructed him. It was better for him to face death now, he figured, in the face, then to always live in

110

fear of it. He tried to lift his chin and walk boldly forward, even increasing his pace and going a few feet out in front of the others. His heart was pounding, but he felt as if he were facing his fears.

"What are we patrolling for exactly?" Thor asked.

As soon as he said it, he realized it might be a dumb question, and he expected Elden to make fun of him.

But to his surprise, there was only silence in return. He looked over and saw the whites of Elden's eyes, and realized he was even more afraid. This, at least, gave Thor some confidence. Thor was younger and smaller than him, and he was not giving in to his fear.

"The enemy, I guess," Reece finally said.

"And who is that?" Thor asked. "What does he look like?"

"There are all sorts of enemies out here," Reece said. "We are in the Wilds now. There are nations of savages, and all manner and races of evil creatures."

"But what is the point of our patrol?" O'Connor asked. "What difference can we possibly make by doing this? Even if we kill one or two, is that going to stop the million behind it?"

"We are not here to make a dent," Reece answered. "We are here to make our presence known, on behalf of our King. To let them know not to come too close to the Canyon."

"I think it would make more sense to wait till they try to cross it and deal with them then," O'Connor said.

"No," Reece said. "It is better to deter them from even approaching. That is why these patrols. At least, that is what my older brother says."

Thor's heart was pounding, as they continued deeper into the forest.

"How far are we supposed to go?" Elden asked, speaking up for the first time, his voice quivering.

"Don't you remember what Kolk said? We have to retrieve the red banner and bring it back," Reece said. "That is our proof that we've gone far enough for our patrol."

"I have not seen a banner anywhere," O'Connor said. "In fact, I can barely see a thing. How are we supposed to get back?"

No one answered. Thor was thinking the same thing. How can they possibly find a banner in the black of night? He started to wonder if this was all a trick, an exercise, another one of the psychological games the Legion played on the boys. He thought again of Erec's words, of his many enemies at court. He had a sinking feeling about this patrol. Were they being set up?

Suddenly there came a horrific screeching noise, followed by movement inside the branches—and something large ran across their path. Thor pulled his sword, and the others did, too. The sound of swords leaving scabbards, of metal on metal, filled the air, as they all stood there, holding their swords out in front of them, looking nervously in every direction.

"What was that?" Elden cried out, his voice cracking with fear.

The animal once again crossed their path, racing from one side of the forest to the other, and this time they got a good look at it.

Thor's shoulders relaxed, as he recognized it.

"Just a deer," he said, greatly relieved. "The strangest looking deer I've seen—but a deer nonetheless."

Reece laughed, a reassuring noise, a laugh too mature for his age. As Thor heard it, he realized it was the laugh of a future King. He felt better having his friend at his side. And then, he laughed, too. All that fear, all for nothing.

"I never knew that your voice cracked when you caved in to fear," Reece mocked Elden, laughing again.

"If I could see you, I would pummel you," Elden said.

"I can see you fine," Reece said. "Come try it."

Elden glared back at him, but didn't dare make a move. Instead he put his sword back in his scabbard, as did the others. Thor admired Reece for giving Elden a hard time; Elden mocked everybody else— he deserved to get some back himself. He admired Reece's fearlessness in doing so: after all, Elden was still twice their size.

Thor finally felt some of the tension leaving his body. They'd had their first encounter, the ice was broken, and they were still alive. He leaned back and laughed, too, happy to be alive.

"Keep laughing, stranger boy," Elden said. "We'll see who has the last laugh."

I'm not laughing at you, as Reece is, Thor thought. *I'm just relieved to be alive.*

But he didn't bother saying it; he knew that nothing he could say would change Elden's hatred for him.

"Look!" O'Connor screamed. "There!"

Thor squinted but could barely see what he was pointing at in the thickening night. Then he saw it: the banner of the Legion. It hung from one of the branches.

They all began to run for it.

Elden ran past all of them, brushing them aside roughly.

"That flag is mine!" he yelled.

"I saw it first!" O'Connor yelled.

"But I will get it first, and I will be the one to bring it back!" Elden yelled.

Thor fumed; he could barely believe Elden's actions. He recalled what Kolk had said—that whoever got the banner would be rewarded, and realized why Elden sprinted. But that did not excuse him: they were supposed to be a team, a group—not every man for himself. Elden's true colors were coming out—none of the others ran for it, tried to outdo the others. It made Thor hate Elden even more.

Elden sprinted past after elbowing O'Connor, and before the others could react, he gained several feet on them and snatched the banner.

As he did, a huge net appeared out of nowhere, rising from the ground, springing up into the air, entrapping Elden and hoisting him up high. He swung back and forth before their eyes, just feet away, like an animal caught in a trap.

"Help me! Help me!" he screamed, terrified.

They all slowed as they walked up close to him; Reece began to laugh.

"Well, who is the coward now?" Reece yelled out, amused.

"Why you little crap!" he yelled. "I will kill you when I'm down from this!"

"Oh really?" Reece retorted. "And when will that be?"

"Set me down!" Elden yelled, turning and spinning in the net. "I command you!"

"Oh, you command us, do you?" Reece said, bursting into laughter.

Reece turned and looked at Thor.

"What do you think?" Reece asked.

"I think that he owes all of us an apology," O'Connor said. "Especially Thor."

"I agree," Reece said. "I'll tell you what," he said to Elden. "Apologize, and make it sincere, and I will consider cutting you down."

"Apologize?" Elden echoed, horrified. "Not in one million suns."

Reece turned to Thor.

113

"Maybe we should just leave this lump here for the night. It would be great food for the animals. What do you think?"

Thor smiled wide.

"I think that's a fine idea," O'Connor said.

"Wait!" Elden screamed out.

O'Connor reached up and snatched the banner from Elden's dangling finger.

"Guess you didn't beat us to the banner after all," O'Connor said.

The three of them turned, and began to walk away.

"No, wait!" Elden cried. "You can't leave me here. You wouldn't!"

The three of them continued to walk away.

"I'm sorry!" Elden began to sob. "Please! I'm sorry!"

Thor stopped, but Reece and O'Connor continued to walk. Finally, Reece turned.

"What are you doing?" Reece asked Thor.

"We can't leave him here," Thor said. As much as Thor disliked Elden, he didn't think it right to leave him there.

"Why not?" Reece asked. "He brought it on himself."

"If the tables were turned," O'Connor said, "you know that he would gladly leave you there. Why should you care?"

"I understand," Thor said. "But that doesn't mean we should act like him."

Reece put his hands on his hips and sighed deeply as he leaned in and whispered to Thor.

"I wasn't going to leave him there all night. Maybe just half the night. But you do have a point. He's not cut out for this. He'd probably piss himself and have a heart attack. You're too kind. That's a problem," Reece said as he put a hand on Thor's shoulder. "But that's why I chose you for a friend."

"And I," O'Connor said, putting his hand on Thor's other shoulder.

Thor turned, marched towards the net, reached out and cut it down.

Elden went flying, hitting the ground hard, with a thud. He scrambled to his feet, threw the net off and frantically searched the ground.

"My sword!" he yelled, frantic. "Where is it?"

Thor looked down at the ground, but it was too dark out. He could not see it.

"It must have went flying into the trees when you were hoisted up," Thor answered.

"Wherever it is, it's gone now," Reece said. "You'll never find it."

"But you don't understand," Elden pleaded. "The Legion. There is just one rule. Never leave your weapon behind. I can't return without it. I would be ousted!"

Thor turned and searched the ground again, searched the trees, looking everywhere. But he could see absolutely no sign of it. Reece and O'Connor just stood there, not bothering to look.

"I'm sorry," Thor said, "I don't see it."

Elden scrambled everywhere, then finally gave up.

"It's *your* fault," he, pointing at Thor. "You got us into this mess!"

"No I didn't," Thor replied. "You did! You ran for the flag. You pushed us all out of the way. You have no one to blame but yourself."

"I hate you!" Elden screamed.

He charged Thor, grabbing him by the shirt, knocking him down to the ground. The weight of him caught Thor off guard. Thor managed to spin around, But Elden spun again and pinned Thor down. Elden was just too big and strong, and it was too hard to hold him back.

Suddenly, though, he let go. Thor heard the sound of a sword being extracted from his scabbard, and looked up and saw Reece standing over Elden, holding the tip of his sword at his throat.

O'Connor reached over and gave Thor a hand, and yanked him quickly to his feet. Thor stood, with his two friends, looking down on Elden, who remained pinned to the ground, Reece's sword at his throat.

"You touch my friend again," Reece, deadly serious, said slowly to Elden, "and I assure you, I will kill you."

CHAPTER SEVENTEEN

Thor, Reece, O'Connor, Elden, and Erec all sat on the ground, before a fire, forming a circle around it. The five of them sat glum and silent, Thor surprised to realize that it could be this cold on a summer night. There was just something about this canyon, the cold, mystical winds that swirled around, down his back, and which mingled with the fog that never seemed to go away, which left him damp to the bone. He leaned forward and rubbed his hands against the fire, unable to get them warm.

Thor chewed on the piece of dried meat that the others were passing around; it was tough and salty, but somehow nourished him. Erec reached over and handed him something and Thor felt a soft wineskin being pressed into his hand, the liquid sloshing in it. It was surprisingly heavy as he raised it to his lips and squirted it into the back of his mouth, for too long a time. He felt warm for the first time.

Everyone was quiet, staring into the flames. Thor was still on edge, being on this side of the Canyon, in enemy territory, still felt as if he should be on guard at every moment, and marveled at how calm Erec seemed to be, as if he were casually sitting in his own backyard. Thor was relieved, at least, to be out of the Wilds, reunited with Erec, and sitting around the reassurance of a fire. Erec watched the forest line, attentive to every little noise, yet confident and relaxed. Thor knew that if any danger was coming, Erec would protect them all.

Thor felt content around the flames, and he looked around and saw that the others seemed content, too—except, of course, for Elden, glum ever since returning from the forest. He had lost his confident swagger from earlier in the day, and he sat there, sour, without his sword. Thor knew that the commanders would never forgive such a mistake, and that Elden would be kicked out of the Legion upon their return. He wondered what Elden would do. He had a feeling he would not go down so easily, that he had some trick, some backup plan, up his sleeve. Thor assumed that, whatever it was, it would not be good.

Thor turned and followed Erec's gaze to the distant horizon, in the southern direction. There was a faint glow, an endless line as far as the eye could see, that lit up the night. Thor wondered.

"What is it?" he finally asked Erec. "That glow? The one you keep staring at?"

Erec was silent for a long time, and the only sound was that of the whipping of the wind. Finally, without turning, he said: "The Gorals."

Thor exchanged a glance with the others, who looked back, fearful. Thor's stomach tightened at the thought of it. The Gorals. So close. There was nothing in between them and him except for a simple forest and a vast plain. There was no longer the great Canyon separating them, keeping them safe. All his life he had heard tales of these violent savages from the Wilds who had no ambition except to attack the Ring. And now, there was nothing between them. He couldn't believe how many of them there were. It was a vast and waiting army.

"Aren't you afraid?" he asked Erec. "There is nothing between us."

Erec shook his head.

"The Gorals move as one. Their army camps out there every night. They have for years. They would only attack the Canyon if they mobilized the entire army and attacked as one. And they wouldn't dare try. The power of the Sword acts as a shield. They know they cannot breach it."

"So then why do they camp out there?" Thor asked.

"It is their way of intimidating. And preparing. There have been many times throughout the course of history, in the time of our fathers, when they attacked, tried to breach the canyon. But it hasn't happened in my time."

Thor looked up at the black sky, the yellow and blue and orange stars twinkling high overhead, and he wondered. He could hardly believe he was out here, on this side of the canyon. It was a place of nightmares, and had been ever since he could walk. The thought of it made him fearful, but he forced fearful thoughts from his mind. He was a member of the Legion now, and knew he had to act like it.

"Do not worry," Erec said, as if reading his thoughts. "They will not attack while we have the Destiny Sword."

117

"Have you ever held it?" Thor asked Erec, suddenly curious. "The Sword?"

"Of course not," Erec retorted sharply. "No one is allowed to grasp it, except for descendants of the King."

Thor looked at him, confused.

"I don't understand? Why?"

Reece cleared his throat.

"May I?" he interceded.

Erec nodded back.

"There is a legend around the Sword. It has never actually been hoisted by anyone. Legend has it that one man, the chosen one, will be able to hoist it by himself. Only the King is allowed to try, or one of the King's descendants, if named King. So there it sits, untouched."

"And what of our current King? Your father?" Thor asked. "Can't he try to hoist it?"

Reece looked down.

"He tried to hoist it once. When he was crowned. So he tells us. He could not. It sits there like an object of rebuke for him. He hates it. It weighs on him like a living thing.

"When the chosen one arrives," Reece added, "he will free the Ring from its enemies all around and lead us to a greater destiny than we've ever known. All wars will end."

"Fairytales and nonsense," Elden interceded. "That sword will be lifted by no one. It is too heavy. It is not possible. And there is no 'chosen one.' It's all hogwash. That legend was invented just to keep the common man down, to keep us all waiting for the supposed 'chosen one.' To embolden the line of MacGils. It is a very convenient legend for them."

"Shut your tongue, boy," Erec snapped. "You will always speak respectfully of your King."

Elden looked down, humbled.

Thor thought about everything, trying to take it all in. It was so much to process at once. All his life he had dreamt of seeing the Destiny Sword. He had heard stories of its perfect shape. It was rumored to be crafted from a material no one understood, was supposed to be a magical weapon. Thor looked around, at the Canyon, and could hardly imagine its energy protected the entire Ring. It made Thor wonder what would happen if they didn't have the sword to protect them. Would the King's army then be vanquished by the Empire? Thor looked out at the glowing fires on the horizon. They seemed to stretch for an eternity.

"Have you ever been out there?" Thor asked Erec. "Far out there? Beyond the forest? Into the Wilds?"

The others all turned and look at Erec, as Thor anxiously awaited his reply. In the thick silence, Erec stared at the flames for a long time—so long that Thor began to doubt he would ever answer. Thor hoped he had not been too nosy; he felt so grateful and indebted to Erec, and certainly didn't want to get on his bad side. Thor also wasn't sure if he wanted to know the answer.

Just when Thor was wishing he could retract his question, Erec responded:

"Yes," he said, solemn.

That single word hung in the air for too long, and in it, Thor heard the gravity that told him all he needed to know.

"What is it like out there?" O'Connor asked.

Thor was relieved that he was not the only one asking the questions.

"It is controlled by one ruthless empire," Erec said. "But the land is vast and varied. There is the land of the savages. The land of the slaves. And the land of the monsters. Monsters unlike any you can imagine. And there are deserts and mountains and hills as far as you can see. There are the marshes and the swamps and the great ocean. There is the land of the Druids. And the land of the Dragons."

Thor's eyes opened wide at the mention of it.

"Dragons?" he asked, surprised. "I thought they didn't exist."

Erec looked at him, deadly serious.

"I assure you, they do. And it is a place you never want to go. A place that even the Garlons fear."

Thor swallowed at the thought. He could hardly imagine venturing out that deep into the empire. He wondered how Erec had ever made it back alive. He made a note mental note to ask him at another time.

There were so many questions Thor wanted to ask him—about the nature of the evil empire, who ruled it; why they wanted to attack; when he had ventured out; when he had returned. But as Thor stared into the flames it grew colder and darker, and as all his questions swirled in his head, he felt his eyes grow heavy. He knew this was not the right time to ask.

Instead, he let sleep carry him away. He felt his eyes grow heavy, and lay his head down on the ground. Before his eyes closed for good, he looked over at the foreign soil, and wondered when—or if—he would ever return home again.

*

Thor opened his eyes, confused, wondering where he was and how he had gotten here. He looked down and saw a thick fog up to his waist, so thick he could not see his feet. He turned and saw dawn breaking over the canyon before him. Far, on the other side, was his homeland. He was still on this side, the wrong side, of the divide. His heart quickened.

Thor looked at the bridge, but strangely, it was now empty of soldiers. The whole place, in fact, seemed desolate. He could not understand what was happening. As he watched the bridge, its wooden planks fell one after another, like dominoes. Within moments the bridge collapsed, dropped down into the precipice. The bottom was so far down, he never even heard the planks hit.

Thor swallowed and turned, looking for the others—but they were nowhere in sight. He had no idea what to do. Now he was stuck. Here, alone, on the other side of the canyon, with no way to get back. He could not understand where everyone had gone.

He heard something and turned and looked into the forest. He detected movement. He rose to his feet and walked towards it, his feet sinking into the earth as he went. As he got closer, he saw a net hanging from a low lying branch. There, inside it, was Elden. He was spinning around and around in circles, the branches creaking as he moved.

A falcon sat perched on his head, a distinct looking creature with a body which gleamed of silver and a single back stripe running down its forehead, between its eyes. It bent over and plucked out his eye, and held it there. It turned to Thor, holding the eye in its mouth.

Thor wanted to look away, but could not. Just as he was realizing that Elden was a corpse, suddenly, the entire wood came to life. Charging out of it, from every direction, came an army of Gorals. Huge, wearing only loins, with immense muscled chests, three noses placed in a triangle on their face, and two long, curved sharp fangs, they hissed and snarled as they sprinted right for him. It was a hair-raising sound, and there was nowhere for Thor to go. He reached

120

down and grabbed for his sword—but looked down to discover it was gone.

Thor screamed.

He woke sitting straight up, breathing hard, looking frantically in every direction. All around him was silence. But it was a real, alive silence, not the silence of his dream. It was then that he realized that he had, indeed, been dreaming.

Beside him, in the first light of dawn, Reece, O'Connor, and Erec slept sprawled out on the ground, the dying embers of the fire near them. On the ground, hopping, there was a falcon. It turned and cocked its head at Thor. It was large and silver and proud, with the single black stripe running down its forehead, and it stared back at him, looking him right in the eye, and screeched. The sound made him shiver. Thor could not believe it: it was the same falcon from his dream.

It was then he realized the bird was a message—that his dream had been more than a dream. That something was wrong. He could feel it, a slight vibration on his back, running up his arms.

He quickly got to his feet, looked all around, wondering what it could be. He heard nothing wrong, and nothing seemed out of place; he turned and saw that the bridge was still there, and in the distance, the soldiers were all on it.

What was it? he wondered.

And then he realized what it was. One of them was missing. Elden.

At first Thor wondered if maybe he had left them, headed back across the bridge to the other side of the Canyon. Maybe he was ashamed over losing his sword, and had left the region altogether.

But then Thor turned and looked to the forest, and he could see the fresh indentation in the moss, the footprints heading towards the trail in the morning dew. There was no doubt that those were Elden's. Elden had not left them. He had gone back into the forest. Alone. Maybe to relieve himself. Or maybe, Thor realized with a shock, to try to retrieve his sword.

It was a stupid move, to go alone like that, and it proved how desperate he was. Thor sensed right away that there was great danger. He could feel that Elden's life was at stake.

The falcon screeched at that moment, as if to confirm Thor's thoughts. Then it picked up and flew, diving right for Thor's face.

Thor ducked his head, and its talons just missed, and it rose in the air, flying away.

Thor leapt into action. Without thinking, without even contemplating what he was doing, he sprinted off into the woods, following the footprints.

Thor didn't stop to feel the fear as he sprinted alone, deep into the Wilds. If he had paused to think how crazy it was, he probably would have frozen, would have felt himself flooded with panic. But instead, he just reacted. He felt a pressing need to help Elden. He ran and ran, alone, deeper into the wood in the early light of dawn.

"Elden!" he screamed.

He couldn't explain it, but somehow he sensed that Elden was about to die. He knew he shouldn't care, based on the way that Elden had treated him, but he couldn't help himself: he did. If it were he in this situation, Elden would certainly not come to rescue him. It was crazy to put his life on the line for someone who cared nothing for him—and, in fact, would gladly see him die. But he could not help it. He'd never felt a sensation like this one before, where his senses were screaming to him to react—especially over something he could not possibly have known. He was changing somehow, and he did not know how. He felt as if his body were being controlled by some new, mysterious power, and it made him feel uneasy, out of control. Was he losing his mind? Was he overreacting? Was it all just from his dream? Should he turn around?

But he did not. He let his feet lead him, and did not give in to fear or doubts. He ran and ran, until his lungs were bursting.

Thor turned a bend, and what he saw made him stop short in his tracks. He stood there, trying to catch his breath, trying to reconcile the image before him, which did not make any sense. It was enough to strike terror into any hardened warrior.

There stood Elden, holding his short sword and looking up at a creature unlike any Thor had ever seen. It was horrific. It towered over them both, at least nine feet tall, and as wide as four men. It leaned back and raised its muscular, red arms, with three long fingers, like nails, at the end of each hand, and a head like that of a demon, with four horns, a long jaw, and a broad forehead. It had two large yellow eyes and fangs curled like tusks. It leaned back and screeched.

Beside him, a thick tree, hundreds of years old, split in two at the sound.

Elden stood there, frozen in fear. He dropped his sword, and the ground beneath him went wet; Thor realized Elden must have peed his pants.

The creature drooled and snarled, and took a step towards Elden.

Thor, too, was filled with fear, but unlike Elden, it did not immobilize him. For some reason, the fear heightened him. It heightened his senses, made him feel more alive. It gave him tunnel vision, allowed him to focus supremely on the creature before him, on its position to Elden, on its width and breadth and strength and speed. On its every movement. It also allowed him to focus on his own body position, his own weapons.

Thor fearlessly burst into action. He charged forward, past Elden, and came between him and the beast. The beast roared, its breath so hot, Thor could feel it even from here. The sound raised every hair on Thor's spine, and made him want to turn around. But he heard Erec's voice in his head, telling him to be strong. To be fearless. To retain equanimity. And he forced himself to stand his ground.

Thor raised his sword high and charged, plunging it into the beast's ribs, aiming for his heart.

The beast shrieked in agony, its blood pouring down Thor's hand as Thor plunged the sword all the way in, to the hilt.

But to Thor's surprise, it did not die. The beast seemed invincible.

Without missing a beat, the beast swung around and swiped Thor so hard that he felt his ribs cracking. Thor went flying, through the air, all the way across the clearing, and smashed into a tree before collapsing to the ground. He felt a terrible headache as he lay there.

Thor looked up, dazed and confused, the world spinning. The beast reach down and extracted Thor's sword from its stomach. The sword seemed tiny in its hands, like a toothpick, and the beast reached back and hurled it; it went flying through the trees, taking down branches, and disappeared into the wood.

It turned its full attention on Thor, and began to bear down on him.

Elden stood there, still frozen in fear. But as the beast charged Thor, suddenly, Elden burst into action. He charged the beast from behind, and jumped onto its back. It slowed the beast just enough for Thor to sit up; the beast, furious, flung back his arms and threw Elden. He went flying across the clearing, smashed into a tree, and slumped to the ground.

The beast, still bleeding, panting heavily, turned its attention back to Thor. It snarled and widened its fangs, as it bore down on him.

Thor was out of options. His sword was gone, and there was nothing between him and the monster. The monster dove down for him, and at the last second, Thor rolled out of the way. The monster hit the tree were Thor had been with such force that it uprooted it from the ground.

The beast raised its foot, and brought it down for Thor's head. Thor rolled out of the way and it left a footprint were Thor's head had been.

Thor rolled to his feet, placed a stone in his sling and hurled.

He hit the monster square between the eyes, a fiercer throw than he had ever made, and the creature staggered back. Thor was certain he had killed it.

But to his amazement, the beast did not stop.

Thor tried his best to summon his power, whatever power it was that he had. He charged the beast, leaping forward, crashing into it, aiming to tackle it and drive it down to the ground with a superhuman power.

But to Thor's shock, this time his power never kicked in. He was just another boy. A frail boy, next to this massive beast.

The beast merely reached down, grabbed Thor by his waist and hoisted him high above its head. Thor felt so helpless, dangling high in the air—and then he was thrown. He went flying like a missile across the clearing, and smashed again into a tree.

Thor lay there, stunned, his head splitting, his ribs feeling cracked in two. The beast raced for him, and he knew that this time he was finished. It raised its red, muscular foot, bringing it down right for Thor's head. Thor looked up, and prepared to die.

Then, for some reason, the beast froze in midair. Thor blinked, trying to understand why.

The beast reached up and clutched its throat, and Thor saw an arrow, piercing through it. A moment later, the beast keeled over, dead.

Erec came running into view, followed by Reece and O'Connor. Thor saw Erec looking down on him, asking if he was okay, and he wanted to answer, more than anything. But the words would not come out. A moment later, his eyes closed on him, and then his world was blackness.

CHAPTER EIGHTEEN

Thor opened his eyes slowly, dizzy at first, trying to figure out where he was. He was laying on straw, and for a moment wondered if he was back in the barracks. He propped himself up on one elbow, on alert, looking for the others.

He realized he was somewhere else. From the looks of it, he was in a very elaborate stone room. It looked as if he were in a castle. A royal castle.

Before he could figure it all out, a large, oak door swung open and in strutted Reece. In the distance, Thor could hear the muted noise of a crowd.

"Finally, he lives," Reece announced with a smile, as he rushed forward and grabbed Thor's hand and yanked him to his feet.

Thor raised a hand to his head, trying to slow his terrible headache from rising too fast.

"Come on, let's go, everyone's waiting for you," he urged, yanking Thor.

"Wait a minute, please," Thor said, trying to collect himself. "Where am I? What happened?"

"We're back in King's Court—and you are about to be celebrated as the hero of the day!" Reece said merrily, as they headed for the door.

"Hero? What do you mean? And…how did I get here?" he asked, trying to remember.

"That beast knocked you out. You've been out for quite a while. We had to carry you back across the Canyon bridge. Quite dramatic. Not exactly how I expected you to return to the other side!" he said with a laugh.

They walked out into the corridors of the castle, and as they went, Thor could see all sorts of people—women, men, squires, guards, knights—staring at him, as if they had been waiting for him to wake. He also saw something new in their eyes, something like respect. It was the first time he had seen it. Up until now, he had seen something

125

else in people's eyes: something like disdain. Now they looked at him as if he were one of them.

"What exactly happened?" Though racked his brain, trying to remember.

"Don't you remember any of it?" Reece asked.

Thor tried to think.

"I remember running into the wood. Fighting with that beast. And then..." He tried to think, but was drawing a blank.

"You saved Elden's life," Reece said. "You ran fearlessly into the wood, on your own. I don't know why you wasted energy on saving that prim's life. But you did. The King is very, very pleased with you. Not because he cares about Elden. But he cares very much about bravery. He loves to celebrate. It's important to him, to celebrate stories like this, to inspire the others. And it reflects well on the king, and on the Legion. He wants to celebrate. You're here because he's going to reward you."

"Reward me?" Thor asked, dumbfounded. "But I didn't do anything!"

"You saved Elden's life."

"I only reacted. I only did what came naturally."

"And that's exactly why the King wants to reward you."

Thor felt embarrassed. He didn't think that his actions deserved rewarding. After all, if it hadn't have been for Erec, Thor would be dead right now. Thor thought about it, and his heart filled with gratitude for Erec, once again. He hoped that one day he could repay him.

"But what about our patrol duty?" Thor asked. "We didn't finish it."

Reece put a reassuring hand on his shoulder.

"Friend, you saved a boy's life. A member of the Legion. That's more important than our patrol." Reece laughed. "So much for an uneventful first patrol!" he added.

They finished walking down yet another corridor, and two guards opened a door for them, and Thor blinked and found himself in the royal chamber. There must have been a hundred knights standing about the room, with its soaring cathedral ceilings, stained glass, its weapons and suits of armor hung everywhere on the walls, like trophies. The Hall of Arms. It was the place where all the greatest warriors met, all the men of the Silver. Thor's heart raced as he surveyed the walls, all the famous weaponry, the armor of heroic and legendary knights. Thor had heard rumors of this place, his entire life. It had been his dream to see it for himself one day. He could hardly believe he was here. He knew that normally no squires were allowed here—no one but the Silver.

Even more surprising, as he entered, real knights turned and looked at him—*him*—from all sides. And they wore looks of admiration. Thor had never seen so many knights in one room, and he had never felt so accepted. It was like walking into a dream. Especially since just moments before, he had been fast asleep.

Reece must have noticed Thor's dumbfounded face.

"The finest of the Silver have gathered here to honor you."

Thor felt himself well with pride and disbelief. "Honor me? But I've done nothing."

"Wrong," came a voice.

Thor turned and felt a heavy hand on his shoulder. It was Erec, grinning down.

"You have displayed bravery and honor and courage, beyond what was expected of you. You nearly gave up your life to save one of your brethren. That is what we look for in the Legion, and this is what we look for in the Silver."

"You saved my life," Thor said to Erec. "If it weren't for you, that beast would have killed me. I don't know how to thank you."

Erec grinned down.

"You already have," he answered. "Don't you remember the joust? I believe we are even."

Thor marched down the walkway towards MacGil's throne, at the far end of the hall, Reece on one side of him and Erec on the other. He felt hundreds of eyes on him, and it all felt like a dream.

Standing around the King were his dozens of counselors, along with his eldest son, Kendrick. As Thor approached, his heart swelled with pride. He could hardly believe the King was granting him an audience for the second time in as many days—and that so many important men were here to witness it.

They reached the king's throne, MacGil stood, and a muted hush overcame the room. MacGil's ponderous expression broke into a wide smile, as he took three steps forward and to Thor's surprise, gave him a hug.

A great cheer rose up in the room.

He pulled back, held Thor firmly by the shoulders, and grinned down.

"You served the Legion well," he said.

A servant handed the king a goblet, and the King raised it and looked all around. In a loud voice, he called out:

"TO COURAGE!"

"TO COURAGE!" shouted back the hundreds of men in the room. An excited murmur followed, then the room once again fell quiet.

"In honor of your exploits today," the King bellowed, "I grant you a great gift."

The King gestured, and an attendant stepped forward, wearing a long, black gauntlet, on which sat a magnificent falcon. It sat there, its claws resting on the gauntlet, and turned, and stared right Thor—as if he knew him.

It took Thor's breath away. He could hardly believe it. It was the exact falcon from his dream, with its silver body and the single black stripe running down its forehead.

"The falcon is the symbol of our kingdom, and of our Royal family," MacGil boomed. "It is a bird of prey, of pride and honor. Yet it is also a bird of skill, of cunning. It is loyal, and fierce, and it soars above all other animals. It is also a sacred creature. It is said that he who owns a falcon is also owned by one. It will guide you on all your ways. It will leave you, but it will always come back. And now, it is yours."

The falconer stepped forward, placed a heavy, chainmail gauntlet onto Thor's hand and wrist, then reached out, picked up the bird, and placed it on Thor's gauntlet. Thor felt electrified, having it on his arm. He could hardly move. He was shocked by its weight, a struggle just to keep it up as it fidgeted on his wrist. He felt its claws digging in, though luckily he only felt pressure, as he was protected by the gauntlet. The bird turned, stared right at him, and screeched. Thor felt it looking into his eyes, and he felt a mystical connection to the animal. He just knew that it would be with him all his days.

"And what shall you name her?" the King asked, in the thick silence of the room.

Thor racked his brain, too frozen to even work.

He tried to think quick. He summoned in his mind all the names of all the famed warriors of the kingdom. He turned and scanned the walls, and saw a series of plaques with all the names of battles, all the places of the kingdom. His eyes rested on one particular place. It was a place in the Ring which he had never been, but which he had always heard was a mystical, powerful place. It sounded right to him.

"I shall call her Estopheles," Thor called out.

"Estopheles!" the crowd echoed, sounding pleased.

The falcon screeched, as if in response.

Suddenly, Estopheles flapped her wings and flew up high, all the way to the peak of the cathedral ceiling, and out an open window. Thor watched her go.

"Don't worry," the falconer said, "she shall always return to you."

Thor turned and looked at the King. He had never been given a gift in his life, much less one of this stature. He hardly knew what to say, how to thank him. He was overwhelmed.

"My liege," he said, lowering his head. "I don't know how to thank you."

"You already have," MacGil said.

The crowd cheered, and the tension in the room was broken. A spirited conversation broke out among the men, and so many knights approached Thor, he hardly knew which way to turn.

"That is Algod, of the Eastern Province," Reece said, introducing him to one.

"And this is Kamera, of the Low Marshes…. And this, Basikold, of the Northern Forts…."

Soon, the names became a blur. Thor was overwhelmed. He could hardly believe that all these knights wanted to meet him. He had never felt so accepted or honored anytime in his life and he had a feeling that a day like this would never come again. It was the first time in his life he had a feeling of self-worth.

And he could not stop thinking of Estopheles.

As Thor turned every which way, greeting people whose names flowed by, names he could hardly grasp onto, a messenger hurried over, slipping between the Knights. He carried a small scroll, which he pressed into Thor's palm.

Thor rolled it open, and read the fine, delicate handwriting. He could hardly imagine who it was from. He had never been handed a message before in his life:

Meet me in the back courtyard. Behind the gate.

Thor could smell the delicate fragrance coming off the pink scroll, and was puzzled as he tried to figure out who it was from. It bore no signature.

Reece leaned over, read it over his shoulder, and laughed.

"It seems my sister has taken a fancy to you," he said, smiling. "I would go if I were you. She hates to be kept waiting."

Thor felt himself blush.

"The rear courtyard is through those gates. Hurry. She's known to change her mind quickly," Reece smiled as he looked at him. "And I'd love to have you in my family."

CHAPTER NINETEEN

Thor tried to follow Reece's directions as he wound his way through the crowded castle, but it was not easy. This castle had too many twists and turns, too many hidden back doors, and too many long corridors that seemed to only lead to more corridors.

He ran through Reece's directions in his head as he descended yet another small set of steps, turned down another corridor, and finally, he stopped before a small arched door with a red handle, the one that Reece had told him about, and pushed it open.

Thor hurried outside and was struck by the strong light of the summer day; it felt good to be outdoors, out of that stuffy castle, breathing fresh air, the sun on his face. He squinted, his eyes adjusting in the bright light, and took in the site: before him sprawled the royal gardens, stretching as far as the eye could see, hedges perfectly trimmed in different shapes, forming neat rows of gardens, trails winding amidst them. There were fountains, unusual trees of all types, fruit orchards, ripe with early summer fruits, and fields of flowers, of every size and shape and color. The site took his breath away. It was like walking into a painting.

Thor looked everywhere for a sign of Gwendolyn, his heart pounding. This rear courtyard was empty, and Thor assumed it was probably reserved for the royal family, set off from the public with its high, stone garden walls. And yet, he looked everywhere and could not find her.

He wondered if her note was a hoax. That was probably it. She was probably just making fun of him, the country bumpkin, amusing herself at his expense. After all, how could someone of her rank, really have any interest in him?

Thor looked down and read her note again, then rolled it back up in shame. He had been made fun of. What a fool he was to get his hopes up like that. It hurt him deeply.

Thor turned and prepared to head back into the castle, head lowered. Just as he reached for the door, a voice rang out.

"And where are *you* going?" came the joyful voice. It sounded like a bird's song.

Thor wondered if he was imagining it. He spun, searching, and there she was, sitting in the shade beneath a castle wall. She smiled back, dressed in her royal finest, layers of white satin dress, with pink trim, and she looked even more beautiful than he'd remembered.

It was her. Gwendolyn. The girl he had been dreaming about since they had met, with her almond, blue eyes and long strawberry hair, with her smile that lit his heart. She wore a large white-and-pink hat, shading her from the sun, beneath which her eyes sparkled; he could hardly believe she was looking at him. For a moment he felt like turning around to make sure that there was no one else standing behind him that she could be looking at.

"Um…" Thor began. "I…um…don't know. I…um…was going inside."

Once again, he was finding himself flustered around her, finding it hard to collect his thoughts and articulate them.

She laughed, and it was the most beautiful sound he had ever heard.

"And why would you be doing that?" she asked, playful. "You just arrived."

Thor was flustered. His tongue was tied.

"I…um…couldn't find you," he said, embarrassed.

She laughed again.

"Well, I'm right here. Aren't you going to come and get me?"

She held out a single hand, and Thor rushed over to her, reached down and took her hand. He was electrified by the touch of her skin, so smooth and soft, her frail hand fitting perfectly inside of his. She looked up at him and let her hand linger there a moment, before slowly rising. He loved the feel of her fingertips in his palm, and hoped she would never take them away.

She withdrew her hand, then placed her arm in his, locking arms. She began to walk, leading the way down the series of winding trails. They walked along a small cobblestone path, and soon they were inside a labyrinth of hedges, protected from outside view.

Thor was nervous. He did not know if he, a commoner, would get in trouble, walking like this with the King's daughter. He felt a light sweat break out on his forehead, and did not know if it was from the heat or from her touch.

He wasn't sure what to say.

132

"You've caused quite a stir here, haven't you?" she asked with a smile. He was grateful that she broke the awkward silence.

Thor shrugged. "I'm sorry. I didn't mean to."

She laughed. "And why wouldn't you mean to? Isn't it good to cause a stir?"

Thor was stymied. He hardly knew how to respond. It seemed as if he always said the wrong thing.

"This place is so stuffy and boring anyway," she said. "It's nice to have a newcomer. My father seems to have taken quite a liking to you. So has my brother."

"Um…thanks," Thor replied.

He was kicking himself, dying inside. He knew he should say more, and he wanted to. He just did not know what to say.

"Do you…" he began, racking his brain for the right thing to say, "like it here?"

She leaned back and laughed.

"Do I like it here?" she. "But I should hope so. I live here!"

She laughed again and Thor felt himself redden. He felt that he was really messing things up. But he wasn't raised around girls, he had never had a girlfriend in his village, and he just did not know what to say to her. What could he ask her? Where are you from? He already knew where she was from. He started to wonder why she bothered with him; was it just for her amusement?

"Why do you like me?" he asked.

She looked back at him, and made a funny sound.

"You are a presumptuous boy," she chuckled. "Who says I like you?" she asked with a huge smile. Clearly, everything he said amused her.

Thor now felt as if he'd gotten himself into deeper trouble.

"I'm sorry. I didn't mean to say that. I was just wondering. I mean…um…I know you don't like me."

She laughed harder.

"You are amusing, I have to give you that. I take it you've never had a girlfriend, have you?"

Thor looked down and shook his head, humiliated.

"I assume no sisters, either?" she pressed.

Thor shook his head.

"I have three brothers," he blurted out. Finally, at least, he had managed to say something normal.

"Do you?" she asked. "And where are they? Back in your village?"

Thor shook his head. "No, they are here, in the Legion, with me."

"Well that must be comforting."

Thor shook his head.

"No. They don't like me. They wish I wasn't here."

It was the first time her smile dropped.

"And why wouldn't they like you?" she asked, horrified. "Your own brothers?"

Thor shrugged. "I wish I knew."

They walked a while more in silence. He was suddenly afraid that he was killing their happy mood.

"But don't worry, it doesn't bother me. It's always been that way. In fact, actually, I've met good friends here. Better friends than I've ever had."

"My brother? Reece?" she asked.

Thor nodded.

"Reece is a good one," she said. "He's my favorite in some ways. I have four brothers, you know. Three are true, and one is not. The eldest is my dad's son from another woman. My half-brother. You know him, Kendrick?"

Thor nodded. "I owe him a great debt. It is thanks to him that I have a spot in the Legion. He's a fine man."

"It's true. He's one of the finest men in the kingdom. I love him, as much as a true brother. And then there's Reece, who I love just as much. The other two…well…. You know how families are. Not everyone gets along. Sometimes I wonder how the four of us all come from the same people."

Now Thor was curious. He wanted to know more about who they were, her relationship to them, why they weren't close. He wanted to ask her, but didn't want to pry. And she didn't seem to want to dwell on it, either. She seemed to be a happy person, a person who only liked to focus on happy things.

As they finished the labyrinth trail, the courtyard opened up, and Thor was amazed to see a new garden, where the grass was perfectly trimmed and designed into shapes, with huge wooden pieces placed on it. It was a massive game board of some sort, sprawling at least fifty feet in each direction, with huge wooden pieces, higher than Thor, placed throughout.

Gwen cried out in delight.

"Will you play?" she asked.

"What is it?" he asked.

She turned, her eyes opened wide in amazement.

"You've never played Racks?" she asked.

Thor shook his head, embarrassed, feeling more like a country rube than ever.

"It is the finest game!" she exclaimed.

She reached out with her two hands and yanked his, dragging him onto the field. She bounded off with delight and he couldn't help but smile himself, as she tugged him. More than anything, more than the field, more than this beautiful place, it was the feel of her hands on his that electrified him. The feeling of being wanted. She *wanted* him to go with her. She *wanted* to spend time with him. He could hardly believe it. Why would anyone care about him? Especially someone like her? He still felt as if this were all a dream.

"Stand over there," she said. "Behind that piece. You have to move it, and you have only ten seconds to do so."

"What do you mean move it?" Thor asked.

"Choose a direction, quickly!" she cried out.

Thor picked up the huge wooden block, surprised at its weight. He carried it several steps, and put it down on another square.

Without hesitating, Gwen pushed her own piece over, and it landed on Thor's, knocking his down to the ground.

She cried out in delight.

"That was a bad move!" she said. "You got right in my way! You lost!"

Thor looked at the two pieces on the ground, puzzled. He didn't understand this game at all.

She laughed, taking his arm as she continued to lead him down the trails.

"Don't worry, I'll teach you," she said.

His heart soared at her words. *She'd teach him.* He could hardly believe it. She would teach him. She wanted to see him again. To spend time with him. Was he imagining all of this?

"So tell me, what do you think of this place?" she asked, as she led him into another series of labyrinths. This one was decorated with flowers, eight feet high, bursting with color, strange insects hovering over their tips.

"It is the most beautiful place I've ever seen," Thor answer truthfully.

"And why do you want to be a member of the Legion?"

"It is all I ever dreamed of," he replied.

"But why?" she asked. "Because you want to serve my father?"

Thor thought about that. He'd never really wondered why—it was always just there.

"Yes," answered. "I do. And the Ring."

"But what about life?" she asked. "Don't you want to have a family? Land? A wife?"

She stopped and looked at him; it threw him. He was frazzled. He had never considered these things before, and he hardly knew how to respond. Her eyes sparkled as she glanced back at him.

"Um…I…I don't know. I never really thought about it."

"And what would your mother say about that?" she asked, playfully.

Thor's smile lowered.

"I don't have a mother," he said.

Her smile dropped, for the first time.

"What happened to her?" she asked.

Thor was about to answer her, to tell her everything. It would be the first time in his life that he had ever spoken about her, to anyone. And the crazy thing was, he wanted to. He wanted, desperately, to open up to her, this stranger, and to let her know everything about his deepest feelings.

But as he opened his mouth to speak, suddenly a harsh voice came from out of nowhere.

"Gwendolyn!" shrieked the voice.

They both spun to see her mother, the Queen, dressed in her finest, accompanied by her handmaids, marching right for her daughter. Her face was livid.

She walked right up to her, grabbed her roughly by the arm, and yanked her away.

"You get back inside right now. What did I tell you? I don't want you speaking to him ever again. Do you understand me?"

Gwen's face reddened, then transformed with anger and pride.

"Get off of me!" she yelled at her mother. But it was no use: her mother kept dragging her away, and her handmaids encircled her, too.

"I said get off of me!" Gwen yelled. She turned and took one look back at Thor, with a desperate, sad look, one of pleading.

Thor understood the feeling. It was one that he felt himself. He wanted to call out to her, and felt his heart breaking as he watched her get dragged away. It was like watching a future life get taken away from him, right before his eyes.

He stood there for long after she disappeared from view, staring, rooted to the place, breathless. He didn't want to leave, didn't want to forget all of this.

Most of all, he did not want to imagine that he might not ever see her again.

*

As Thor ambled back to the castle, still reeling from his encounter with Gwen, he was barely even aware of his surroundings. His mind was consumed by thoughts of her; he could not stop seeing her face. She was magnificent. The most beautiful and kind and sweet and gentle and loving and funny person he had ever met. He needed to see her again. He actually felt pained at the absence of her presence. He didn't understand his feelings for her, and that scared him. He barely knew her, yet he knew already that he could not be without her.

Yet at the same time, he thought back to her mother, yanking her way, and his stomach sank to think of the powerful forces standing between them. Forces that did not want them to be together, for some reason.

As he racked his brain, trying to get to the bottom of it, suddenly he felt a stiff hand on his chest, stopping him hard in his tracks.

He looked up to see a boy, maybe a couple of years older than him, tall and thin, dressed in the most expensive clothes he had ever seen—in royal purple and green and scarlet silks, with an elaborate feathered hat—grimacing down. The boy looked dainty, spoiled, as if raised in the lap of luxury, with softened hands and high arched eyebrows that peered down disdainfully.

"They call me Alton," the boy began. "I am the son of Lord Alton, first cousin to the King. We have been lords of the realm for seven centuries. Which entitles me to be a Duke. You, by contrast, are a *commoner*," he said, nearly spitting the word. "The royal court is for royalty. And for men of rank. Not for your kind."

Thor stood there, having no idea who this boy was or what he had done to upset him.

"What do you want of me?" Thor asked.

Alton snickered.

"Of course, you would not know. You probably don't know anything, do you? How dare you barge in here and pretend to be one of us!" he spat.

Thor hardly knew how to respond.

"I'm not pretending anything," he said.

"Well, I don't care whatever wave you washed in on. I just want to warn you, before you get any more fantasies in your head, that Gwendolyn is mine."

Thor stared back, shocked. *His?* He hardly knew what to say.

"Our marriage has been arranged since birth," Alton continued. "We are of the same age, and of the same rank. Plans are already in motion. Don't you dare think, even for instant, that it will be any different."

Thor felt as if the wind had been knocked out of him; he didn't even have the strength to respond.

Alton took a step closer, and stared down.

"You see," he said in a soft voice, "I allow Gwen her flirtations. She has many. Every once in a while she'll take pity on a commoner, or perhaps a servant. She will allow them to be her entertainment, her amusement. You might have come to the conclusion that it is something more. But that's all it is for Gwynn. You are just another acquaintance, another amusement. She collects them, like dolls. They don't mean anything to her. She's excited by the newest commoner, and after a day or two, she gets bored. She shall drop you quickly. You're nothing to her, really. And by year's end she and I will be wed. Forever."

The boy's eyes opened wide, and Thor could see his fierce determination.

Thor felt his heart breaking at his words. Were they true? Was he really nothing to Gwynn? Now he was confused; he hardly knew what to believe. She had seemed so genuine. But maybe Thor had just been jumping to the wrong conclusion?

"You're lying," Thor finally said back.

Alton sneered, and then raised a single, pampered finger, and jabbed it into Thor's chest.

"If I see you near your again, I'll use my authority to call the royal guard. They will have you imprisoned!"

"On what grounds!?" Thor asked.

"I need no grounds. I have rank here. I will make one up, and it is me they will believe. By the time I'm done slandering you, half the kingdom will believe you are a criminal."

Alton smiled, self-satisfied; Thor felt sick.

"You lack honor," Thor said, uncomprehending that anyone could act with such indecency.

Alton laughed, a high-pitched sound.

"I never had it to begin with," he said. "Honor is for fools. I have what I want. You can keep your honor. And I will have Gwendolyn."

CHAPTER TWENTY

Thor walked with Reece out the arched gate of King's Court and onto the country road that led to the Legion's barracks. The guards stood at attention for them as they passed and Thor felt a great sense of belonging. He was finally starting to feel like he wasn't such an outsider. He thought back to just a few days before, when a guard had chased him out of here. How much had changed, so quickly.

Thor heard a screeching and looked up to see, high overhead, Estopheles, circling, looking down. She dove, and Thor, excited, held out his wrist, still wearing the metal gauntlet. But she rose again, and flew off. She flew higher and higher, never completely out of sight. Thor wondered. She was a mystical animal, and he felt an intense connection to her that was hard to explain.

Thor and Reece continued in silence, keeping a quick pace towards the barracks. Thor knew his brethren would be awaiting him, and wondered what sort of reception he would receive. Would there be envy, jealousy? Would they be mad that he got all this attention? Would they make fun of him for being carried back across the canyon? Or would they finally accept him?

Thor hoped it was the latter. He was tired of struggling with the rest of the Legion and just wanted, more than anything, to belong. To be accepted as one of them.

The barracks came into sight in the distance, and Thor's mind began to be preoccupied with something else.

Gwendolyn.

Thor didn't know how much he could talk to Reece about this, given that it was his sister. But he could not get her out of his mind. He couldn't stop thinking of his encounter with that menacing royal, Alton, and wondered how much of what he said was true. A part of him feared to discuss it with Reece, not wanting to risk upsetting him somehow and losing his new friend over his sister. But another part of him had to know what he thought.

"Who is Alton?" Thor finally asked, hesitant.

"Alton?" Reece repeated. "Why do you ask of him?"

Thor shrugged, unsure how much to say.

Luckily, Reece continued.

"He's but a menacing, lesser royal. Third cousin to the king. Why? Has he been after you about something?" Then Reece narrowed his eyes. "Gwen? Is that it? I should've warned you."

Thor turned and looked at Reece, eager to hear more.

"What do you mean?"

"He's a lout. He's been after my sister since he could walk. He's certain the two of them will be wed. My mother seems to think so, too."

"Will they?" Thor asked, surprised by the urgency in his own voice.

Reece looked at him and smiled.

"My, my, you have fallen for her, haven't you?" He chuckled. "That was fast."

Thor reddened, hoping it wasn't so obvious.

"Whether or not they do would depend on my sister's feelings for him," Reece finally answered. "Unless they forced her into marriage. But I doubt my father would do that."

"And how does she feel for him?" Thor pressed, afraid he was being too nosy, but needing to know.

Reece shrugged. "You'd have to ask her, I guess. I never talk to her about it."

"But would he force her into marriage?" Reece pressed. "Could he really do such a thing?"

"My father can do anything he wants. But that's between him and Gwyn."

Reece turned and looked at Thor.

"Why all these questions? What did you talk about?"

Thor blushed, unsure what to say.

"Nothing," he said finally.

"Nothing!" Reece laughed. "Sounds like a lot of nothing to me!"

Reece laughed harder, and Thor was embarrassed, wondering if he was just imagining that Gwen liked him. Reece reached over and put a firm hand on his shoulder.

"Listen old mate," Reece said, "the only thing you can know for sure about Gwen is that she knows what she wants. And she gets what she wants. That's always been the case. She's as strong-willed as my father. No one can force her to do anything—or like anyone—she doesn't want. So don't worry. If she chooses you, trust me, she'll let you know. Okay?"

Thor nodded, feeling better, as always, after he talked to Reece.

He looked up and saw the huge gates to the Legion's barracks before him. He was surprised to see several of the other boys standing at the gate, as if waiting for them, and even more surprised to see them grinning, and let out a cheer at the sight of him. They rushed forward, grabbed Thor by the shoulders, draped their arms around him, and pulled him inside. Thor was amazed as he was swept inside in an embrace of goodwill by the others.

"Tell us about the Canyon. What's it like on the other side?" one asked.

"What was the creature like? The one that you killed?" another asked.

"I didn't kill him," Thor protested. "Erec did."

"I heard you saved Elden's life," one said.

"I heard you attacked the creature head-on. Without any real weapons."

"You're one of us now!" one yelled out, and the other kids cheered, ushering him along, as if he were their long-lost brother.

Thor could hardly believe it. The more he heard their words, the more he realized that maybe they did have a point. Maybe he had been brave after all. He never really thought about it. For the first time in a long while, he was starting to feel good about himself. Most of all because now, finally, he felt like he belonged with these boys. He felt tension releasing from his shoulders.

Thor was ushered out into the main training ground, and before him stood dozens more of the legion, along with dozens of the Silver. They, too, let out a cheer at the sight of him. They all came forward, and patted him on the back.

Thor was amazed. He hardly knew how to react.

Kolk stepped forward, and the others quieted. Thor braced himself, since Kolk never had anything but contempt for Thor. But now, to Thor's surprise, he looked down at him with a different sort of expression. While he still couldn't quite bring himself to smile, he wasn't scowling, either. And Thor could have sworn he detected something like admiration in his eyes.

Kolk stepped forward, held up a small pin of a black falcon, and pinned it on Thor's chest.

Thor looked down and could hardly believe it. The pin of the Legion. He had been accepted. Finally, he was one of them.

"Thorgrin of the Southern Province of the Western Kingdom," Kolk said, gravely. "We welcome you to the Legion."

The boys let out a shout, then all rushed in, draping their arms around Thor and swaying him this way and that.

Thor couldn't even take it all in. He tried not to. He just wanted to enjoy this moment. Now, finally, there was somewhere he belonged.

Kolk turned and faced the other boys.

"Okay boys, calm yourselves," he commanded. "Today is a special day. No more pitchforks and polish and horse crap for you. Now it's time to really train. It's weapons day."

The boys returned an excited shout, and followed Kolk as he trotted across the training field, towards a huge circular building made of oak, with shining bronze doors. Thor walked with the group as they approached, an excited buzz in the air. Reece was by his side, and O'Connor came up and joined them.

"Never thought I'd see you alive again," O'Connor said, smiling and clapping a hands on his shoulder. "Next time, let me wake up first, will you?"

Thor smiled back.

"What is that building?" Thor asked Reece, as they got closer. There were immense iron rivets all over the door, and the place had an imposing presence.

"The weapons house," Reece answered. "It's where they store all our arms. Every once in a while they let us get a peek, even train with some of them. Depends what lesson they want to impart."

Thor's stomach tightened as he noticed Elden, coming over to them. Thor braced himself, expecting a threat—but this time, to Thor's amazement, Elden wore a look of appreciation.

"I have to thank you," he said, looking down, humbled. "For saving my life."

Thor was stumped: he had never expected this from him.

"I was wrong about you," Elden added. "Friends?" he asked.

He held out a hand.

Thor was not one to hold a grudge, and he gladly reached over and met his hand.

"Friends," Thor said.

"I don't take that word lightly," Elden said. "I will always have your back. And I owe you one."

With that, he turned and hurried off, back into the crowd.

Thor barely knew what to make of it. He was amazed at how quickly things had changed.

"I guess he's not a complete creep," O'Connor said. "Maybe he's okay after all."

They reached the weapons house, the immense doors swung open, and Thor was in awe as he entered. He walked slowly, neck craned, surveying the place in a broad circle, taking it all in. There were hundreds of weapons, weapons he didn't even recognize, hanging on the walls. The other kids hurried forward in an excited rush, running up to weapons, picking them up, handling them, examining them. Thor followed their example, and felt like a kid in a candy store.

He hurried over to a large halberd, hoisted the wooden shaft with two hands, and felt its weight. It was massive, well oiled. The blade was worn and notched, and he wondered if it had killed any men in battle.

He set it down and picked up a mace, a studded metal ball attached to a short staff by a long chain. He held the studded wooden shaft, and felt the metal spike dangle on the end of the chain. Beside him, Reece handled a battle ax, and beside him, O'Connor tested the weight of a long pike, jabbing into the air at an imaginary enemy.

"Listen up!" Kolk yelled, and they all turned.

"Today we will learn about fighting your enemy from a distance. Can anyone here tell me what weapons can be used? What can kill a man from thirty paces away?"

"A bow and arrow," somebody yelled.

"Yes," Kolk answered. "What else?"

"A spear!" someone shouted.

"What else? There are more than just these. Let's hear them."

"A slingshot," Thor added.

"What else?"

Thor racked his brain, but was running out of options.

"Throwing knives," Reece yelled.

"What else?"

The other boys hesitated. No one had any ideas left.

"There are throwing hammers," Kolk yelled, "and throwing axes. There is the crossbow. Pikes can be thrown. So can swords."

Kolk paced the room, looking over the faces of the boys, who stood rapt with attention.

"That is not all. A simple rock from the ground can be your best friend. I've seen a man, big as a bull, a war hero, killed on the spot by a throw from a rock by a craftier soldier. Soldiers often don't realize that armor can be used as a weapon, too. The gauntlet can be taken off and thrown in an enemy's face. This can stun him, several feet away. In that moment, you can kill him. Your shield can be thrown, too."

Kolk took a breath.

"It is crucial that when you learn to fight, you don't just learn to fight in the distance between you and your opponent. You must expand your fight to a much greater distance. Most people fight with three paces. A good warrior fights with thirty. Understood?"

"Yes sir!" came the chorus of shouts.

"Good. Today, we will sharpen your throwing skills. Canvas the room and grab what throwing devices you see. Each grab one and be outside in thirty seconds. Now move!"

The room erupted into a scramble, and Thor ran for the wall, searching for something to grab. He was bumped and pushed every which way by other excited boys, until he finally saw what he wanted and grabbed it. It was a small throwing axe. O'Connor grabbed a dagger, Reece a sword, and the three of them raced out, with the other boys, into the field.

They followed Kolk to the far side of the field, where there were lined up a dozen shields on posts.

All the boys, holding their weapons, gathered around Kolk expectantly.

"You will stand here," he boomed out, gesturing to a line in the dirt, "and aim for those shields when throwing your weapons. You will then run to the shields, grab a weapon that was not yours, and practice throwing that. Never choose the same weapon. Always aim for the shield. For those of you who miss a shield, you will be required to run one lap around the field. Begin!"

The boys lined up, shoulder to shoulder, behind the dirt line, and began to throw their weapons at the shields, which must have been a good thirty yards away. Thor fell in line with them. The boy beside him reached back and threw his spear, and it missed by a hair.

The boy turned and began to jog around the arena. As he did, a member of the King's men ran up beside him, and laid a heavy mantle of chainmail over his shoulders, weighing him down.

"Run with that, boy!" he ordered.

The boy, weighed down, already sweating, continued to run in the heat.

Thor did not want to miss the target. He leaned back, concentrated, pulled his throwing axe back, and let it go. He closed his eyes and hoped it hit its mark, and was relieved to hear the sound of it embedding itself in the leather shield. He barely made it, hitting a lower corner, but at least he did. All around him, several boys missed and broke off into laps. The few that hit raced for the shields to grab a new weapon.

Thor reached the shields and found a long, slim throwing dagger, which he extracted, then ran back to the throwing line.

They continued to throw for hours, until Thor's arm was killing him and he had run one too many laps himself. He was dripping in sweat, as were others around him. It was an interesting exercise, to throw all sorts of weapons, to get used to the feel and weight of all different shafts and blades. Thor felt himself getting better, more used to it, with each throw. But still, the heat was oppressive, and he was getting tired. There were only a dozen boys still standing before the shields, with most of them broken off into laps. It was just too hard to hit so many times, with so many different weapons, and the laps and the heat were making accuracy even worse. Thor was gasping, and didn't know how much longer he could go on. Just when he felt he was about to collapse, suddenly, Kolk stepped forward.

"Enough!" he yelled.

The boys returned from their laps and collapsed on the grass. They lay there, panting, breathing hard, removing the heavy coats of chain mail that had been draped on them. Thor, too, sat down in the grass, arm exhausted, dripping with sweat. Some of the King's men came around with buckets of water and dropped them on the grass. Reece reached out, grabbed one, drank from it, then handed it to O'Connor, who drank and handed it to Thor. Thor drank and drank, the water dripping down his chin and chest. The water felt amazing. He breathed hard as he handed it back to Reece.

"How long can this go on?" he asked.

Reece shook his head, gasping. "I don't know."

"I swear they're trying to kill us," came the voice. Thor turned and saw Elden, who had come up and sat beside him. Thor was surprised to see him there, and it sank in that Elden truly wanted to be friends. It was odd to see such a change in his behavior.

"Boys!" Kolk yelled, walking slowly between them. "More of you are missing your marks now, late in the day. As you can see, it is harder to be accurate when you're tired. That's the point. During battle, you will not be fresh. You will be exhausted. Some battles can go on for days. Especially if you are attacking a castle. And it is when you're at your most tired that you must make your most accurate throw. Often you will be forced to throw whatever weapon is at your disposal. You must be an expert in every weapon, and in every state of exhaustion. Is that understood?"

"YES SIR!" they shouted back.

"Some of you can throw a knife, or a spear. But that same person is missing with a hammer or axe. Do you think you can survive by throwing one weapon?"

"NO SIR!"

"Do you think this is just a game?"

"NO SIR!"

Kolk grimaced as he paced, kicking boys in the back who he felt were not sitting up straight enough.

"You've rested long enough," he said. "Back on your feet!"

Thor scrambled to his feet with the others, his legs weary, not sure how much more of this he could stand.

"There are two sides to distance fighting," Kolk continued. "You can throw—but so can your enemy. He may not be safe at thirty paces away—but you may not be, either. You must learn how to defend yourself at thirty paces. Is that understood?"

"YES SIR!"

"To defend yourself from a throwing object, you will need to not only be aware and quick on your feet, to duck, or roll, or dodge—but to also be adept at protecting yourself with a large shield."

Kolk gestured, and a soldier brought out a huge, heavy shield. Thor was amazed: it was nearly twice the size of him.

"Do I have a volunteer?" Kolk asked.

The group of boys was quiet, hesitant, and without thinking, Thor, swept up in the moment, raised his hand.

Kolk nodded, and Thor hurried forward.

"Good," Kolk said. "At least one of you is dumb enough to volunteer. I like your spirit, boy. A stupid decision. But good."

Thor was beginning to wonder if he had made a bad decision as Kolk handed him the huge metal shield. He fastened it to one arm, and could not believe how heavy it was. He was barely able to lift it.

"Thor, your mission is to run from this end of the field to the other. Unscathed. See those fifty boys facing you?" Kolk said to Thor. "They are all going to throw weapons at you. Real weapons. Do you understand? If you do not use your shield to protect you, you may die before you make it to the other side."

Thor stared back, unbelieving. The crowd of boys grew very quiet.

"This is not a game," Kolk continued. "This is very serious. Battle is serious. It is life-and-death. Are you sure you still want to volunteer?"

Thor nodded, too frozen in terror to say anything else. He could hardly change his mind at this point, not in front of everyone.

"Good."

Kolk gestured to an attendant, who stepped forward and blew a horn.

"Run!" Kolk screamed.

Thor hoisted the heavy shield with two hands, grasping it with all that he had. As he did, he felt a resounding thud, so severe it shook his skull. It must have been a metal hammer. It didn't pierce the shield, but it sent an awful shock throughout his system. He nearly dropped the shield, but forced himself to grasp it, and to move on.

Thor began to run, hobbling as fast as he could with the shield. As weapons and missiles flew past him, he forced himself to huddle within the shield as best he could. The shield was his lifeline. And as he ran, he learned how to stay within it.

An arrow flew by him, missing him by a fraction of an inch, and he pulled his chin back tighter. Another heavy object slammed against the shield, hitting him so hard that he stumbled back several feet and collapsed to the ground. But Thor stumbled back to his feet, and continued to run. With a supreme effort, gasping for air, finally he crossed the field.

"Yield!" Kolk yelled.

Thor dropped the shield, dripping in sweat. He was beyond grateful that he had reached the other side: he didn't know if he could've held that shield for another moment.

Thor hurried back to the others, many of whom gave him looks of admiration. He wondered how he had survived.

"Nice work," Reece whispered to him.

"Any other volunteers?" Kolk called out.

There was dead silence among the boys. Clearly, after watching Thor, no one else wanted to try.

Thor felt proud of himself. He wasn't sure if he would have volunteered knowing what was entailed, but now that it was over, he was glad that he did it.

"Fine. Then I will volunteer for you," Kolk yelled. "You! Saden!" he called out, pointing to someone.

An older, thin boy stepped forward, looking terrified.

"Me?" Saden said, his voice cracking.

The other boys laughed at him.

"Of course you. Who else?" Kolk said.

"I'm sorry sir, but I would rather not."

A horrified gasp arose among the Legion.

Kolk stepped forward, approaching him, grimacing.

"You don't do what you want," Kolk growled. "You do what I tell you to do."

Saden stood there, frozen, looking scared to death.

"He shouldn't be here," Reece whispered to Thor.

Thor turned and looked at him. "What do you mean?"

"He comes from a noble family, and they placed them here. But he doesn't want to be here. He's not a fighter. Kolk knows that. I think they're trying to break him. I think they want him out."

"I'm sorry sir, but I cannot," Saden said, sounding terrified.

"You can," Kolk screamed, "and you will!"

There was a frozen, tense standoff.

Saden looked down to the ground, hanging his chin in shame.

"I am sorry, sir. Give me some other task, and I will gladly do it."

Kolk turned red in the face, storming towards him until he was inches from his face.

"I *will* give you another task, boy. I don't care who your family is. From now on, you will run. You will run around this field until you collapse. And you will not come back until you volunteer to take up this shield. Do you understand me?"

Saden looked as if he were about to burst into tears, as he nodded back.

A soldier came over, draped chainmail over Saden, and then a second arrived and draped another set of chainmail on him. Thor could not understand how he could bear the weight of it. He could barely run with one of them on.

Kolk leaned back and kicked Saden hard in the rear, and he went stumbling forward and began his long, slow jog around the field. Thor felt bad for him. As he watched him hobble around, he couldn't help but wonder if the boy would survive the Legion.

Suddenly a horn was sounded, and Thor turned to see a company of the King's men ride up on horseback, a dozen of the Silver with them, holding long spears, wearing feathered helmets. They rode up and stopped before the legion.

"In honor of the king's daughter's wedding day, and in honor of the summer solstice, the king has declared the rest of today a hunting day!"

All the boys around Thor erupted into a huge cheer. As one, they all broke off into a sprint, following the horses as they turned and charged across the field.

"What's happening?" Thor asked Reece, as he began to run with the others.

Reece wore a huge smile on his face.

"It's a godsend!" he said. "We're off for the day! We get to hunt!"

CHAPTER TWENTY ONE

Thor jogged down the forest trail with the others, holding the spear that had been handed to him for the hunt. Beside him were Reece, O'Connor and Elden, along with at least fifty other members of the Legion. In front of them rode a hundred Silver, on horseback and in light armor, some carrying short spears, but most with bows and arrows slung over their backs. Running on foot amongst them were dozens of squires and attendants.

Riding at the front was King MacGil, looking as huge and proud as ever, an excited grin on his face. He was flanked by his sons, Kendrick and Gareth, and, Thor was surprised to see, even Godfrey. Dozens of pages ran amidst them, a few of them leaning back and blowing horns made of long ivory tusks; others yanked at baying dogs, who anxiously ran forward to keep up with the horses. It was complete mayhem. As the huge group charged through the forest, they began to split off in every direction, and Thor hardly knew where they were going, or which group to follow.

Erec rode close by, and Thor and the others decided to follow his trail. Thor came running up beside Reece.

"Where are we going?" he asked Reece, out of breath as they ran.

"Deep into the wood," Reece called back. "The King's men aim to bring back days' worth of foul."

"Why are some of the Silver on horses and others on foot?" O'Connor asked Reece.

"Those on horses are hunting the easier kill, such as deer and fowl," Reece responded. "They use their bows. Those on foot aim for the more dangerous animals. Like the yellowtail boar."

Thor was both excited and nervous at the mention of the animal. He had seen one growing up: it was a nasty and dangerous creature, known to tear a man in two with little provocation.

"The oldest warriors tend to stay on horseback and go after deer and birds," Erec added, looking down. "The younger tend to stay on foot, and go after the bigger game. You have to be in better shape for it, of course."

"Which is why we allow this hunt for you boys," Kolk, running with the others, not far away, yelled out, "it is training for you, too. You will have to be on foot the entire hunt, keep up with the horses. As we go, you will break off into smaller groups, and each fork down your own path, and each hunt down your own animal. You will find the most vicious animal you can—and you will fight it to the death. These are the same qualities that make you a soldier: stamina, fearlessness, and not backing down from your adversary, no matter how big or how vicious. Now go!" he screamed.

Thor ran faster, as did all of his brethren, racing to catch up to the horses as they tore through the forest. He hardly knew which way to go, but he figured if he stuck close to Reece and O'Connor, he would be okay.

"An arrow, quick!" Erec yelled down.

Thor burst into action, running up beside Erec's horse, grabbing an arrow from the quiver on the saddle, and handing it up to him. Erec placed it on his bow as he rode, slowed and took steady aim at something in the woods.

"The dogs!" Erec screamed.

One of the King's attendants released a barking dog, which dove into the bushes. To Thor's surprise, a large bird flew up, and as it did, Erec let loose the arrow.

It was a perfect shot, right to the neck, and the bird fell down, dead. Thor was amazed at how Erec had spotted it.

"The bird!" Erec yelled out.

Thor ran, grabbed the dead bird, warm, blood still oozing from its neck, and ran back to Erec. He slung it on Erec's saddle, and it hung there as he rode.

All around Thor, many knights on horseback were doing the same, flushing birds and shooting at them, their squires retrieving them. Most used arrows; some used spears. Thor watched as Kendrick pulled back his spear, took aim and hurled it at a deer. It was a perfect strike, right into its throat, and it fell, too.

Thor was amazed at the abundance of game in these woods, the amount of bounty they would be bringing home. It would be enough to feed King's Court for days.

"Have you been on a hunt before?" Thor called out to Reece, narrowly avoiding being trampled by one of the King's men as they ran. It was hard to hear, with the barking of the dogs, the horns sounding, the screams of men, laughing, victorious, as they took down animal after animal.

Reece had a big smile on his face as he jumped over a log and continued running.

"Many times! But only because of my father. They don't let us join the hunt until a certain age. It's a thrilling thing—although no one tends to get out of it unscathed. More than one man has been hurt, or killed, chasing boar."

Reece gasped as he ran. "But I've always ridden on horseback," he added. "I've never been allowed to be on foot before, with the Legion, never allowed to hunt boar. It is a first for me!"

The forest suddenly changed, with dozens of trails stretching out before them, splitting in a dozen ways. Another horn sounded, and the huge group began to break up into smaller groups.

As they all split up, Thor stuck close to Erec, and Reece and O'Connor joined them; they all turned onto a narrow path that curved sharply downward. They ran and ran, Thor clutching his spear and jumping a small creak. Their small group comprised Erec and Kendrick on horseback, Thor, Reece, O'Connor, and Elden on foot, making six of them—and as Thor turned, he noticed two more members of the legion running up behind them, joining them. They were large and broad, with wavy sandy hair that fell past their eyes, and big smiles. They looked to be a couple of years older than Thor—and they were identical twins.

"I am Conval," one of them called out to Thor.

"And I Conven."

"We are brothers," Conval said.

"Twins!" Conven added.

"Hope you don't mind if we join you," Conval said to Thor.

Thor had seen them around, in the Legion, but had never met them before. He was happy to meet new members, especially members who were friendly to him.

"Happy to have you," Thor called out.

"The more hands the better," Reece echoed.

"I hear the boars in this wood are huge," Conval remarked.

"And deadly," Conven answered.

Thor looked at the long spears that the twins carried, three times longer than his, and wondered. He noticed them looking at his short spear

"That spear won't be long enough," Conval said

"These boars have big tusks. You need something longer," Conven said.

"Take mine," Elden said, and ran over beside him, and tried to hand it to him.

"I can't take yours," Thor said. "What would you use?"

Elden shrugged. "I'll be okay."

Thor was touched at his generosity, and marveled at how different their friendship was now.

"Take one of mine," ordered a voice.

Thor looked up and saw Erec ride up beside him, gesturing to the saddle, which held two long spears.

Thor reached out and grabbed a long spear from the saddle, so grateful to have it. It was heavier, and more awkward to run with— but he did feel more protected, and it sounded like he would need it.

They ran and ran, until the air burned in Thor's lungs and he did not know if he could go any farther. He was alert, looking about him for any sign of an animal. He felt protected with these other men around him, and invincible with a long spear. But he was still very much on edge. He had never hunted a boar before, and had no idea what to expect.

As his lungs burned, the forest broke open into a clearing and thankfully, Erec and Kendrick pulled their horses to a stop. Thor assumed that granted them all permission to stop, too. They all stood there, the eight of them in the forest clearing, the boys on foot gasping for air, and Erec and Kendrick dismounting from their horses. The horses panted, but otherwise it was quiet, the only sound the wind in the trees. The noise of the hundreds of other men racing through the forest was now gone, and Thor realized they must be very far from the others.

He stood there, panting, looking around the clearing.

"I haven't seen any markings of animals," Thor said to Reece. "Have you?"

Reece shook his head.

"The boar is a crafty animal," Erec said, stepping forward. "He won't always show himself. Sometimes he'll be the one watching you. He might wait until you're caught off guard, and then he'll charge. Always keep your guard up."

"Look out!" O'Connor yelled.

Thor spun and suddenly a large animal burst out it into the clearing with a huge commotion; Thor flinched, thinking they were

154

being attacked by a boar. O'Connor screamed, and Reece turned and hurled a spear at it. It missed, and the animal flew up into the air. It was then that Thor realized it was just a turkey, disappearing back into the wood.

They all laughed, the tension broken. O'Connor reddened, and Reece laid a reassuring hand on his shoulder.

"Don't worry, friend," he said.

O'Connor looked away, embarrassed.

"There are no boar here," Elden said. "We chose a bad path. The only thing down this path are fowl. We will come back empty-handed."

"Maybe that's not a bad thing," said Conval. "I hear a boar fight can be life-and-death."

Kendrick stood there, calmly surveying the wood, and Erec did the same. Thor could see on the faces of these two men that something was out there. He could tell from their experience and wisdom that they were on guard.

"Well, the trail seems to end here," Reece said. "So if we go on, the wood will be unmarked. We won't find our way back."

"But if we go back, our hunt is over," O'Connor said.

"What would happen if we should return empty-handed?" Thor asked. "Without a boar?"

"We would be the laughing stock of the others," Elden said.

"No we wouldn't," Reece said. "Not everyone finds a boar. In fact, it's more rare to find one than not."

As the group of them stood there in silence, breathing hard, watching the woods, Thor suddenly realized that he had drank too much water. He had been holding it in the entire hunt and now he had such a pain in his bladder, he could barely contain it.

"Excuse me," he said, and began make to his way into the woods.

"Where are you going?" Erec asked, cautious.

"I just have to relieve myself. I'll be right back."

"Don't go far," Erec cautioned.

Thor, self-conscious, hurried into the woods and went about twenty paces from the others, until he found a spot just out of view.

Just as he finished relieving himself, suddenly, he heard a twig snap. It was loud and distinct, and he knew, he just knew, it was from no human.

He turned slowly, the hair rising on the back of his neck, and looked. Up ahead, maybe another ten paces, was another small

155

clearing, a boulder in its center. And there, at the base of the boulder, was movement. A small animal, he could not tell what.

Thor stood there, debating whether to go back to his people or to see what it was. Without thinking, he crept forward. Whatever the animal was, he didn't want to lose it, and if he headed back, it might be gone when he returned.

Thor stepped closer, hairs on edge as the woods got thicker and there was less room to maneuver. He could see nothing but dense woods, the sun cutting at sharp angles. Finally, he reached the clearing. As he approached, he loosened his grip on his spear, and lowered it down to his hip. He was taken aback by what he saw before him, in the clearing, in a patch of sunlight.

There, squirming in the grass, beside the rock, was a small leopard cub. It sat there, squirming and whining, squinting into the sun. It looked as if it had just been born, barely a foot long, small enough to fit inside Thor's shirt.

Thor stood there, amazed. The pup was all white, and he knew it must be the pup of the White Leopard, the rarest of all animals.

He heard a sudden rustling of leaves behind him, and turned to see the entire group rushing towards him, Reece out front, looking worried. In moments, they were upon him.

"Where did you go?" he demanded. "We thought you were dead."

As they all came up beside him and looked down at the pup, he could hear them gasp in shock.

"A momentous omen," Erec said to Thor. "You have found the find of a lifetime. The rarest of all animals. It has been left alone. It has no one to care for it. That means it's yours. It is your obligation to raise it."

"Mine?" Thor asked, perplexed.

"It is your obligation," Kendrick added. "You found it. Or, I should say, it found you."

Thor was baffled. He had tended sheep, but he had never raised an animal in his life, and he had no idea what to do.

But at the same time, he already felt a strong kinship with the animal. Its small, light blue eyes opened and seemed to stare only at him.

He approached it, bent down, and picked it up in his arms. The animal reached up and licked his cheek.

"How does one care for a leopard cub?" Thor asked, overwhelmed.

"I suppose the same way one cares for anything else," Erec said. "Feed it when it's hungry."

"You must name it," Kendrick said.

Thor racked his brain, amazed that this was his second time having to name an animal in as many days. He remembered a story from his childhood, about a lion that terrorized a village.

"Krohn," Thor said.

The others nodded back in approval.

"Like the legend," Reece said.

"I like it," O'Connor said.

"Krohn it is," Erec said.

As Krohn lowered its head into Thor's chest, Thor felt a stronger connection to it than to anything he'd ever had. He couldn't help but feel as if he'd already known Krohn for lifetimes as the animal squirmed and squealed at him.

Suddenly there came a distinct sound, one that raised the hair on the back of Thor's neck, and made him turn quickly and stare up at the sky.

There, high above, was Estopheles. It suddenly dove down low, right for Thor's head, screeching as it did, before lifting at the last second.

At first Thor wondered if it was jealous of Krohn. But then, with a split second to spare, Thor realized: his falcon was warning him.

A moment later there came a distinct noise from the other side of the wood. It was a rustling, followed by a charging—and it all happened too fast.

Because of the warning, Thor had an advantage: he saw it coming and leapt out of the way with a second to spare, as a massive boar charged right for him. It missed him by a hair.

The clearing broke into chaos. The boar charged the others, ferocious, swinging its tusks every which way. In one swipe, it managed to slice O'Connor's arm, and blood burst out as he clutched it, screaming.

It was the biggest and most ferocious animal Thor had ever seen. It was like trying to fight a bull, but without the proper weapons. Elden tried to jab it with his long spear, but the boar merely turned its head, clamp down on it, and in one clean motion snapped it in two.

Then it turned and charged Elden, hitting him in the ribs; luckily for Elden, he narrowly missed its tusks tearing him apart.

This boar was unstoppable. It was out for blood, and it would clearly not leave them alone until it had it.

The others rallied and broke into action. Erec and Kendrick extracted their swords, as did Thor, Reece and the others.

They all encircled it, but it was hard to hit, especially with its three-foot long tusks that kept them from getting anywhere close to it. It ran in circles, chasing them around the clearing. As they each took turns attacking, Erec scored a direct hit, slashing it on its side; but this boar must have been made of steel, because it just kept going.

That was when everything changed. For a brief moment, something caught Thor's eyes, and he turned and looked into the forest. In the distance, hidden behind the trees, he could have sworn he saw a man with a black, hooded cloak; he saw him raise a bow and arrow, and aim it right for the clearing. He seemed to be aiming not at the boar, but at the men.

Thor wondered if he were seeing things. He could hardly believe it. Could they be under attack? Here? In the middle of nowhere? By who?

Thor allowed his instincts to take over. He sensed that the others were in danger, and he raced for them. He saw the man aiming his bow for Kendrick.

Thor dove for Kendrick. He tackled him hard, knocking him to the ground, and as he did so, a moment later the arrow flew by, just missing him.

Thor immediately looked back to the forest, looking for signs of the attacker. But he was gone.

But he had no time to think: the boar was still sprinting madly about the clearing, only feet away from them. Now it turned in their direction, and Thor had no time to react. He braced himself for the impact, as the long, sharp tusks bore down directly for him.

A moment later there came a high-pitched squeal; Thor turned to see Erec, leaping onto the beast's back, raising his sword high with both hands, and plunging it into the back of its neck. The beast roared, blood squirting from its mouth, as it buckled to its knees, then crashed down to the ground, Erec on top of it. It ground to a halt, just feet away from Thor.

All of them stood there, frozen in place, looking at each other— and wondering what on earth just happened.

CHAPTER TWENTY TWO

Thor, carrying Krohn inside his shirt, was overwhelmed by the noise as Reece opened the door to the alehouse. A huge group of waiting Legion members and soldiers, crammed inside, met them with a shout. It was packed, and hot in here, and Thor was immediately sandwiched in between his brethren, shoulder to shoulder. It had been a long day of hunting, and they had all gathered here, at this alehouse deep in the woods, to celebrate. The Silver had led the way, and Thor, Reece and the others followed.

Behind Thor, the twins, Conval and Conven, carried their prize possession, the boar, bigger than anyone else's, on a long pole over their shoulders. They had to set it down outside the tavern doors before coming in. As Thor took a last glance back, it looked so fierce, it was hard to conceive they had killed it.

Thor felt a squirm inside his jacket, and he looked down to see his new companion, Krohn. He could hardly believe that he was actually carrying a white leopard pup. It stared up at him with its crystal blue eyes, and squeaked. Thor sensed that he was hungry.

Thor was jostled inside the alehouse, dozens more men streaming in behind him, and he proceeded deeper into the small, crowded place, which must have been twenty degrees warmer in here—not to mention, more humid. He followed Erec and Kendrick, and he in turn was followed by Reece, Elden, the twins and O'Connor, whose arm was bandaged from the boar's slice, and had finally stopped bleeding. O'Connor seemed more dazed than hurt, his good spirits had returned, and their whole group shuffled deep into the room.

It was packed shoulder to shoulder, so tight that there was barely room to even turn. There were long benches, and some men stood, while others sat, singing drinking songs and banging their casks into their friends', or banging them on the table. It was a rowdy, festive environment, and Thor had never seen anything like it.

"First time in an alehouse?" Elden asked, practically shouting to be heard.

Thor nodded back, feeling like a rube once again.

"I bet you've never even had a cask of ale, have you?" asked Conven, clapping him on the shoulder with a laugh.

"Of course I have," Thor shot back defensively.

He was blushing, though, and hoped no one could tell, because, in fact, he never had. His father had never allowed it. And even if he did, he was sure he couldn't afford it.

"Very good then!" cried out Conval. "Bartender, give us a round of your strongest. Thor here is an old pro!"

One of the twins put down a gold coin, and Thor was amazed at the money these boys carried; he wondered what family they hailed from. That coin could have lasted his family a month back in his village.

A moment later a dozen casks of foaming ale were slid across the bar, and the boys pushed their way through and grabbed them; a cask got shoved into Thor's hand. The foam dripped over the side of his hand, and his stomach twisted in anticipation. He was nervous.

"To our hunt!" Reece called out.

"TO OUR HUNT!" the others echoed.

Thor followed the others, trying to act natural as he raised the foaming cask to his lips. He took a sip, and hated the taste, but saw the others gulping theirs down, not removing them from their lips until they finished. Thor felt obliged to do the same, or else look like a coward. He forced himself to drink it, gulping it down as fast he could, until finally, halfway through, he set it down, coughing.

The others looked at him, and roared with laughter. Elden clapped him on the back.

"It *is* your first time, isn't it?" he asked.

Thor reddened as he wiped foam from his lips. Luckily, before he could reply, there came a shout in the room, and they all turned to see several musicians shove their way in. They started playing on lutes and flutes, clanging cymbals, and the rowdy atmosphere heightened.

"My brother!" came a voice.

Thor turned to see a boy a few years older than him, with a small belly yet broad shoulders, unshaven, looking somewhat slovenly, step forward and embrace Reece in an awkward hug. He was joined by three companions, who seemed equally slovenly.

"I never thought I'd find you here!" he added.

"Well, once in a while I need to follow in my brother's footsteps, don't I?" Reece shouted back with a smile. "Thor, do you know my brother, Godfrey?"

160

Godfrey turned and shook Thor's hand, and Thor could not help but notice how smooth and plump it was. It was not a warrior's hand.

"Of course I know the newcomer," Godfrey said, leaning in too close and slurring his words. "The whole kingdom is alive with talk of him. A fine warrior I hear," he said to Thor. "Too bad. What a waste of a talent for the alehouse!"

Godfrey leaned back and roared with laughter, and his three companions joined him. One of them, a head taller than the others, with a huge belly, bright red cheeks, and flush with drink, leaned forward and clamped a hand on Thor's shoulder.

"Bravery is a fine trait. But it sends you to the battlefield, and keeps you cold. Being a drunk is a better trait: it keeps you safe and warm—and assures a warm lady by your side!"

He roared with laughter, as did the others, and the bartender set down fresh casks of ale for all of them. Thor hoped he wouldn't be asked to drink; he could already feel the ale rushing to his head.

"It was his first hunt today!" Reece yelled out to his brother.

"Was it then?" Godfrey replied. "Well then that calls for a drink, doesn't it?"

"Or two!" his tall friend echoed.

Thor looked down as another cask was shoved into his palm.

"To firsts!" Godfrey called out.

"TO FIRSTS!" the others echoed.

"May your life be filled with firsts," the tall one echoed, "except for the first time being sober!"

They all roared with laughter, as they drank their casks.

Thor sipped his, then tried to get away with lowering it—but Godfrey caught him.

"That's not the way you drink it boy!" Godfrey yelled. He stepped forward, grabbed the cask, put it to Thor's lips, and pushed it down his mouth. The men all laughed as Thor gulped it down. He set it down, empty, and they cheered.

Thor felt lightheaded. He was beginning to feel out of control, and it was harder to focus. He didn't like the feeling.

Thor felt another squirm in his shirt, as Krohn reared his head.

"Well, what have we here!" Godfrey shouted in delight.

"It's a leopard cub," Thor said.

"We found it on the hunt," Reece added.

"He's hungry," Thor said. "I'm not sure what to feed him."

"Why, of course, ale!" the tall man yelled.

"Really?" Thor asked. "Is that healthy for him?"

"Of course!" Godfrey yelled. "It is just hops, boy!"

Godfrey reached out, dipped his finger into the foam, and held it out; Krohn leaned forward and licked it up. He licked again and again.

"See, he likes it!"

Godfrey suddenly retracted his finger with a scream. He held it up and showed blood.

"Sharp teeth on that one!" he yelled out—and the others all broke into laughter.

Thor reached down, stroked Krohn's head, and tilted the remnant of his cask into his mouth. Krohn lapped it up, and Thor resolved to find him real food. He hoped that Kolk would let him stay in the barracks, and hoped none of the Legion objected.

The musicians changed their song, and several more friends of Godfrey's appeared. They came over, joined them in a fresh round of drinks, and led Godfrey away, back into the crowd.

"I will see you later young man," Godfrey said to Reece, before leaving. Then he turned to Thor: "Hopefully, you'll spend more time in the alehouse!"

"Hopefully you'll spend more time on the battlefield," Kendrick called back.

"I very much doubt that!" Godfrey said and roared with laughter with the rest of his compatriots, as he disappeared into the crowd.

"Do they always celebrate like this?" Thor asked Reece.

"Godfrey? He's been in the alehouse since he could walk. A disappointment to my father. But he's happy with himself."

"No, I mean the King's men. The Legion. Is there always a trip to the alehouse?"

Reece shook his head.

"Today is a special day. The first hunt, and the summer solstice. This doesn't happen that often. Enjoy it while it does."

Thor was feeling increasingly disoriented as he looked around the room. This was not where he wanted to be. He wanted to be back in the barracks, training. And his thoughts drifted, once again, to Gwendolyn.

"Did you get a good look at him?" Kendrick asked, as he came up to Thor.

Thor looked at him, puzzled.

"The man, in the woods, who shot the arrow?" Kendrick added.

The others crowded around close, trying to hear as the mood grew serious.

Thor tried again to remember, but he could not. Everything was fuzzy.

"I wish I did," he said. "It all happened so fast."

"Maybe it was just one of the king's other men, shooting in our direction by accident," O'Connor said.

Thor shook his head.

"He wasn't dressed like the others. He wore all-black, and a cloak and hood. And he only shot one arrow, aimed right for Kendrick, then disappeared. I'm sorry. I wish I saw more."

Kendrick shook his head, trying to think.

"Who would want you dead?" Reece asked Kendrick.

"Was it an assassin?" O'Connor asked.

Kendrick shrugged. "I have no enemies that I know of."

"But father has many," Reece said. "Maybe someone wants to kill you to get to him."

"Or maybe someone wants you out of the way for the throne," Elden postulated.

"But that's absurd! I'm illegitimate! I cannot inherit the throne!"

While they all shook their heads, sipping their ale and trying to figure it out, there came another shout in the room, and all the men's attention turned towards the staircase leading upstairs. Thor looked up, and saw a string of ladies walk out of an upper hallway, stand by a bannister, and look down at the room. They were all scantily dressed, and wore too much makeup.

Thor blushed.

"Well, hello men!" called the lady in front, with a large bosom and wearing a red lace outfit.

The men cheered.

"Who's got money to spend tonight?" she asked.

The men cheered again.

Thor's eyes opened wide in surprise.

"Is this also a brothel?" he asked.

The others turned and looked at him in stunned silence, then all broke into laughter.

"My God, you are naïve, aren't you!" Conval said.

"Tell me you've never been to a brothel?" Conven said.

"I bet he's never been with a woman!" Elden said.

Thor felt them all looking at him, and he felt his face turn red as a beet. He wanted to disappear. They were right: he had never been with a woman. But he would never tell them that. He wondered if it was obvious from his face.

Before he could respond, one of the twins reached up, clasped a firm hand on his back, and threw a gold coin up to the woman on the stairs.

"I believe you have your first customer!" he yelled.

The room cheered, and Thor, despite his pushing and pulling and resisting, felt himself shoved forward by dozens of men, through the crowd, and up the staircase. As he went, his mind filled with thoughts of Gwen. Of how much he loved her. Of how he didn't want to be with anyone else.

He wanted to turn and run. But there was literally no escape. Dozens of the biggest men he had ever seen shoved him forward, and did not allow retreat. Before he knew it, he was up the steps, on the landing, staring at a woman taller than he, who were too much perfume, and smiled down at him. Making matters worse, Thor was drunker than he had ever been. The room was positively spinning out of control, and he felt that in another moment he would collapse.

The woman reached down, pulled Thor's shirt, led him firmly into a room, and slammed the door behind them. Thor was determined *not* to be with her. He held in his mind thoughts of Gwen, forcing them to the front. This was not how he wanted his first experience to be.

But his mind was not listening. He was so drunk, he could barely see now. And the last thing he remembered, before he blacked out, was being led across the room, towards a lady's bed, and hoping he made it before he hit the floor.

CHAPTER TWENTY THREE

MacGil peeled open his eyes, awakened by the relentless pounding on his door, and immediately, he wished he hadn't. His head was splitting. Harsh sunlight shone in through the open castle window, and he realized his face was planted in his sheepskin blanket. Disoriented, he tried to remember. He was home, in his castle. He tried to summon the night before. He remembered the hunt. Then, an alehouse, in the woods. Drinking way too many casks. Somehow, he must have made it back here.

He looked over and saw his wife, the Queen, sleeping beside him, under the covers and slowly rousing.

The pounding came again, the awful noise of an iron knocker slamming.

"Who could that be at this hour?" she asked, annoyed.

MacGil was wondering the same thing. He specifically remembered leaving instructions with his servants not to wake him—especially after the hunt. There'd be hell to pay for this.

It was probably his steward, with another petty financial matter.

"Stop that bloody banging!" MacGil finally bellowed, rolling out of bed, sitting with his elbows on his knees, hand in his head. He ran his hands through his unwashed hair and beard, then over his face, trying to wake himself up. The hunt—and the ale—had taken a lot out of him. He wasn't as limber as he used to be. The years had taken their toll; he was exhausted. At this moment, he felt like never drinking again.

With a supreme effort he pushed himself off his knees, and to his feet. Dressed only in his robe, he quickly crossed the room, and finally reached the door, a foot thick, grabbing the iron handle and yanking it back.

Standing there was his greatest general, Brom, flanked by two attendants. They lowered their heads in deference, but his general stared right at him, a grim look on his face. MacGil hated it when he wore that look. It always meant somber news. It was at moments like these that he hated being King. He had been having such a good day yesterday, a great hunt, and it had reminded him of when he was young, carefree. Especially wasting the night away like that in the alehouse. Now, to be rudely awakened like this, it took away any illusion of peace he had had.

"My liege, I am sorry to wake you," Kolk said.

"You should be sorry," MacGil growled. "This better be important."

"It is," he said.

He spotted the seriousness of his face, and turned and checked back over his shoulder for his queen. She was still asleep.

MacGil gestured for them to enter, then led them through his vast bedroom, and through another arched door, to a side chamber, shutting the door behind them so as not to disturb her. He sometimes used this smaller room, no greater than twenty paces in each direction, with a few comfortable chairs and a big stained-glass window, when he didn't feel like going down to the Great Hall.

"My liege, our spies have told us of a McCloud contingent of men, riding east, for the Fabian Sea. And our scouts in the south report a caravan of empire ships, heading north. Surely they must be heading there to meet the McClouds."

MacGil tried to process this information, his brain moving too slowly in his drunken state.

"And?" he prodded, impatient, tired. He was so exhausted by the endless machinations and speculations and subterfuges of his court.

"If the McClouds are truly meeting with the Empire, there can only be one purpose," Brom continued. "To conspire to breach the Canyon and overthrow the Ring."

MacGil looked up at his old commander, a man who we had fought with for thirty years, and could see the deadly seriousness in his eyes. He could also see fear. That disturbed him: this was not a man he had ever seen fear anything.

MacGil slowly rose, to his full height, which was still considerable, and turned and walked across the room, until he reached the window. He looked out, surveying his court below, empty in the early morning, and thought to himself. He knew, all along, that one day a day like this would come. He just had not expected it to come so soon.

"That was quick," he said. "It's been but hours since I married off my daughter to their prince. And now you think they already conspire to overthrow us?"

"I do, my liege," Brom responded sincerely. "I see no other reason. All indications are it is a peaceful meeting. Not a military one."

MacGil slowly shook his head.

"But it does not make sense. They could not let the Empire in. Why would they? Even if for some reason they managed to help lower the Shield on our side and open a breach, then what would happen? The Empire would overwhelm them as well. They would not be safe, either. Surely, they know this."

"Maybe they are going to strike a deal," Brom retorted. "Maybe they will let the Empire in, in return for their attacking us only, so that the McClouds can control the Ring."

MacGil shook his head.

"The McClouds are too smart for that. They are crafty. They know that the Empire cannot be trusted."

His general shrugged.

"Maybe they want control of the Ring so badly, they are willing to take that chance. Especially now that they have your daughter as their queen."

MacGil thought about this. His head was pounding. He did not want to deal with this now. Not so early in the morning.

"So then what do you propose?" he asked, short with him, tired of all the speculation.

"We could preempt this, sire, and attack the McClouds. The time is now."

MacGil could hardly believe it.

"Right after I gave my daughter to them in a wedding? I don't think so."

"If we don't," Brom countered, "we allow them to dig our grave. Surely they will attack us. If not now, then later. And if they join with the empire, we would be finished."

"They cannot cross the Highlands so easily. We control all the choke points. It would be a slaughter. Even with the empire in tow."

"The empire have millions of men to spare," Kolk responded. "They can afford to be slaughtered."

"Even with the shield down," MacGil said, "it would not be so easy to just march millions of soldiers across the Canyon—or across the Highlands, or to approach by ship. We would spot such mobilization far in advance. We would have warning."

MacGil thought.

"No, we will not attack. But for now, we can take a prudent step: double our patrols at the Highlands. Strengthen our fortifications. And double our spies. That will be all."

"Yes, my liege," Brom said, turning, with his lieutenants and hurrying from the room.

MacGil turned back to the window, his head pounding. He sensed war on the horizon, coming at him with the inevitability of a winter storm. He sensed, further, that there was nothing he could do about it. He looked all around him, at his castle, at the stone, at the pristine royal court spread out beneath him, and he could not help but wonder how long all of this would last.

What he would give now for another drink.

CHAPTER TWENTY FOUR

Thor felt a foot nudging him in his ribs, and he slowly peeled opened his eyes. He lay face down, on a mound of straw, and for a moment had no idea where he was. His head felt like it weighed a million pounds, his throat was drier than it had ever been, and his eyes and head were killing him. He felt as if he'd fallen off a horse.

He was nudged again, and he sat up, the room spinning violently. He leaned over and threw up, gagging again and again.

A chorus of laughter erupted all around him, and he looked up to see Reece, O'Connor, Elden and the twins hovering close by, looking down.

"Finally, sleeping beauty wakes!" Reece called out, smiling.

"We didn't think you'd ever rise," O'Connor said.

"Are you okay?" Elden asked.

Thor sat up, wiping his mouth with the back of his hand, trying to process it all. As he did, Krohn, lying a few feet away, whimpered and ran over to him, jumping into his arms and burying his head in his shirt. Thor was relieved to see him, and happy to have him at his side. He tried to remember.

"Where am I?" Thor asked. "What happened last night?"

The three of them laughed.

"I'm afraid you had one drink too many, my friend. Someone can't hold his ale. Don't you remember? The alehouse?"

Thor closed his eyes, rubbing his temples, and tried to bring it all back. It came in flashes. He remembered the hunt...entering the alehouse...the drinks. He remembered being led upstairs...the brothel. After that, it was all black.

His heart quickened, as he thought of Gwendolyn. Had he done anything stupid with that girl? Had he ruined his chances with Gwen?

"What happened?" he pressed Reece, serious, as he clasped his wrist. "Please, tell me. Tell me I didn't do anything with that woman."

The others laughed, but Reece stared back at his friend earnestly, realizing how upset he was.

169

"Don't worry, friend," he answered. "You did nothing at all. Except for throw up and collapse on her floor!"

The others laughed again.

"So much for your first time," Elden said.

But Thor felt deeply relieved. He had not alienated Gwen.

"Last time I buy you a woman!" said Colven.

"Perfectly good waste of money," said Caven. "She wouldn't even return it!"

The boys laughed again. Thor was humiliated, but so relieved he had not ruined anything.

He took Reece's arm and pulled him aside.

"Your sister," he whispered, urgently. "She doesn't know about any of this, does she?"

Reece broke into a slow smile, as he put an arm around his shoulder.

"Your secret is safe with me, even though you didn't do anything. She doesn't know. And I can see how deeply you care for her, and I appreciate that," he said, his face morphing into a serious expression. "I can see now that you really do care for her. If you had gone whoring, that would not be the kind of brother-in-law I would want. In fact, I have been asked to deliver you this message."

Reece shoved a small scroll into Thor's palm, and Thor looked down, confused. He saw the royal stamp on it, the pink paper, and he knew. His heart quickened.

"From my sister," Reece added.

"Whoa!" came a chorus of voices.

"Someone's got a love letter!" O'Connor said.

"Read it to us!" Elden yelled.

The others chimed in with laughter.

But Thor, wanting privacy, hurried off to the side of the barracks, away from the others. His head was splitting, and the room still spun—but he didn't care anymore. He unrolled the delicate parchment and read the note with trembling hands.

"Meet me at Forest Ridge at midday. Don't be late. And don't call attention to yourself."

Thor stuffed the note into his pocket.

"What does it say, lover boy?" Calven called out.

Thor hurried over to Reece, knowing he could trust him.

"The Legion has no exercises today, right?" Thor asked.

Reece shook his head. "Of course not. It's a holiday."

170

"Where is Forest Ridge?" Thor asked.

Reece smiled. "Ah, Gwen's favorite place," he said. "Take the eastern road out of the court and stay right. Climb the hill, and it begins after the second knoll."

Thor looked at Reece.

"Please, I don't want anyone to know."

Reece smiled.

"I'm sure she does not either. If my mother found out, she would kill you both. She would lock my sister in her room, and exile you to the southern end of the kingdom."

Thor gulped at the thought of it.

"Really?" he asked

Reece nodded back.

"She doesn't like you. I don't know why, but her mind is set. Go quickly, and don't tell a soul. And don't worry," he said, clasping his hand. "I won't either."

*

Thor walked quickly in the early morning, Krohn trotting along beside him, trying his best not to be seen. He followed Reece's directions as best he could, repeating them in his head, as he hurried past the outskirts of the royal court, up a small hill, and along the edge of a thick forest. To his left, the ground fell off below him, leaving him walking on a narrow trail on the edge of a steep ridge, a cliff to his left, and the forest to his right. Forest Ridge. She had told him to meet her there. Was she serious? Or was she just playing with him?

Was that prissy royal, Alton, right? Was he just entertainment for her? Would she tire of him soon? He hoped, more than anything, that that was not the case. He wanted to believe her feelings for him were genuine; yet he still had a hard time conceiving how that could be the case. She barely knew him. And she was royalty. What interest could she possibly have in him? Not to mention that she was a year or two older, and he had never had an older girl take an interest in him; in fact, he had never had *any* girl take an interest in him. Not that there were many girls to choose from in his small village.

Thor had never thought about girls that much. He hadn't been raised with any sisters, and there weren't many girls to choose from in his village. At his age, none of the other boys seemed too concerned. Most of the boys seemed to wed around their eighteenth year, in arranged marriages—really, more like business arrangements. Those of high rank, who weren't married off by their twenty fifth year, reached their Selection Day: they were obligated to either choose a bride, or go out and find one. But that did not apply to Thor. He was of poor means, and people of his rank usually were just married off in ways that benefited the families. It was like trading cattle.

But when Thor had seen Gwendolyn for the first time, all that had changed. For the first time, he had been struck by something, a feeling so deep and strong and urgent, that it allowed him to think of nothing else. Every time he saw her, that feeling deepened. He hardly understood it, but it pained him to be away from her.

Thor doubled his pace along the ridge, looking for her everywhere, wondering exactly where she would meet him—or if she would meet him at all. The sun grew higher and the first bead of sweat formed on his forehead, he still feeling ill from the effects of the night before, queasy. As the sun grew even higher, and his search for her was proving futile, he began to wonder if she was really going to meet him at all. He also began to wonder just how much danger he was putting them in: if her mother, the Queen, really was so against this, would she truly have him deported from the kingdom? From the Legion? From everything he's come to know and love? Then what would he do?

As he thought about it, he realized that it was still all worth it, for the chance to be with her. He was willing to risk it all for that chance. He only hoped he wasn't being made a fool of, or rushing to any premature conclusions about how strong her feelings were for him.

"Were you just going to walk right by me?" came a voice, followed by a giggle.

Thor jumped, caught off guard, and stopped and turned. He could hardly believe it: there, standing in the shade of a huge pine tree, smiling back, was Gwendolyn. His heart lifted at that smile. He could see the love in her eyes, and all his worries and fears instantly melted away. He chided himself for how he could have been so stupid to ever second-guess her.

Khron squeaked at the sight of her.

"And what do have we here!?" she cried out in delight.

She knelt down and Khron came running to her, leaping into her arms with a whimper; she picked him up and held him, caressing him.

"He's so cute!" she said, hugging him. She leaned back, and he licked her face. She giggled, and kissed him back.

"And what's your name, little fellow?" she asked.

"Khron," Thor said. Finally, this time, he was not as tongue-tied as before.

"Khron," she echoed, looking into the cub's eyes.

"And is it every day that you travel with a leopard friend?" she asked Thor with a laugh.

"I found him," Thor said, feeling self-conscious beside her, as he always did. "In the wood—on the hunt. Your brother said I should keep him, because I found him. That it was destined."

She looked at him, and her expression became serious.

"Well, he is right. Animals are very sacred things. You don't find them. They find you."

"I hope you don't mind if he joins us," Thor said.

She giggled.

"I would be sad if he didn't," she answered.

She looked both ways, as if to make sure no one was watching, then reached out, grabbed Thor's hand and pulled him into the wood.

"Let's go," she whispered. "Before someone spots us."

Thor was exhilarated at the feel of her touch, as she yanked him onto the forest trail. They headed quickly into the woods, the path twisting and turning amidst the huge pines. She let go of his hand, but he did not forget the feel of it.

He was beginning to feel more confident that she actually liked him, and it was obvious that she did not want to be spotted, either, probably by her mother. Clearly she took this seriously, because she had something to risk by seeing him, too.

Then again, Thor thought, maybe she just didn't want to be spotted by Alton—or by any other boys she might be with. Maybe Alton had been right. Maybe she was ashamed to be seen with Thor.

Thor felt all these mixed emotions swirl within him, and hardly knew what to do.

"Cat has your tongue, does it?" she asked, finally breaking the silence.

Thor felt torn: he didn't want to risk messing things up by telling her what was on his mind—but at the same time he felt like he needed to put all his worries to rest. He needed to know where she really stood. He could contain it no longer.

"When I left you last time, I ran into Alton. He confronted me."

Gwendolyn's expression darkened, her high spirits suddenly ruined—and Thor immediately felt guilty that he had brought it up.

He cherished her good nature, her joy, and he wished he could take it back. He wanted to stop, but it was too late. There was no turning back now.

"And what did he say?" she said, her voice dropping.

"He told me to stay away from you. He told me you didn't really care about me. He told me that I was just amusement for you. That you would tire of me in a day or two. He also said that you and he were set to be wed, and that your marriage was already arranged."

Gwendolyn let out an angry, mocking laugh.

"Did he then?" she snorted. "That boy is the most arrogant, unbearable little pip," she added, angry. "He's been a thorn in my side since the time I could walk. Just because our parents are cousins, he thinks he's part of the royal family. I've never met anyone so entitled who deserved it less. Making things worse, he's got it into his head somehow that the two of us are destined to wed. As if I would just go along with whatever my parents forced me to do. Never. And certainly not with him. I can't stand the sight of him."

Thor felt so relieved at her words, he felt a million pounds lighter; he felt like singing from the rooftops. It was exactly what he had needed to hear. Now he felt sorry he had darkened their mood, all over nothing. But he wasn't completely satisfied yet; he noticed she still hadn't said anything about whether she truly liked him, Thor.

"As far as *you* are concerned," she said, stealing a glance him, then looking away. "I barely know you. I hardly need to be pressed to commit my feelings now. But I would say that I don't think I would be spending time with you if I hated you that much. Of course it is my right to change my mind as I wish, and I can be fickle—but not when it comes to love."

That was all Thor needed to hear. He was impressed by her seriousness, and even more impressed by her choice of word: "love." He felt restored.

"And incidentally, I might also ask the same of you," she said, turning the tables. "In fact, I think I have a lot more to lose than you do. After all, I am royalty, and you are commoner. I am older and you are younger. Don't you think I should be the one who is more guarded? Whispers come to me in the court of your agenda, your social climbing, of your just using me, being hungry for rank. Your wanting favor with the King. Should I believe all this?"

Thor was horrified.

"No, my lady. Never. These things never even entered my mind. I'm with you only because I cannot think of being anywhere else. Only because I want to be. Only because when I'm *not* with you, I think of nothing else."

A small smile played at the corner of her mouth, and he could see her expression starting to lighten.

"You are new here," she said. "You are new to King's Court, to royal life. You need time to see how things really work. Here, nobody means what they say. Everyone has an agenda. Everyone is angling for power—or rank or wealth or riches or titles. No one can ever be taken for face value. Everyone has their own spies, and factions, and agendas. When Alton told you that my marriage has already been arranged, for instance, what he was really doing was trying to find out how close you and I are. He is threatened. And he might be reporting to someone. For him, marriage doesn't mean love. It means a union. Purely for financial gain, for rank. For property. In our royal court, nothing is what it seems."

Suddenly, Khron sprinted past them, down the forest trail, and into a clearing.

Gwen looked at Thor and giggled; she reached out, grabbed his hand, and ran with him.

"Come on!" she yelled, excited.

The two of them ran down the trail, and burst into the huge clearing, laughing. Thor was taken aback by the site: it was the most beautiful place he had ever seen, a forest meadow, filled with wildflowers of every possible color, up to their knees. Birds and butterflies of every color and size danced and flew in the air, and the meadow was alive with the sound of chirping. The sun shone down brilliantly, and it felt like a secret place, hidden here in the midst of this tall dark wood.

"Have you ever played Hangman's Blind?" she asked with a laugh.

Thor shook his head, and before he could respond, she took a handkerchief from her neck, reached up, and wrapped it over Thor's eyes, tying it behind him. He couldn't see, and she giggled loudly in his ear.

"You're it!" she said.

Then he heard her run away in the grass.

He smiled.

"But what do I do?" he called out.

175

"Find me!" she called back.

Her voice was already far away.

Thor, blindfolded, began to run after her, tripping as he went. He listened carefully to the rustle of her dress, trying to follow her direction. It was hard, and he ran with his hands out before him, thinking always that he might run into a tree, even though he knew it was an open meadow. Within moments, he was disoriented, and felt as if he were running in circles.

But he continued to listen, and heard the sound of her giggle, far away, and kept adjusting, running for it. Sometimes it seemed to get closer, then farther. He was beginning to feel dizzy.

He heard Khron running beside him, yelping, and he listened instead to Khron, following his footsteps. As he did, Gwyn's giggle got louder, and Thor realized that Krohn was leading him to her. He was amazed at how smart Khron was, to join in their game.

Soon he could hear her just feet away from him, and he chased her, zigzagging every which way, through the field. He reached out, and she screamed in delight as he caught the corner of her dress. As he grabbed her, he tripped, and the two of them went crashing down, into the soft field. He spun at the last second, so that he would fall first and she on top of him, cushioning her fall.

Thor landed on the ground, and she on top of him, screaming out in surprise. She was still giggling as she reached up and pulled back the kerchief.

Thor's heart was pounding as he saw her face just inches from his. He felt the weight of her body on his, in her thin summer dress, felt every contour of her body. The full weight of her pressed down on him, and she made no move to resist. She was staring into his eyes, their breathing shallow, and she did not look away. He did not either. Thor's heart pounded so fast, he was having a hard time focusing.

Suddenly, she leaned in and planted her lips on his. They were softer than he could possibly imagine, and as they met, for the first time in his life, he felt truly alive.

He closed his eyes, and she closed hers, and they did not move, their lips meeting for he did not know how long. He wanted to freeze this time.

Finally, slowly, she pulled away. She still smiled, as she slowly opened her eyes, and she still lay there, her body on his.

They lay like that for a long time, staring into each other's eyes.

"Where did you come from?" she asked, softly, smiling.

He smiled back. He did not know how to answer.

"I'm just a regular boy," he said.

She shook her head and smiled.

"No you are not. I can sense it. I suspect you are far, far more than that."

She leaned in and kissed him again, and his lips met hers, this time, for a much longer time. He reached up and ran his hand through her hair, and she ran hers through his. He could not stop his mind from racing.

He already wondered how this would end. Could they possibly be together, with all the forces between them? Was it possible for them to really be a couple?

Thor hoped, more than anything in his life, that they could. He wanted to be with her now, even more than he wanted to be in the Legion.

As he was thinking these thoughts, there came a sudden rustling in the grass, and the two of them, startled, turned. Khron leapt through the grass, just feet away, and there came another rustling noise. Khron yelped, then growled—then their came a hissing noise. Finally, it was quiet.

Gwen rolled off Thor as they both sat up and looked. Thor jumped to his feet, protective of Gwen, wondering what it could be. He didn't see anyone for miles. But someone—or something—must be there, just feet away, in the tall grass.

Khron appeared before them, and in his mouth, in his small, razor-sharp teeth, there dangled a huge, limp white snake. It must have been ten feet long, its hide a brilliant, shining white, as thick as a large tree branch.

Thor realized in an instant what had happened: Khron had spared the two of them from an attack by this deadly animal. His heart rushed with gratitude for the cub.

Gwen gasped.

"A Whiteback," she said. "The most lethal animal of the entire kingdom."

Thor stared at it, in awe.

"I thought this snake did not exist. I thought it was just a legend."

"It is very rare," Gwen said. "I've only see one in my lifetime. The day my father's father was killed. It is an omen."

She turned and looked at Thor.

"It means a death is coming. A death of someone very close."

177

Thor felt a chill on his spine. A sudden cold breeze ran through the meadow on this summer day, he knew, with absolute certainty, that she was right.

CHAPTER TWENTY FIVE

Gwendolyn walked alone through the castle, taking the spiral staircase, twisting and turning her way to the top. Her mind raced with thoughts of Thor. Of their walk. Of their kiss. And then, of that snake.

She burned with conflicting emotions. On the one hand, she had been elated to be with him; on the other, she was terror-stricken by that snake, and she knew it meant a death was coming. But she did not know for whom, and she could not get that out of her mind either. She feared it was for someone in her family. Could it be one of her brothers? Godfrey? Kendrick? Could it be her mother? Or, she shuddered to even think, her father?

The site of that snake had cast a somber shadow on their joyous day, and once their mood had been shattered, they had been unable to get it back. They had made their way back together to the court, parting ways right before they came out of the woods, so they would not be seen. The last thing she wanted was for her mother to catch them together. But Gwen would not give up Thor so easily, and she would find a way to combat her mother; she needed time to figure out her strategy.

It had been painful to part with Thor; thinking back on it, she felt badly. She had meant to ask him if he would see her again, had meant to make a plan for another day. But she had been in a daze, so distraught by the site of that snake that she had forgotten. Now she wondered if he thought she didn't care for her.

The second she had arrived at King's Court, her father's servants had summoned her. She had been ascending the steps ever since, her heart beating, wondering why he wanted to see her. Had she had been spotted with Thor? There could be no other reason her father wanted to see her so urgently. Was he, too, going to forbid her to see him? She could hardly imagine that he would. He had always taken her side.

Gwen, nearly out of breath, finally reached the top. She hurried down the corridor, passed the attendants who snapped at attention and opened the door for her to her father's chamber. Two more servants, waiting inside, bowed at her presence.

"Leave us," her father said to them.

They bowed and hurried from the room, closing the door behind them with a reverberating echo.

Her father rose from his desk, a big smile on his face, and ventured towards her across the vast chamber. She felt at ease, as she always did, at the sight of him, and felt relieved to see no anger in his expression.

"My Gwendolyn," he said.

He held out his arms and embraced her in a big hug. She embraced him back, and he directed her to two huge chairs, placed on an angle beside the roaring fire. Several large dogs, wolfhounds, most of whom she had known since childhood, got out of their way as they walked towards the fire. Two of them followed her, and rested their heads in her lap. She was glad the fire was on: it had become unusually cold for a summer day.

Her father leaned in towards the fire, staring at the flames as the fire crackled before them.

"You know why I have summoned you?" he asked.

She searched his face, but still was not sure.

"I do not, father."

He looked back in surprise.

"Our discussion the other day. With your siblings. About the kingship. That is what I wanted to discuss with you."

Gwen's heart soared with relief. This was not about Thor. It was about politics. Stupid politics, which she could care less about. She sighed in relief.

"You look relieved," he said. "What did you think we were going to discuss?"

Her father was too perceptive; he always had been. He was one of the few people who could read her like a book. She had to be careful around him.

"Nothing, father," she said quickly.

He smiled again.

"So, then tell me. What do you think of my choice?" he asked.

"Choice?" she asked.

"For my heir! To the kingdom!"

"You mean me?" she asked.

"Who else?" he laughed.

180

She blushed.

"Father, I was surprised, to say the least. I am not the firstborn. And I am a woman. I know nothing of politics. And care nothing for them—or for ruling a kingdom. I have no political ambition. I do not know why you chose me."

"It is precisely for those reasons," he said, his expression deadly serious. "It is because you don't aspire to the throne. You don't want the kingship. And you know nothing of politics."

He took a deep breath.

"But you know human nature. You are very perceptive. You got it from me. You have your mother's quick wit, but my skill with people. You know how to judge them; you can see right through them. And that is what a king needs. To know human nature. There is nothing more you need. All else is artifice. Know who your people are. Understand them. Trust your instincts. Be good to them. This is all."

"Surely, there must be more to ruling a kingdom than that," she said.

"Not really," he said. "It all stems from that. Decisions stem from that."

"But father, you are forgetting that, first, I have no desire to rule, and second, you're not going to die. This is all just a silly tradition, on your eldest's wedding day. Why dwell on this? I'd rather not even speak of it, or think of it. I hope the day should never come when I see you pass—so this is all irrelevant."

He cleared his throat, looking grave.

"I have spoken to Argon, and he sees a dark future for me. I have felt it myself. I must prepare," he said.

Gwen felt her stomach tighten.

"Argon is a fool. A sorcerer. Half of what he says doesn't come to pass. Ignore him. Don't give in to his silly omens. You are fine. You will live forever."

But he slowly shook his head, and she could see the sadness in his face, and she felt her stomach tighten even more.

"Gwendolyn, my daughter, I love you. I need you to be prepared. I want you to be the next ruler of the Ring. I am serious in what I say. It is not a request. It is a command."

He looked at her with such seriousness, his eyes darkening, it scared her. She had never seen that look on her father's face before.

She felt herself tearing up, and reached up and brushed back a tear.

"I am sorry to have upset you," he said.

"Then stop talking of this," she said, crying. "I don't want you to die."

"I am sorry, but I cannot. I need you to answer me."

"Father, I do not want to insult you."

"Then say yes."

"But how can I possibly rule?" she pleaded.

"It is not as hard as you think. You will be surrounded by advisors. The first rule is to trust none of them. Trust yourself. You can do this. Your lack of knowledge, your naïveté—that is what will make you great. You will make genuine decisions. Promise me," he insisted.

She looked into his eyes, and saw how much this meant to him. She wanted to get off this topic, if for no other reason than to appease his morbidity and cheer him up.

"Okay, I promise you," she said in a rush. "Does that make you feel better?"

He leaned back, and she could see him greatly relieved.

"Yes," he said. "Thank you."

"Good, now can we talk of other things? Things that might actually happen?" she asked.

Her father leaned back and roared with laughter; he seemed a million pounds lighter.

"That is why I love you," he said. "Always so happy. Always able to make me laugh."

He examined her, and she could sense he was searching for something.

"You seem unusually happy yourself," he said. "Is there a boy in the picture?"

Gwen blushed. She stood up and walked to the window, turning from him.

"I'm sorry father, but that is a private affair."

"It is not private if you will be ruling my kingdom," he said. "But I won't pry. However, your mother has requested an audience with you, and I assume she will not be so lenient. I will let it go. But prepare yourself."

Her stomach tightened, and she turned away, looking out the window. She hated this place. She wished she were anywhere but here.

In a simple village, on a simple farm, living a simple life with Thor. Away from all of this, from all of these forces trying to control her.

She felt a gentle hand on her shoulder, and turned to see her father standing there, smiling down.

"Your mother can be fierce. But whatever she decides, know that I will take your side. In matters of love, one must be allowed to choose freely."

Gwen reached up and hugged her dad. At that moment, she loved him more than anything. She tried to push the omen of that snake from her mind, and prayed, with all she had, that it was not meant for her father.

*

Gwen twisted and turned down corridor after corridor, past rows of stained-glass, heading towards her mother's chamber. She hated being summoned by her mother, hated her controlling ways. In many ways, her mother was really the one who ruled the kingdom. She was stronger than her father in many ways, stood her ground more, gave in less easily. Of course the kingdom had no idea: he put on a strong face, seemed to be the wise one. But when he returned to the castle, behind closed doors, it was she who he turned to for advice. She was the wiser one. The colder one. The more calculating one. The tougher one. The fearless one. She was the rock. And she ruled their large family with an iron fist. When she wanted something, especially if she got it into her head that it was for the good of the family, she made sure it happened.

And now, Gwen sensed, her mother's iron will was about to be turned towards her; she was already bracing herself for the confrontation. She sensed it had something to do with her romantic life, and feared she had been spotted with Thor. But she was resolved not to back down. No matter what it took. If she had to leave this place, she would. Her mother could put her in the dungeon for all she wanted.

As Gwen approached her mother's chamber, the large oak door was opened by her servants, who stepped out of the way as she entered and closed it behind her.

Her mother's chamber was much smaller than her father's, more intimate, with large rugs, a small tea set and gaming board set up beside a roaring fire, several delicate, yellow velvet chairs beside them.

Her mother sat in one of the chairs, her back to Gwen, even though she was expecting her. She faced the fire, sipped her tea, and moved one of the pieces on the game board. Behind her were two ladies in waiting, one tending her hair, and the other tightening her strings on the back of her dress.

"Come in, child," came her mother's stern voice.

Gwen hated when her mother did this—held court in front of her servants. She wished she would dismiss them, like her father did when they spoke. It was the least she could do for privacy and decency. But her mother never did. Gwen concluded it was a power-play, keeping her servants hovering around, listening, in order to keep Gwen on edge.

Gwen had no choice but to cross the room and take a seat in one of the velvet chairs opposite her mother, too close to the fire. Another one of her mother's power plays: it kept her company too warm, caught off guard by the flames.

Her mother did not look up; rather she stared down at her board game, pushing one of the ivory pieces in the complex maze.

"Your turn," her mother said.

Gwen looked down at the board; she was surprised her mother still had this game going. She recalled she had the brown pieces, but she hadn't played this game with her mother in weeks. Her mother was an expert at Pawns—but Gwen was even better. Her mother hated to lose, and she clearly had been analyzing this board for quite a while, hoping to make the perfect move. Now that Gwen was here, she moved.

But, unlike her mother, Gwen didn't need to study the board. She merely glanced at it and saw the perfect move in her head. She reached up and moved one of the brown pieces sideways, all the way across the board. It put her mother one move away from losing.

Her mother stared down, expressionless except for a flicker of her eyebrow, which Gwen knew indicated dismay. Gwen was smarter, and her mother would never accept that.

Her mother cleared her throat, studying the board, still not looking at her.

"I know all about your escapades with that common boy," she said derisively. "You defy me." Her mother looked up at her. "Why?"

Gwen took a deep breath, feeling her stomach tighten, trying to frame the best response. She would not give in. Not this time.

"My private affairs are not your business," Gwen responded.

"Aren't they? They are very much by business. Your private affairs will affect kingships. The fate of this family. Of the Ring. Your private affairs are political—as much as you would like to forget. You are not a commoner. *Nothing* is private in your world. And nothing is private from me."

Her mother's voice was steely and cold, and Gwen resented every moment of it. There was nothing Gwen could do but sit there and wait for her to finish. She felt trapped.

Finally, her mother cleared her throat.

"Since you refuse to listen to me, I will have to make decisions for you. You will not see that boy ever again. If you do, I will have him transferred out of the Legion, out of King's Court, and back to his village. Then I will have him put in stocks—along with his whole family. He will be cast out in disgrace. And you will never know him again."

Her mother looked at her, her lower lip trembling in rage.

"Do you understand me?"

Gwen breathed in sharply, for the first time comprehending the evil her mother was capable of. She hated her more than she could say. Gwen also caught the nervous glances of the attendants. It was humiliating.

Before she could respond, her mother continued.

"Furthermore, in order to prevent more of your reckless behavior, I have taken steps to arrange a rational union for you. You will be wed to Alton, on the first day of next month. You may begin your wedding preparations now. Prepare for life as a married woman. That is all," her mother said dismissively, turning back to the board as if she had just mentioned the most common of matters.

Gwen seethed and burn inside, and wanted to scream.

"How dare you," Gwen said back, a rage building inside. "Do you think I am some puppet on a string, to be played by you? Do you really think I will marry whomever you tell me to?"

"I don't think," her mother replied. "I *know*. You are my daughter, and you answer to me. And you will marry exactly who I say you will."

"No I won't!" Gwen screamed back. "And you can't make me! Father said you can't make me!"

"Arranged unions are still the right of every parent in this kingdom—and they are certainly the right of the king and queen. Your father postures, but you know as well as I do that he will always concede to my will. I have my ways."

Her mother glared at her.

"So, you see, you will do as I say. Your marriage is happening. Nothing can stop it. Prepare yourself."

"I won't do it," Gwen responded. "Never. And if you talk to me anymore of this, I will never speak to you again."

Her mother looked up and smiled at her, a cold, ugly smile.

"I don't care if you never speak to me. I'm your mother, not your friend. And I am your Queen. This may very well be our last encounter together. It does not matter. At the end of the day you will do as I say. And I will watch you from afar, as you live out the life I plan for you."

Her mother turned back to her game.

"You are dismissed," she said with a wave of her hand, as if Gwen were another servant.

Gwen so boiled over with rage, she could not take it anymore. She took three steps, marched to her mother's game board, and threw it over with both hands, sending the ivory pieces and the big ivory table crashing down and shattering in pieces.

Her mother jumped back in shock as it did.

"I hate you," Gwen hissed.

With that, Gwen turned, red-faced, and stormed from the room, brushing off the attendants' hands, determined to walk out on her own volition—and to never see her mother's face again.

Thor was beginning to have second thoughts, but forced himself to stay on the path. As he approached the door, he felt the energy in the air, so thick he could hardly breathe. His heart beat faster with trepidation as he reached out to knock with his fist.

Before he could touch it, the door opened by itself, a crack. It looked black in there, and Thor could not tell if only the wind had pushed it open. It was so dark, he could not see how anyone could be inside.

Thor reached out, gently pushed open the door, and stuck his head in:

"Hello?" he called out.

He pushed it wider. It was black in here, save for a soft glow on the far side of the dwelling.

"Hello?" he called out, louder. "Argon?"

Beside him, Krohn whined. It seemed obvious to Thor that this was a bad idea, that Argon was not at home. But still he forced himself to look. He took two steps in, and as he did, the door slammed close behind him.

Thor spun, and there, standing on the far wall, was Argon.

"I'm sorry to have disturbed you," Thor said, his heart pounding.

"You come uninvited," Argon said.

"Forgive me," Thor said. "I did not mean to intrude."

Thor looked around, as his eyes adjusted to the darkness, and saw several small candles, laid out in a circle, around the periphery of the stone wall. The room was lit mostly by a single shaft of light, which came in through a small, circular opening in the ceiling. This place was overwhelming, stark and surreal.

"Few people have been here," Argon replied. "Of course, you would not be here now unless I allowed you to be. That door only opens for whom it is intended. For whom it is not, it would never open—not with all the strength of the world."

Thor felt better, and yet he also wondered how Argon had known he was coming. Everything about this man was mysterious to him.

"I had an encounter I did not understand," Thor said, needing to let it all out, and to hear Argon's opinion. "There was a snake. A Whiteback. It nearly attacked us. We were saved by my leopard, Krohn."

"We?" Argon asked.

Thor flushed, realizing he had said too much. He didn't know what to say.

189

"I was not alone," he said.

"And who were you with?"

Thor bit his tongue, not knowing how much to say. After all, this man was close to her father, the king, and perhaps he would tell.

"I don't see how that is relevant to the snake."

"It is entirely relevant. Have you not wondered if that is why the snake came to begin with?"

Thor was completely off guard.

"I don't understand," he said.

"Not every omen you see is meant for you. Some are meant for others."

Thor examined Argon in the dim light, starting to understand. Was Gwen fated for something evil? And if so, could he stop it?

"Can you change fate?" Thor asked.

Argon turned, slowly crossing his room.

"Of course, that is the question we have been asking for centuries," Argon replied. "Can fate be changed? On the one hand, everything is destined, everything is written. On the other hand, we have free will. Our choices also determine our fate. It seems impossible for these two—destiny and free will—to live together, side by side, yet they do. It is where these two intercede—where destiny meets free will—that human behavior comes into play. Destiny can't always be broken, but sometimes it can be bent, or even changed, by a great sacrifice and a great force of free will. Yet most of the time, destiny is firm. Most of the time, we are just bystanders, put her to watch it play out. We think we play a part in it, but usually we don't. We are mostly observers, not participants."

"So then why does the universe bother showing us omens, if there's nothing we can do about them?" Thor asked.

Argon turned and smiled.

"You are quick boy, I will give you that. Mostly, we are shown omens to prepare ourselves. We are shown our fate to give us time to prepare. Sometimes, rarely, we are given an omen to enable us to take action, to change what will be. But this is very rare."

"Is it true that the Whiteback foretells death?"

Argon examined him.

"It is," he said, finally. "Without fail."

Thor's heart pounded at the response, at the confirmation of his fears. He was also surprised by Argon's straightforward response.

"I encountered one, today," Thor said, "but I don't know who will die. Or if there is some action I can take to prevent it. I want to put it out of my mind, but I cannot. Always, that image of the snake's head is with me. Why?"

Argon examined him a very long time, and sighed.

"Because whomever will die, it will affect you directly. It will affect your destiny."

Thor was increasingly agitated; he felt that every answer bred more questions.

"But that's not fair," Thor said. "I need to know who it is that will die. I need to warn them!"

Slowly, Argon shook his head.

"It may not be for you to know," he answered. "And if you do know, there may still be nothing you can do about it. Death finds its subject—even if someone is warned."

"Then why was I shown this?" Thor asked, tormented. "And why can't I get it from my head?"

Argon stepped forward, so close, inches away; the intensity of his eyes burned bright in this dim place, and it frightened Thor. It was like looking into the sun, and it was all he could do not to look away. Argon raised a hand and placed it on Thor's shoulder. It was ice to the touch and sent a chill through him.

"You are young," Argon said, slowly. "You are still learning. You feel things too deeply. Seeing the future is a great reward. But it can also be a great curse. Most humans who live out their destiny have no awareness of it. Sometimes the most painful thing is to have an awareness of your destiny, of what will be. You have not even begun to understand your powers. But you will. One day. Once you understand where you are from."

"Where I'm from?" Thor asked, confused.

"Your mother's home. Far from here. Beyond the Canyon, on the outer reaches of the Wilds. There is a castle, high up in the sky. It sits alone on a cliff, and to reach it, you walk along a windy stone road. It is a magical road—like ascending into the sky itself. It is a place of profound power. That is where you hail from. Until you reach that place, you will never fully understand. Once you do, all your questions will be answered."

Thor blinked, and when he opened his eyes, he found himself, to his amazement, standing outside Argon's dwelling. He had no idea how he got here.

The wind whipped through the rocky crag, and Thor squinted at the harsh sunlight. Beside him stood Krohn, whining.

Thor went back to Argon's door and pounded on it with all his might. There came nothing but silence in return.

"Argon!" Thor screamed.

He was answered only by the whistling of the wind.

He tried the door, even putting his shoulder to it—but it would not budge.

Thor waited a long time, he was not sure how long, until finally the day grew late. Finally, he realized that his time here was over.

He turned and began to walk back down the rocky slope, wondering. He felt more confused than ever, and also felt more certain that a death was coming—yet more helpless to stop it.

As he hiked in that desolate place, he began to feel something cold on his ankles and he looked down and saw a thick fog forming. It rose, growing thicker and rising higher by the moment. Thor did not understand what was happening. Krohn whined.

Thor tried to speed up, to continue his way back down the mountain, but in moments the fog grew so thick, he could barely see before his eyes. At the same time, he felt his limbs grow heavy, and, as if by magic, the sky grew dark. He felt himself growing exhausted. He could not take another step. He curled up in a ball on the ground, right where he stood, enveloped in the thick fog. He tried to open his eyes, to move, but he could not. In moments, he was fast asleep.

*

Thor saw himself standing at the top of a mountain, staring out over the entire kingdom of the Ring. Before him was King's Court, the castle, the fortifications, the gardens, the trees and rolling hills as far as he could see—all in full bloom of summer. The fields were filled with fruits and colored flowers, and there was the sound of music and festivities.

But as Thor turned slowly, surveying everything, the grass began to turn black. Fruits fell off the trees. Then the trees themselves shriveled up to nothing. All the flowers dried up to crisps, and, to his horror, one building after the next crumbled, until the entire kingdom was nothing but desolation, heaps of rubble and stone.

Thor looked down and suddenly saw a huge Whiteback, slithering between his legs. He stood there, helpless, as it coiled around his legs, then his waist, then arms. He felt himself being suffocated, the life squeezed out of him, as the snake coiled all the way around and stared at him in the face, inches away, hissing, its long tongue nearly touching Thor's cheek. And then it opened its mouth so wide, revealing huge fangs, leaned forward, and swallowed Thor's face.

Thor shrieked, and then found himself standing alone inside the king's castle. The castle was completely empty, no throne left where one used to be, and the Destiny Sword lying on the ground, untouched. The windows were all shattered, stained-glass lying in heaps on the stone. He heard distant music and turned and walked through empty room after empty room. Finally he reached huge double doors, a hundred feet tall, and he opened them with all his might.

Thor stood at the entrance to the royal feasting hall. Before him were two long feasting tables, stretching across the room, overflowing with food—yet empty of men. At the far end of the hall sat one man. King MacGil. He sat on his throne, staring right at Thor. He seemed so far away.

Thor felt he had to reach him. He began to walk through the great room, towards him, between the two feasting tables. As he went, all the food on either side of him went bad, becoming rotten with each step he took, turning black and covered with flies. Flies buzzed and swarmed all around him, tearing apart the food.

Thor walked faster. The king was getting close now, hardly ten feet away, when a servant appeared out of a side chamber carrying a huge, golden goblet of wine. It was a distinct goblet, made of solid gold and covered in rows of rubies and sapphires. While the king wasn't looking, Thor saw the servant slip a white powder into the goblet. Thor realized it was poison.

The servant brought it closer, and MacGil reached down and grabbed it with both hands.

"No!" Thor screamed.

Thor lunged forward, trying to knock the wine away from the king.

But he was not fast enough. MacGil leaned back and drank the wine in big gulps. It poured down his cheeks, down his chest, as he finished it.

MacGil then turned and looked at Thor, and as he did, his eyes opened wide. He reached up and grabbed his throat until, gagging, he keeled over and fell off his throne; he fell sideways, landing on the hard stone floor. His crown rolled off it, hit the stone floor with a clang, and rolled several feet.

He lay there, motionless, eyes open, dead.

Ephistopheles swooped down, landed on MacGil's head. It sat there, looked right at Thor and screeched. The sound was so shrill, it sent a shiver up Thor's spine.

"No!" Thor screamed.

*

Thor woke screaming.

He sat up, looking all around, sweating, breathing hard, trying to figure out where he was. He was still lying on the ground, on Argon's mountain. He could not believe it: he must have fallen asleep here. The fog was gone, and as he looked up and saw that it was daybreak. A blood red sun was breaking over the horizon, lighting up the day. Beside him, Khron whined, jumped into his lap and licked his face.

Thor hugged Khron with one hand as he breathed hard, trying to figure out if he was awake or asleep. It took him a long time to realize it had just been a dream. It had felt so real.

Thor heard a screech and turned to see Ephistopheles, perched on a rock, just a foot away. He looked right at him and screeched, again and again.

The sound sent a chill up Thor's spine. It was the sound from his dream, and at that moment he knew, with every ounce of his body, that his dream had been a message. The king was going to be poisoned.

Thor jumped to his feet and, in the breaking light of dawn, sprinted down the mountain, heading for King's Court. He had to get to the king. He had to warn him. The king might think he was crazy, but he had no choice: he would do whatever he could to save the king's life.

*

Thor raced across the drawbridge, sprinting for the castle's outer gate, and luckily, the two guards recognized him from the Legion. They let him through without stopping him, and he continued running, Khron by his side.

Thor sprinted across the royal courtyard, past the fountains, and ran right to the inner gate of the king's castle. There stood four guards, who blocked his way.

Thor stopped, gasping for air.

"What is your purpose, boy?" one of them asked.

"You don't understand, you have to let me in," Thor gasped. "I need to see the King."

The guards looked at each other, skeptical.

"I am Thorgrin, of the King's Legion. You must let me through."

"I know who he is," one guard said to the other. "He's one of us."

But the lead guard stepped forward.

"What business have you with the king?" he pressed.

Thor still fought to catch his breath.

"Very urgent business. I must see him at once."

"Well he must not be expecting you, because you are ill-informed. Our King is not here. He left with his caravan hours ago, on court business. They won't be returning until tonight, until the royal feast."

"Feast?" Thor asked, his heart thumping. He remembered his dream, the feasting tables, and eerily felt it all coming to life.

"Yes, feast. If you are of the Legion, I am sure you will be there. But now he is gone, and there is no way you can see him. Come back tonight, with the others."

"But I must get him a message!" Thor insisted. "Before the feast!"

"You can leave the message with me if you like. But I can't deliver it any sooner than you."

Thor did not want to leave such a message with a guard; he realized it would seem crazy. He had to deliver it himself, tonight, before the feast. He only prayed it would not be too late.

CHAPTER TWENTY SEVEN

Thor hurried back to the Legion's barracks at the crack of dawn, luckily arriving before the day's training began. He was winded when he arrived, Khron at his side, and he ran into the other boys just as they were waking, beginning to file out for the day's assignments. He stood there, gasping, more troubled than ever. He hardly knew how he would make it through the day's training; he would be counting down the minutes until the night's feast, until he could warn the king. He felt certain that the omen came to him so that he could warn him, that the fate of the kingdom rested on his shoulders.

Thor ran up beside Reece and O'Connor as they made their way out to the field, looking exhausted, and began to line up.

"Where were you last night?" Reece asked.

Thor wished he knew how to respond—but he didn't really know where he had been himself. What was he supposed to say? That he had fallen asleep outside on the ground, on Argon's mountain? It made no sense, not even to him.

"I don't know," he answered, not knowing how much to tell them.

"What do you mean you don't know?" O'Connor asked.

"I got lost," Thor said.

"Lost?"

"Well you're lucky you made it back when you did," Reece said.

"If you had come back late for the day's assignments, they wouldn't have let you back into the Legion," Elden added, coming up beside them, clapping a beefy hand on his shoulder. "Good to see you. You were missed yesterday."

Thor was still shocked at the difference in how Elden treated him since their time on the far side of the Canyon.

"How did things go with my sister?" Reece asked, in hushed tones.

Thor blushed, unsure how to respond.

"Did you see her?" Reece prodded.

"Yes, I did," he began. "We had a great time. Although we had to leave abruptly."

"Well," Reece continued, as they all lined up side-by-side before Kolk and the King's men, "you will get to see more of her tonight. Put on your finest. It's the King's feast."

Thor's stomach dropped. He thought of his dream and felt as if destiny were dancing before his eyes—and that he was helpless, fated to do nothing but just watch it unfold.

"QUIET!" screamed Kolk, as he began to pace before the boys.

Thor stiffened, with the others, as they all fell silent.

Kolk walked slowly up and down the lines, surveying them all.

"You had your fun yesterday. Now it's back to training. And today, you will learn the ancient art of ditch digging."

A collective groan rose up among the boys.

"SILENCE!" he yelled.

The boys fell quiet.

"Ditch digging is hard work," Kolk continued. "But it is important work. You will one day find yourself out there, protecting our kingdom, in the wilderness, with no one to help you. It will be freezing, so cold you can't feel your toes, the black of night, and you will do anything to keep warm. Or you may find yourself in a battle, in which you need to take cover, to save yourself from the enemies' arrows. There may be a million reasons why you need a ditch. And a ditch may be your best friend.

"Today," he continued, clearing his throat, "you will spend all day digging, until your hands are red with calluses and your back is breaking, and you can't take it anymore. Then, on the day of battle, it will not seem as bad.

"FOLLOW ME!" Kolk yelled.

There came another groan of disappointment as the boys broke down into a line of two, and began marching across the field, following Kolk.

"Great," Elden said. "Ditch digging. Exactly how I wanted to spend the day."

"Could be worse," O'Connor said. "It could be raining."

They looked up at the sky, and Thor spotted threatening clouds overhead.

"It just might," Reece said. "Don't jinx it."

"THOR!" came a shout.

Thor turned to see Kolk glaring at him, off to the side. He ran over to him, wondering what he had done wrong.

"Yes, sire."

"Your knight has summoned you," he said, curt. "Report to Erec at the castle grounds. You're lucky: you're off-duty for today. You will serve your knight instead, as all good squires should. But don't think you're getting out of ditch digging: when you return tomorrow, you will be digging ditches by yourself. Now go!" he yelled.

Thor turned and saw the envious looks of the others, then ran from the field, heading for the castle. What could Erec want from him? Had it something to do with the King?

*

Thor ran through King's Court, turning down a path he had never gone down before: towards the barracks of the Silver. Their barracks were much more grand than those of the Legion's, their buildings twice the size, lined with copper, and their pathways paved with new stone. To get there, Thor had to pass through an arched gate twice the size of any other, a dozen of the King's men standing guard. The path then broadened, stretching out across a huge, open field, and culminating in a complex of stone buildings, encircled by a fence, and guarded by dozens more knights. It was an imposing site, even from here.

Thor raced down the path, conspicuous in the open field, and knights already prepared for his approach, even though he was so far away, stepping forward and crossing their lances, looking straight ahead, ignoring him, as they blocked his path.

"What business have you here?" one of them asked.

"I am reporting for duty," Thor responded. "I am Erec's squire."

The knights exchanged a wary look, but another knight stepped forward and nodded. They stepped back, uncrossed their weapons, and the gate slowly opened, its metal spikes rising, creaking. The gate was immense, at least two feet thick, and Thor thought that this place was even more fortified than even the King's Castle.

"The second building on the right." the knight yelled. "You'll find him in the stables."

Thor turned and hurried down the path through the courtyard, passing a compound of stone buildings, taking it all in. Everything was gleaming here, spotless, perfectly maintained. The whole place exuded an aura of strength.

Thor found the building, and was dazzled by the sight before him: dozens of the biggest and most beautiful horses he'd ever seen were tied up in neat rows outside the building, most of them covered in armor. The horses gleamed. Everything here was bigger, grander. He was inside the Silver's home; he could hardly believe it.

Real knights trotted by in every direction, carrying various weapons, passing through the courtyard on their way in or out of various gates. It was a busy place, and Thor could feel the presence of battle here. This place was not about training: it was about war. Life and death.

Thor passed through a small, arched entranceway, down a darkened corridor of stone, and continued hurrying through, passing by stable after stable, searching for Erec. But he reached the end of it, and he was nowhere to be found.

"Looking for Erec, are you?" a guard asked.

Thor turned and nodded.

"Yes, sire. I am his squire."

"You are late. He is already outside, preparing his horse. Move quickly, then."

Thor ran down the corridor and burst out of the stables into an open field. There was Erec, standing before a giant, valiant stallion, a gleaming black horse with a white nose. The horse snorted as Thor arrived, and Erec turned.

"I am sorry, sire," Thor said, out of breath. "I came as fast as I could. I did not mean to be late."

"You are just in time," Erec said with a gracious smile. "Thor, meet Lannin," he added, gesturing to the horse.

Lannin snorted and pranced, as if in response. Thor stepped up and reached out a hand and stroked his nose; he whinnied softly in return.

"He is my journey horse. A knight of rank has many horses, as you will learn. There is one for jousting, one for battle, and one for the long, solitary journey. This is the one you forge the closest friendship with. He likes you. That is good."

Lannin leaned forward and stuck his nose in Thor's palm. Thor was overwhelmed by the magnificence of this creature. He could see intelligence shining in his eyes. It was eerie: he felt as if he understood everything.

But something Erec said threw Thor off.

"Did you say a journey, sire?" he asked surprised.

Erec stopped tightening the harness, turned and looked at him.

"Today is the day of my birth. I have reached my twenty fifth year. That is a special day. Do you know about Selection Day?"

Thor shook his head. "Very little, sire; only what others tell me."

"We knights of the Ring must always continue on, generation after generation," Erec began. "We have until our twenty fifth year to choose a bride. If one is not chosen by then, law dictates for us to find one. We are given one year to find her, and to bring her back. If we return without one, then one is given to us by the king, and we forfeit our right to choose.

"So today, I must embark on my journey to find my bride."

Thor stared back, speechless.

"But sire, you are leaving? For one year?"

Thor's stomach dropped at the thought of it. He felt his world crumbling around him. It wasn't until this moment that he realized what a liking he had taken to Erec; in some ways, he had become like a father to him—certainly more of a father than the one he'd had.

"But then who shall I be squire to?" Thor asked. "And where will you go?"

Thor recalled how much Erec had stuck up for him, how he had saved his life. His heart sank at the idea of his leaving.

Erec laughed, a carefree laugh.

"Which question shall I answer first?" he said. "Do not worry. You have been assigned a new knight. You will be squire to him until my return. Kendrick, the king's eldest son."

Thor's heart soared to hear that; he felt an equally strong attachment to Kendrick who, after all, was the first one to look out for him and assure him a spot in the Legion.

"As far as my journey…." Erec continued, "…I do not yet know. I know I will head south, towards the kingdom that I hail from, and search for a bride in that direction. If I do not find one within the Ring, then I may even cross the sea to my own kingdom to search for one there."

"Your own kingdom, sire?" Thor asked.

Thor realized that he didn't really know that much about Erec, about where he came from. He had always just assumed he had come from within the Ring.

Erec smiled. "Yes, far from here, across the sea. But that is a tale for another time. It will be a far journey, and a long one, and I must prepare. So help me now. Time is quick. Harness my horse, and stock it with all manner of weapons."

Thor's head was spinning as he sprang into action, running to the stables, to the horse armory, and grabbing the distinct black and silver armor he knew belonged to Lannin. He ran back with one piece at a time, first placing the mailcoat on the horse's back, reaching up to drape it around his huge body. Then Thor ran and grabbed the shaffron, the thin, plated metal for the horse's head.

200

Lannin whinnied as he did so, and he seemed to like it. He was a noble horse, a warrior, Thor could tell, and he seemed just as comfortable in armor as a knight would.

Thor ran back and retrieved Erec's golden spurs, and helped attach one to each foot as Erec mounted the horse.

"Which weapons will you need, sire?" Thor asked.

Erec looked down, seeming huge from this perspective.

"It's hard to anticipate what battles I might encounter throughout a year. But I need to be able to hunt, and to defend myself. So of course, I need my longsword. I also should bring my shortsword, a bow, a quiver of arrows, a short spear, a mace, a dagger, and my shield. I suspect that will do."

"Yes, sire," Thor said, and broke into action. He ran to Erec's weapons rack, beside Lannin's stable, and looked over the dozens of weapons. There was an impressive arsenal to choose from.

He carefully removed all the weapons that Erec needed, and brought them back one at a time, handing them to Erec or placing them securely in the harness.

As Erec sat there, tightening his leather gauntlets, preparing to leave, Thor could not stand to watch him go.

"Sire, I feel it is my duty to accompany you on this journey," Thor said. "I am your squire after all."

Erec shook his head.

"It is a journey I must take alone."

"Then may I at least accompany you to the first crossing?" Thor pressed. "If you are heading south, those are roads that I know well. I am from the south."

Erec looked down, considering.

"If you want to accompany me to the first crossing, I see no harm in that. But it is a hard day's ride, so we must leave now. Take my squire's horse, in the rear of the stable. The brown one, with the red mane."

Thor ran back to the stable and found the horse. As he mounted it, Khron stuck his head out of his shirt and looked up and whined.

"It's okay, Khron," Thor reassured.

Thor leaned forward, kicked the horse, and they burst out of the stable. Erec had barely waited for him to catch up when he kicked Lannin and raced off at a gallop. Thor kicked his horse and followed Erec as best he could.

They rode together out of King's Court, through the gate, as several guardsmen pulled it back and stood to the side. Several members of the Silver were lined up, watching, waiting, and as Erec rode by, they raised their fists in salute.

Thor was proud to ride beside him, to be his squire, and excited to accompany him, even if it was only to the first crossing.

There was so much Thor had left to say to Erec, so many things he wanted to ask him—and so much he wanted to thank him for. But there wasn't time, as the two of them galloped south, bursting across the plains, the terrain constantly changing as their horses charged down the King's road in the late morning sun. As they passed a hill, in the distance Thor could see all the Legion members on a field, breaking their backs as they dug trenches. Thor was glad he was not among them. As Thor looked, in the distance he saw one of them stop, raise a fist in the air, towards him. It was hard to see in the sun, but he felt sure it was Reece, saluting. Thor raised a fist back, as they rode on.

The well-paved roads gave way to untended country roads. The roads became more narrow, rougher, and eventually became hardly more than well-trodden paths, cutting through the countryside. Thor knew it was dangerous for common folk to ride these roads alone— especially at night, with all the thieves that lurked on them. But Thor had little worry of this himself, especially with Erec at his side—in fact, if a robber should confront them, Thor feared more for the robber's life. Of course, it would be crazy for any thief to attempt to stop a member of the Silver.

They rode all day, hardly taking a break, until Thor was exhausted, out of breath. He could hardly believe Erec's stamina—yet he dared not let Erec know he was tired, for fear of seeming weak.

They passed a major crossroads, and Thor recognized it. He knew that if they bore right, it would bring them to his village. For a moment, Thor felt overwhelmed with nostalgia, and a part of him wanted to take the road, to see his father, his village. He wondered what his father was doing right now, who was tending the sheep, how irate his father must have been at his not returning. Not that he cared for him much. He just, momentarily, missed what was familiar. He was, in fact, relieved he had escaped from that small village, and another part of him wanted to never return.

They continued galloping on, farther and farther south, to territory even Thor had never been to. He had heard of the southern crossing, though he had never had reason to be there himself. It was one of three major crossroads that led to the southern reaches of the Ring. He was a good half day's ride now from King's court, and already the sun was getting long in the sky. Thor, sweating, out of breath, was starting to wonder, with trepidation, if he would make it back in time for the king's feast tonight. Had he made a mistake to accompany Erec this far?

They rounded a hilltop, and finally Thor saw it, there on the horizon: the unmistakable sign of the first crossing. It was marked by a large, skinny tower, the King's flag draped from it in all four directions, and members of the Silver standing guard atop its parapets. At the site of Erec, the knight atop the tower blew his trumpet. Slowly, the gatehouse rose.

They were but a few hundred yards away, and Erec slowed his horse to a walk. Thor had a knot in his stomach as he realized these were his last few minutes with Erec until who knew how long. Who knew, indeed, if he would even return. One year is a long time, and anything could happen. He was glad, at least, that he had had this chance to accompany him. He felt as if he had fulfilled his duty.

The two of them walked side-by-side, their horses breathing hard, the men breathing hard, as they approached the tower.

"I may not see you for many moons," Erec said. "When I return, I will have a bride in tow. Things may change. Though no matter what happens, know that you will always be my squire."

Erec took a deep breath.

"As I leave you, there are some things I want you to remember. A knight is not forged by strength—but by intelligence. Courage alone does not make a knight, but courage and honor and wisdom together. You must work always to perfect your spirit, your mind. Chivalry is not passive—it is active. You must work on it, better yourself, every moment of every day.

"Over these moons, you will learn all manner of weapons, all manner of skills. But remember: there is another dimension to our fighting. The sorcerer's dimension. Seek out Argon. Learn to develop your hidden powers. I have sensed them in you. You have great potential. It is nothing to be ashamed of. Do you understand me?"

"Yes, sire," Thor answered, welling with gratitude for his wisdom and understanding.

"I chose to take you under my wing for a reason. You are not like the others. You have a greater destiny. Greater, perhaps, even than mine. But it remains unfulfilled. You must not take it for granted. You must work at it. To be a great warrior, you must not only be fearless and skilled. You must also have a warrior's spirit, and carry that always in your heart and your mind. You must be willing to lay down your

203

life for others. The greatest knight does not quest for riches or honor or fame or glory. The greatest knight takes the hardest quest of all: the quest to make yourself a better person. Every day, you must strive to be better. Not just better than others—but better than yourself. You must quest to take up the cause of those lesser than yourself. You must defend those who cannot defend themselves. It is not a quest for the light-hearted. It is a quest of heroes."

Thor's mind spun as he took it all in, pondering Erec's words carefully. He was overwhelmed with gratitude for him, and hardly knew how to respond. He sensed that it would take many moons for the full message of these words to sink in.

They reached the gate of the first crossing, and as they did, several members of the Silver came out to greet Erec. They rode up to him, big grins on their faces, and as he dismounted they clapped him hard on the back, as old friends.

Thor jumped down, took Lannin's reins and led him to the keeper at the gate, to feed and wash him down. Thor stood there, as Erec turned and looked at him, one last time.

In their final goodbye, there was too much Thor wanted to say. He wanted to thank him. But he also wanted to tell him everything. Of the omen. Of his dream. Of his fears for the king. He thought maybe Erec would understand.

But he could not bring himself to. Erec was already surrounded by knights, and Thor feared that Erec—and all of them—would think him crazy. So he stood there, tongue-tied, as Erec reached up and clasped his shoulder one last time.

"Protect our King," Erec said firmly.

The words sent a chill up Thor's spine, as if Erec had read his mind.

Erec turned, walked through the gate with the other knights, and as they passed through, their backs to him, Thor watched as the metal spikes slowly lowered behind him.

Erec was gone now. Thor could hardly believe it, felt a pit in his stomach. It could be an entire year until he saw him again.

Thor mounted his horse, tightened its reins, and kicked hard. The sun was nearly falling, and he had a good half day's ride to make it back for the feast. He felt Erec's final words reverberating in his head, like a mantra.

Protect our king.

Protect our king.

CHAPTER TWENTY EIGHT

Thor rode hard in the darkness, racing through the final gate of King's Court, barely slowing his horse as he jumped off it, breathing hard, and handed the reins to an attendant. He had been riding all day, the sun had fallen hours before, and he could see immediately from all the torchlight inside, hear from all the reverie behind the gates, that the king's feast was in full swing. He kicked himself for being away for as long as he did, and only prayed that he was not too late.

He ran to the nearest attendant.

"Is all in order inside?" he asked in a rush. He had to know that the king was okay—though of course he couldn't directly ask if he had been poisoned.

The attendant looked at him, baffled.

"And why shouldn't it be? All is in order, except that you are late. Members of the King's Legion should always be on time. And your clothes are filthy. You reflect poorly on your peers. Wash your hands, and hurry inside."

Thor rushed through the gate, sweating, put his hands in a small stone lavender of water, splashed it on his face, and ran it through his longish hair. He had been in constant motion since early in the morning, he was covered in dust from the road, and it felt as if it had been ten days in one. He took a deep breath, tried to calm himself and seem orderly, and strode quickly down corridor after corridor, towards the vast doors of the feasting hall.

As he stepped inside, through the huge arched doors, it was just like his dream: before him were the two feasting tables, at least a hundred feet long, at the far end of which sat the king, at the head of his own table, surrounded by men. The noise struck Thor like a living thing, the hall absolutely packed with people. There were not only the King's men, members of the Silver and of the Legion seated at the feasting tables, but also hundreds of others, bands of traveling musicians, groups of dancers, of clowns, dozens of women from the brothels…. There were also all manners of servants, of guards, dogs running about. It was a madhouse.

Men drank from huge casks of wine and beer, and many of them stood, singing drinking songs, arms about each other, clinking casks. There were heaps of food laid out on the tables, and boar and deer and all sorts of animals roasting on spits before the fireplace. Half the room gorged themselves, while the other half mingled about the room. Looking at the chaos in the room, seeing how drunk the men were, Thor realized that if he'd arrived earlier, when it began, it would have been more orderly. Now, at this late hour, it seemed to have evolved into more of a drunken bash.

Thor's first reaction, aside from being overwhelmed, was deep relief to see that the king was alive. He breathed a sigh of relief. He was okay. He wondered again if that omen meant nothing, if his dream meant nothing, if he was just overreacting to fancies, making something bigger in his head than it should be. But still, he just could not shake the feeling. He still felt a pressing urgency to reach the king, to warn him.

Protect our king.

Thor pushed his way into the thick crowd, trying to make it the long way towards the king. It was slow going. The men were drunk and rowdy, packed shoulder to shoulder, and MacGil sat hundreds of feet away.

Thor managed to get about halfway through the crowd when he stopped, suddenly spotted Gwendolyn. She sat at one of the small tables, off to the side of the hall, surrounded by her handmaids. She looked glum, and it seemed unlike her. Her food and drink were untouched, and she sat off to the side, separated from the others. Thor wondered what could be wrong.

Thor broke from the crowd and hurried over to her.

She looked up and saw him coming, but instead of smiling, as she always did, her face darkened. For the first time, Thor saw anger in her eyes.

Gwen slid her chair, got up, turned her back, and began to march away.

Thor felt as if a knife had been plunged into his heart. He could not understand her reaction. Had he done something wrong?

He raced around the table, hurrying over to her, and grabbed her wrist gently.

She surprised him by throwing it off roughly, turning and scowling at him.

"Don't you touch me!" she screamed.

Thor took a step back, shocked at her reaction. Was this the same Gwendolyn he knew?

"I'm sorry," he said. "I meant you no harm. And no disrespect. I just wanted to talk to you."

"I have no words left for you," she seethed, her eyes aglow with fury.

Thor could hardly breathe; he had no idea what he had done wrong.

"My lady, please tell me, what have I done to offend you? Whatever it is, I apologize."

"What you have done is beyond remedy. No apology will suffice. It is who you are."

She started to walk away again, and a part of Thor thought he should let her be; but another part of him couldn't stand to just walk away, not after what they'd had. He had to know; he had to know the reason why she hated him so much.

Thor ran in front of her, blocking her way. He could not let her go. Not like this.

"Gwendolyn, please. Just please give me one chance to at least know what it is that I have done. Please, just give me this."

She stared back, seething, hands on her hips.

"I think you know. I think you know very well."

"I do not," Thor stated earnestly.

She stared, as if summing him up, and finally, seemed to believe him.

"The night before you saw me, I am told that you visited the brothels. That you had your way with many women. And you delighted in them all night long. Then, as the sun broke, you came to me. Does that remind you? I'm disgusted by your behavior. Disgusted that I ever met you, that you ever touched me. I hope I shall never see your face again. You've made a fool of me—and *no one* makes a fool of me!"

"My lady!" Thor yelled out, trying to stop her, wanting to explain. "It isn't true!"

But a band of musicians got between them, and she darted off, slipping through the crowd so fast that he could not find her. Within moments, he completely lost trace of her.

Thor was burning inside. He could not believe that someone had gotten to her, had told her these lies about him, had turned her against him. He wondered who was behind it. It hardly mattered: his chances with her were now ruined. He felt that he was dying inside.

Thor turned and began to stagger through the room, remembering the King, feeling hollowed out, as if he had nothing left to live for.

Before he'd gone a few feet, Alton suddenly appeared, blocked his way, and sneered down with a satisfied smile. He wore silk leggings, a velvet blazer, and a feathered hat. He looked down at Thor, with his long nose and chin, and with the utmost arrogance and self-pride.

"Well well," he said. "If it's not the commoner. Have you found your bride-to-be here yet? Of course you have not. I think rumors have spread already far and wide of your exploits in the brothel." He smiled and leaned in close, revealing small, yellow teeth. "In fact, I'm sure they have."

"You know what they say: if there's a glimmer of truth, it helps spark a rumor. I found that glimmer. And now your reputation is ruined, boy."

Thor, seeing with rage, could take it no longer. He charged and punched Alton in the gut, making him keel over.

Moments later, bodies were on him, fellow Legion members, soldiers, getting in their way, pulling them apart.

"You have overstepped your bounds, boy!" Alton yelled out, pointing at him over the bodies. "No one touches a royal! You will hang in the stocks for the rest of your life! I will have you arrested! Be sure of it! At first light I will have them come from you!" Alton yelled, and turned and stormed away.

Thor could care less about Alton, or his guards. He thought only of the King. He brushed the Legion members off, and turned back for MacGil. He shoved people out of the way as he hurried for the King's table. His mind was swimming with emotions, and he could hardly believe this turn of events. Here he was, just as his reputation was rising, only to have it ruined by some malignant snake, to have his love cheated away from him. And now, tomorrow, the threat of his being imprisoned. And with the Queen aligned against him, he feared that just maybe he would be.

But Thor didn't care about any of that now. All he cared about was protecting the King.

He pushed harder as he weaved his way through the crowd, bumping into a jester, walking right through his act, and finally, after pushing through three more attendants, making it to the King's table.

MacGil sat there, in the center of the table, a huge sack of wine in one hand, his cheeks red, laughing at the entertainment. He was surrendered by all of his top generals, and Thor stood before them, pushing his way right up to the bench, until finally, the King noticed him.

"My liege," Thor yelled out, hearing the desperation in his own voice. "I must speak with you! Please!"

A guard came to pull Thor away, but the King raised a palm.

"Thorgrin!" MacGil bellowed in his deep, kingly voice, drunk with wine. "My boy. Why have you approached our table? The Legion's table is there."

Thor bowed low.

"My king, I am sorry. But I must speak with you."

A musician clanged a cymbal in Thor's ear, and finally, MacGil gestured for him to stop.

The music quieted, and all the generals turned and looked at Thor. Thor could feel all the attention on him.

"Well, young Thorgrin, now you have the floor. Speak. What is it that cannot wait till tomorrow?" MacGil said.

"My liege," Thor began, but then stopped. What could he say exactly? That he had a dream? That he saw an omen? That he felt the King would be poisoned? Would it sound absurd?

But he had no choice. He had to press on.

"My liege, I had a dream," he began. "It was about you. In this feasting hall, in this place. The dream was…that you should not drink."

The King leaned forward, eyes opened wide.

"That I should not drink?" he repeated, slowly and loudly.

Then, after a moment of stunned silence, MacGil leaned back and roared with laughter, bellowing, shaking the whole table.

"That I should not drink!" MacGil repeated. "What a dream is this! I should call it a nightmare!"

The King leaned back and bellowed with laughter, and all of his men joined in. Thor reddened, but he could not back down.

MacGil gestured, and a guard stepped forward and grabbed Thor and began to take him away—but Thor roughly yanked the guard off of him. He was determined. He had to give the King this message.

Protect our King.

"My King, I demand that you listen!" Thor screamed, red-faced, pressing forward and banging the table with his fist.

It shook the table, and all the men's turned and stared at Thor.

There was a stunned silence, as the King's face dropped into a scowl.

"YOU demand?" MacGil yelled. "You demand nothing of me boy!" he screamed, his anger rising.

The table quieted even more, and Thor felt his cheeks redden in humiliation.

"My king, forgive me. I mean no disrespect. But I am concerned for your safety. Please. Do not drink. I dreamt you were poisoned! Please. I care very much about you. That is the only reason for my saying so."

Slowly, MacGil's scowl lifted. He stared deeply into Thor's eyes and took a deep breath.

"Yes, I can see that you do care. Even if you are foolish boy. I forgive you your disrespect. Go on now. And don't let me see your face again until the morning."

He gestured to his guards, and they yanked Thor away, strongly this time. The table slowly resumed its merriment, as they all went back to drinking.

Thor, dragged several feet away, burned with indignation. He feared for what he had done here tonight, and had a sinking feeling that tomorrow he would pay the price. Maybe even be asked to leave this place. Forever.

As the guards gave him one last shove, Thor found himself at the Legion's table, maybe twenty feet away from the King. He felt a hand on his shoulder and spun to see Reece standing there.

"I've been searching for you all day. What happened to you?" Reece asked. "You look as if you have seen a ghost!"

Thor was too overwhelmed to respond. He hardly knew what to do now.

"Come sit with me—I saved you a seat," Reece said.

Reece pulled Thor down beside him, at a table set aside for the King's family. He saw Reece's brother, Godfrey, drinking with both hands, and beside him sat Gareth, watching with shifting eyes. Thor hoped beyond hope that Gwendolyn might be there, too, but she was not.

"What is it, Thor?" Reece prodded, as he sat down beside him. "You stare at this table as if it will bite you."

Thor shook his head.

"If I told you, you would not believe me. So best I just keep my mouth shut."

"Tell me. You can tell me anything," Reece urged with intensity.

Thor saw the look in his eyes, and realized, that finally, someone was taking him seriously. He took a deep breath, and began. He had nothing to lose.

"The other day, in the forest, with your sister, we saw a Whiteback. She said it was an omen of death, and I believe it is. I saw Argon, and he confirmed that a death is coming. Shortly after, I had a dream that your father would be poisoned. Here. Tonight. In this hall. I know it in my bones. He will be. Someone is trying to assassinate him," Thor said.

He said it all in a rush, and it felt good to get it off his chest. It felt good to have someone actually listen.

Reece was quiet as he stared back into his eyes for a long time. Finally, he spoke.

"You seem genuine. I have no doubt. And I appreciate your caring for my father. I believe you. I do. But dreams are tricky things. Not always what we think."

"I told the King," Thor said. "And they laughed at me. Of course, he will drink tonight."

"Thor, I believe you dreamt this. And I believe you feel this. But I've had terrible dreams, too, my entire life. The other night, I dreamt I was pushed out the castle, and I woke feeling that I was. But I was not. Do you understand? Dreams are strange things. And Argon speaks in riddles. You must not take it all so seriously. My father is fine. I am fine. We're all fine. Try to just sit back and drink and relax. And enjoy."

With that, Reece leaned back in his chair, covered in furs, and drank. He flagged a waiter, who put a huge portion of venison before Thor, along with a drinking goblet.

But Thor just sat there, staring at his food He felt his whole life dissolving around him. He didn't know what to do.

He could still think of nothing but his dream. It was like being in a waking nightmare, sitting there, watching everyone drink and feast around him. All he could do was watch the servers, all the drinks, all

211

the goblets, heading for the King. He watched closely every server, every goblet of wine. Every time the King drank, Thor flinched.

But Thor was obsessed. He could not look away. He watched and watched, for what felt like hours.

Finally, Thor spotted one particular server. He approached the king with a goblet unlike the others. It was large, made of a very distinct gold, covered in rows of rubies and sapphires.

It was the exact goblet of Thor's dream.

Thor, his heart pounding in his chest, watched as if in slow motion as the servant came closer to the king. When he was just feet away, Thor could stand it no longer. Every ounce of his body screamed that this was the poisoned chalice.

Thor leapt from his table, shoved his way through the thick crowd, elbowed everyone roughly who was in his way.

Just as the King took the chalice into his hands, Thor leapt up onto his table, reached out, and swiped the goblet from the king's hands.

A horrified gasp filled the entire hall as the goblet flew from the king's hands, landed on the stone with a hard clink.

The entire hall went dead silent. Every musician, every juggler, stopped. Hundreds of men and women all turned and stared.

The king slowly stood, and glowered down at Thor.

"How dare you!" shrieked the King. "You insolent little boy!" he screamed. "I will put you in the stocks for this!"

Thor stood there, horrified, hardly believing what he had just done. He felt the entire world crashing down on him. He just wanted to disappear.

Suddenly, a hound walked over to the puddle of wine now forming on the floor, and lapped it up. Before Thor could respond, before the room could move again, all eyes went to the hound, who started making awful, horrible noises.

A moment later, the hound froze up, and fell on its side, dead. The entire room looked at the dog with a horrified gasp.

"You knew the drink was poison!" yelled a voice.

Thor turned and saw the Prince Gareth, standing there, coming up beside the king, pointing accusingly at Thor.

"How could you have possibly have known it was poisoned? Unless you are the one who did it! Thor tried to poison the king!" Gareth yelled out.

The entire crowd cheered in outrage.

"Take him to the dungeon," the king commanded.

A moment later, Thor felt guards grabbing him hard from behind, dragging him through the hall. He squirmed, and tried to protest.

"No!" he screamed out. "You don't understand!"

But no one listened. He was dragged through the crowd, fast and quick, and as he went, he watched them all disappear from him, his whole life disappear from him. They crossed the hall and out a side door, a door slamming shut behind them.

It was quiet here. A moment later, Thor felt himself descending. He was being pulled by several hands down a winding stone staircase. It grew darker and darker, and soon he could hear the cries of prisoners.

An iron cell door opened, and he realized where he was being taken. The dungeon.

He squirmed, trying to protest, to break free.

"You don't understand!" he yelled.

Thor looked up and saw a guard step forward, a large, crude man with an unshaven face, and yellow teeth.

He scowled down at Thor.

"Oh I understand very well," came his raspy voice.

He reached back his fist, and the last thing Thor saw was his fist, coming down right for his face.

Then his world was blackness.

NOW AVAILABLE!

A MARCH OF KINGS
(Book #2 in the Sorcerer's Ring)

"A breathtaking new epic fantasy series. Morgan Rice does it again! This magical saga reminds me of the best of J.K. Rowling, George R.R. Martin, Rick Riordan, Christopher Paolini and J.R.R. Tolkien. I couldn't put it down!"
--Allegra Skye, Bestselling author of SAVED

A MARCH OF KINGS takes us one step further on Thor's epic journey into manhood, as he begins to realize more about who he is, what his powers are, and as he embarks to become a warrior.

After he escapes from the dungeon, Thor is horrified to learn of another assassination attempt on King MacGil. When MacGil dies, the kingdom is set into turmoil. As everyone vies for the throne, King's Court is more rife than ever with its family dramas, power struggles, ambitions, jealousy, violence and betrayal. An heir must be chosen from among the children, and the ancient Dynasty Sword, the source of all their power, will have a chance to be wielded by someone new. But all this might be upended: the murder weapon is recovered, and the noose tightens on finding the assassin. Simultaneously, the MacGils face a new threat by the McClouds, who are set to attack again from within the Ring.

Thor fights to win back Gwendolyn's love, but there may not be time: he is told to pack up, to prepare with his brothers in arms for The Hundred, a hundred grueling days of hell that all Legion members must survive. The Legion will have to cross the Canyon, beyond the protection of the Ring, into the Wilds, and set sail across the Tartuvian Sea for the Isle of Mist, said to be patrolled by a dragon, for their initiation into manhood.

Will they make it back? Will the Ring survive in their absence? And will Thor finally learn the secret of his destiny?

With its sophisticated world-building and characterization, A MARCH OF KINGS is an epic tale of friends and lovers, of rivals and suitors, of knights and dragons, of intrigues and political machinations, of coming of age, of broken hearts, of deception, ambition and betrayal. It is a tale of honor and courage, of fate and destiny, of sorcery. It is a fantasy that brings us into a world we will never forget, and which will appeal to all ages and genders.

About Morgan Rice

Morgan is author of the #1 Bestselling THE SORCERER'S RING, a new epic fantasy series, currently comprising eleven books and counting, which has been translated into five languages. The newest title, A REIGN OF STEEL (#11) is now available!

Morgan Rice is also author of the #1 Bestselling series THE VAMPIRE JOURNALS, comprising ten books (and counting), which has been translated into six languages. Book #1 in the series, TURNED, is now available as a FREE download!

Morgan is also author of the #1 Bestselling ARENA ONE and ARENA TWO, the first two books in THE SURVIVAL TRILOGY, a post-apocalyptic action thriller set in the future.

Among Morgan's many influences are Suzanne Collins, Anne Rice and Stephenie Meyer, along with classics like Shakespeare and the Bible. Morgan lives in New York City.

Please visit www.morganricebooks.com to get exclusive news, get a free book, contact Morgan, and find links to stay in touch with Morgan via Facebook, Twitter, Goodreads, the blog, and a whole bunch of other places. Morgan loves to hear from you, so don't be shy and check back often!

Books by Morgan Rice

THE SORCERER'S RING
A QUEST OF HEROES (BOOK #1)
A MARCH OF KINGS (BOOK #2)
A FEAST OF DRAGONS (BOOK #3)
A CLASH OF HONOR (BOOK #4)
A VOW OF GLORY (BOOK #5)
A CHARGE OF VALOR (BOOK #6)
A RITE OF SWORDS (BOOK #7)
A GRANT OF ARMS (BOOK #8)
A SKY OF SPELLS (BOOK #9)
A SEA OF SHIELDS (BOOK #10)
A REIGN OF STEEL (BOOK #11)

THE SURVIVAL TRILOGY
ARENA ONE (Book #1)
ARENA TWO (Book #2)

the Vampire Journals
turned (book #1)
loved (book #2)
betrayed (book #3)
destined (book #4)
desired (book #5)
betrothed (book #6)
vowed (book #7)
found (book #8)
resurrected (book #9)
craved (book #10)

RECEIVED APR 2014

Rice, Morgan, author.
A quest of heroes

RECEIVED APR - - 2014

CPSIA information can be obtained at www.ICGtesting.com
Printed in the USA
LVOW06s1526070414

380670LV00001B/71/P

9 781939 416209